HARD TWISTED

HARD TWISTED

A Novel

C. Joseph Greaves

B L O O M S B U R Y
New York   London   New Delhi   Sydney

FEB 1 3 2013

Copyright © 2012 by Charles J. Greaves

Published by Bloomsbury USA, New York

All papers used by Bloomsbury USA are natural, recyclable products made from wood grown in well-managed forests. The manufacturing processes conform to the environmental regulations of the country of origin.

LIBRARY OF CONGRESS CATALOGING-IN-PUBLICATION DATA HAS BEEN APPLIED FOR.

ISBN: 978-1-60819-855-9

First U.S. Edition 2012

1 3 5 7 9 10 8 6 4 2

Typeset by Westchester Book Group
Printed in the U.S.A. by Quad/Graphics, Fairfield, Pennsylvania

This book is for my parents, Charles Alan Greaves and Jane Anne Greaves.

Dearly beloved, we are God's children now;
what we shall later be has not yet come to light.

—I JOHN 3:2

PART ONE

Chapter One

A ROOSTER AIN'T NO JOB

THE COURT: Back on the record in Case No. 7421/6150. All jurors are present and the defendant is present. Mr. Pharr?

BY MR. PHARR: Thank you, Your Honor. The People call Lottie Lucile Garrett.

(THE WITNESS, LUCILE GARRETT, IS DULY SWORN.)

BY MR. PHARR: Now, Miss Garrett, you understand that you're under oath, do you not?

A: Yes, sir.

Q: And therefore required to tell the truth?

A: Yes, sir.

Q: Now then, would you please tell the gentlemen of the jury how it was that you first came to meet Clint Palmer?

A: Well, we was camped out on the Gay Road—

BY MR. HARTWELL: Objection, Your Honor. At this time we would renew our motion regarding the testimony of this witness.

THE COURT: All right. I suppose there's no avoiding this. Henry?

BY MR. PHARR: Miss Garrett, were you ever married to the accused?

BY MR. HARTWELL: Objection. Calls for a conclusion. Lay opinion also.

THE COURT: Overruled. You may answer.

A: No, sir. I ain't never been married to nobody.

(PROCEEDINGS INTERRUPTED.)

THE COURT: Order. We'll have none of this. One more outburst and I'll clear the courtroom. Henry?

BY MR. PHARR: You never went through any kind of wedding ceremony with the accused?

A: No, sir.

Q: He never gave you a ring?

A: No, sir.

Q: You never stood up before a preacher?

A: Never did. Never would, neither.

(PROCEEDINGS INTERRUPTED.)

THE COURT: Order. Do not test me.

BY MR. PHARR: Submitted, Your Honor.

THE COURT: Very well. Does counsel wish to voir dire?

BY MR. HARTWELL: Thank you, Your Honor. Isn't it true that you and Mr. Palmer cohabited together over a period of several months during the years 1934 and 1935?

A: Did what?

Q: Cohabited. Lived under the same roof.

A: Well. There weren't no roof to speak of.

(PROCEEDINGS INTERRUPTED.)

THE COURT: Order. Not another peep, I warn you. And the witness will answer counsel's questions without gratuitous exposition.

BY MR. HARTWELL: You lived together as man and wife.

BY MR. PHARR: Objection.

THE COURT: Sustained.

BY MR. HARTWELL: You shared a bed? Or a bedroll?

A: It weren't never my idea.

Q: But isn't it true that you held yourselves out to the public as man and wife?

A: That's a lie. I never done no such thing.

Q: In Monticello, state of Utah, on December the thirty-first of 1934—

BY MR. PHARR: Objection. This is too much, Your Honor. I would remind the court—

THE COURT: All right, all right. That's enough, both of you. I can see where this is heading. The defense motion is denied.

BY MR. HARTWELL: But, Your Honor—

THE COURT: For Christ sake, L.D., these men got crops planted. I said motion denied.

BY MR. HARTWELL: Exception.

THE COURT: Noted. Henry, you may proceed.

BY MR. PHARR: Thank you, Your Honor. Miss Garrett, I think we were by the side of a road somewhere.

They followed the Frisco tracks with their bodies bent and hooded, the pebbling wind audible on the back of her father's old mackinaw. To the west, a line of T-poles stretched to a dim infinity before a setting sun that melted and bled and blended its sanguinary light with the red dirt and with the red dust that rose up like hell's flame in towering streaks and whorls to forge together earth and sky.

Great deal on land! her father called over his shoulder. Bring your own jar!

They came out to the highway and paused there before turning west, the windblown dust in spectral fingers reaching across the blacktop before them. First one car passed without stopping, then another.

You gettin hungry?

No, sir.

The next vehicle that passed was a slat-sided Ford truck that slowed and shimmied and veered crazily onto the shoulder, and as they hurried to meet it, she saw through the swirling grit the crates of pinewood and twist-wire stacked beneath its flapping canvas tarpaulin.

Her father worked the latches and lowered the endgate and vaulted into the truckbed. She reached a blind hand for him and felt herself rising, weightless in a grip as hard as knotted applewood, his mangled finger biting into the soft flesh of her wrist.

A bonging sound on the cab roof riled the chickens, and a voice called out from the lowered window, Get on up front, you dumb Okies!

The man looked across her lap and studied her father's shoes. He said his name was Palmer, and that he was a Texan, and a cowboy. He wore sharp sideburns and a clean Resistol hat cocked forward over pallid eyes gone violet in the fading glow of sunset, and she could see that he was small—perhaps no taller than she—and that something fiercely defiant, something feral, was in his smallness.

You get a gander at them gamecocks? the man asked without taking his eyes from the roadway.

Look like right fine birds, her father allowed.

The man chuckled. Mister, them's the gamest fightin roosters this side of the Red, for your information.

That a fact.

Damn right that's a fact. The man nodded once. Damn right it is. You know fightin birds?

Her father did not respond, and the man leaned forward to study his profile before dropping his eyes first to her sweater and then to her lap, returning at last and again to her father's shoes.

How long you been outside, cousin?

How's that?

The stranger's smile was sudden, and unnaturally brilliant, and hot on the side of her neck.

So that's how it is.

Do I know you? her father asked, leaning now to face the man.

Maybe you do and maybe you don't, the man said, his ghost reflection grinning in the darkened windscreen. But I surely do know you.

They'd built a fire in the lee of the ruined house, and her father squatted before it stirring red flannel hash with a spoon. The temperature had dropped with the sun and she wore his mackinaw now like a mantle while he sat his heels and rubbed his hands and warmed them over the skillet, the tumbled walls around them shifting and changing, moving inward and then outward again as though breathing in the soft orange glow like a living thing.

Embers popped, running and skittering with the wind. To the north she saw other fires speckling the void, and she studied their positions as an astronomer might chart the nighttime heavens.

More tonight, she said.

Her father followed her gaze. These is hard times, honey. Ain't nobody hirin. Least not in Hugo, anyways. I was thinkin I might light a shuck for Durant come sunrise. Man said a mill there was lookin for hands. Miz Upchurch could mind you for a day.

I don't need no mindin.

He paused and studied her burnished profile, her cheek and lashes luminous in the fireglow.

Tell you what then. You can mind Miz Upchurch. Haul her water and such. You tell her I'll be back by nightfall.

She wielded a broken twig, tracing random patterns in the dirt. Somewhere beyond the firelight, a car passed on the highway.

Who was that man?

Just a man.

He said he knowed you.

He didn't mean like that. More like my kind is what he meant.

What's your kind?

Her father stirred the skillet, and paused, and stirred it again. He tapped the spoon on the iron rim.

Only the good Lord knows what's in a man's heart, Lottie. Happy is the man who follows not the counsel of the wicked nor walks in the way of sinners. He wiped his nose with his wrist. That there's from Psalms.

She poked her stick into the fire and withdrew it and blew out the flame. Then she wrote a secret in the air, and studied it, and watched it disappear in the ravenous wind.

The sun was two fingers off the horizon by the time she awoke. The wind had stilled and the sky had hardened to a diamond blue the weight of which lay upon her in her blankets like some vast and shoreless ocean.

She turned, shielding her eyes with a hand. The white ash of a kindling fire warmed the coffeepot beside her father's bedroll.

She sat up yawning, and then rose to gather some yellowed newsprint from their cache before heading to the creekbed. On her return to the campsite she bent and snapped an aloe spine, spreading the sticky unguent onto her blistered ankle the way the Choctaws did, then she tiptoed back to the fire. There she brushed her hair in long, measured strokes, staring out to the north where the night fires had been, but where nothing now stirred.

Among her father's things she found his small leather Bible, and she sat in the shade of the broken house and read from Exodus about the command to the midwives until, setting the book aside, she closed her eyes and touched the slender cross at her throat, praying aloud, Dear Lord, first for her mother's eternal soul, and then for her uncle Mack, and lastly for a Little Buttercup doll with the blue ruffle dress and the matching bonnet with genuine lace trim, her head bowed as she spoke the words, her voice a tin voice in the still and wilted air.

A vulture kited overhead, its shadow rippling darkly over the ground, over the house, over the day.

Over her life.

She replaced the book and stood and stretched again before walking into the sunlight, where she shook the grit from her socks and boots and pulled them on and walked a tentative circle. Then she sat and removed the one boot, folding a strip of newsprint into her sock and replacing the boot and walking another circle.

She hadn't gone but a hundred yards toward the Upchurch

farm when she caught sight of the truck. It was parked beside the highway, and the man was standing behind it like an exclamation point after a shouted command.

She looked to the farmhouse, small yet on the horizon, and back again to the truck.

He was leaning on the fender, the heel of one boot resting in the crook of the other. The sun was to his back, and his hat flapped listlessly against his thigh. He followed her approach until she'd reached the edge of the bar ditch, where she stopped and studied with lowered eyes whatever grew within.

What's the matter, I'm too ugly to look at?

You ain't ugly.

The man worked a matchstick in the corner of his smile.

If you're lookin for my pa, you're too late. He's over to Durant.

That's his bad luck then, ain't it. Here I come all this way to offer him a job.

What job?

He gestured toward the truckbed. Brought him a rooster.

A rooster ain't no job.

He shook his head sadly, grinning into his hat crown.

What all's he supposed to do with it then?

Hey, you remind me of someone, do you know that? Was you ever in the movin pictures?

Not hardly.

Then it was one of them photo magazines. Am I right?

She lowered her gaze, the heat prickling her face.

What's your name, anyways?

Lucile. Lottie to my friends.

His eyes left hers to scan the field behind her, settling on the spavined house and the broken windmill and the cold thread of woodsmoke hanging above them.

I got friends.

How old are you, anyways? Fourteen?

Thirteen.

Thirteen. He nodded once. I got me a niece name of Johnny Rae, and she's just about your age. She's my sister's youngest.

Lottie shaded her eyes. Does she live in these parts?

He nodded again. Matter of fact, she and me, we was gonna take us a drive down to Peerless tomorrow to visit my daddy. You ever been to Texas?

I don't know.

My daddy's got him a farm down there with cows and goats and pony horses. It's too bad you all couldn't come with us, cuz them horses need to get worked. He looked south, far beyond the horizon. Could use us another hand tomorrow, that's for damn sure.

She studied the stranger's profile. His tooled boots and his new Levi's and his polished oval belt buckle.

My pa wouldn't let me go noways.

How come? Why, you and me and Johnny Rae and her mama, we all could have us a day. Maybe eat us a picnic dinner. You like fried chicken?

I suppose.

And they's a swimmin hole for you girls if the weather holds. Hell, we all'd be back by sunset.

Well.

You want I should talk to your pa?

She shrugged. I don't know.

What's your pa's name, anyways?

Dillard Garrett.

Dillard Garrett, he said. As if weighing it.

They faced each other in the silence that followed, his corn-flower eyes locked on to hers. She looked away, fists thrust into pockets.

I got to go.

You need a ride somewheres?

No, sir.

Don't *sir* me. I ain't your daddy.

All right.

Clinton Palmer. That's my name. Clint to my friends.

Now you're funnin me.

Grinning again, he removed the matchstick and slid himself upright.

Tell you what. Come over here and take this rooster for your pa. I'll come by in the mornin, and him and me'll have us a little talk.

He climbed into the truckbed and, without bending, slid the lone crate toward the endgate with his boot.

Careful now. That's one rank bird.

The cock was rust over black, and the black of it held a greenish cast in the gridded sunlight. It fanned its ruff and pecked at the wire where she reached her hand.

Does he got a name?

No, ma'am, but I reckon you could give him one.

She tipped the crate carefully with her forearm, hiking it onto her hip. The bird was all but weightless, its pink talons balled and its pink head rooting in short and halting jerks.

He sure is fancy, but he don't weigh nothin a'tall.

She carried the crate across the ditch and hiked it again as she walked, pausing but once to turn and face the slender figure still skylighted in the truckbed.

I got me a notion to name him Clint.

The mill jobs in Durant had been but two jobs, for which over a hundred men had applied. Her father's voice quavered as he told the story, and between long tugs of bonded whiskey he cursed the day and he cursed the mill foreman and he cursed Mr. and Mrs. Roosevelt for good measure.

The rooster stirred in its cage.

It's got to where a white man can't find a honest day's work for a honest day's wages, he rasped, his hands trembling, his dark eyes shining in the firelight. It's got to where a Christian man is treated no better than a godless goddamn nigger.

Lottie listened, chewing and nodding in mute commiseration, waiting until at last her father had stoppered the bottle and rolled a smoke and leaned back into his bedroll. Only then did she broach the subject of Peerless, but his answer was curt, and emphatic, and so she let the matter drop.

The truck sat shimmering in the roadside sun as Lottie emerged barefoot from the creekbed. Before it were two figures in backlight, one tall and one short, the shape that was her father listening with folded arms while the smaller man spoke and gestured, first to the truck and then to the highway, and then in a sweeping arc that encompassed the broken house and the field where Lottie crouched in the pokeweed, her eyes closed, her lips moving in swift and silent prayer.

★ ★ ★

Where's Johnny Rae?

Lottie paused with her foot on the running board as Palmer held the door.

Packin her kit bag, I reckon. We'll fetch her up in Hugo.

He closed the door and circled the truck, clapping dust from his hands, his eyes scanning the highway in both directions.

The cab where she waited was spare and tidy and bore the masculine smells of motor oil and leather and old cigarettes. A spider crack stippled the corner of the windscreen. A cowhide valise, like a doctor's bag, rested on the seat beside her.

Palmer clambered in and slammed the door, setting his hat atop the valise and raking his hair with a hand. He looked at her and smiled. He turned the ignition and pressed the starter and mashed the pedals, working the shift lever up and back until the gears ground and caught and the truck lurched forward, rocking and wheeling southbound onto the empty highway.

That weren't too difficult.

What all'd you tell him?

Oh, let's see. That I was Clyde Barrow and needin me a gun moll, and that we all was gonna rob us some banks and shoot our way down to Mexico.

She giggled. You're crazy.

He said to bring him one of them sombrero hats is all.

The day was warm, and the warmth of it rippled on the scrolling blacktop. She watched him in stolen glances; the line of his nose and the set of his jaw and the dance of his hair in the breeze.

What is it?

Nothin, she replied.

You was smilin at somethin.

It weren't nothin to talk about.

They passed beanfields and cornfields and grazing cattle, and then the ironworks and the cotton compress, slowing only at the stockyard where the roadway and the rail line crossed. Palmer pointed out the railmen's barracks, and the ice plant, and a gated cemetery where he swore that elephants and circus clowns had been buried.

A redbrick bank was on the main street, and a general store, and they passed them both before turning left at midblock down a narrow alley.

Wait here a minute, Palmer said, setting the brake and collecting his hat and sliding from under the wheel.

She sat and watched as cars and trucks and occasional horses plodded past the alley mouth like targets in a carnival shooting gallery. She fingered the knobs on the dashboard. She hummed. When a man approached the truck and removed his hat to ask if she could spare a dime, she told the man that she had no dime to spare.

When Palmer returned, he was swinging a brown paper sack that he tucked between his legs as he resumed his place at the wheel.

Change in plans, he announced breezily, releasing the brake and reversing the gears and slinging his arm over the seatback. Looks like Johnny Rae and her mama done already left. We'll have to meet 'em down there, if that's okay with you?

I guess.

He turned to her and winked. Bigger shares for you and me if we hit us a bank on the way.

They passed the Methodist church and the Baptist church, and outside of town they passed the tie-treating plant, where Lottie pinched her nose against the treacle smell of creosote. Beyond these, the countryside opened and the highway rose and fell and she saw in the rising a jagged suture of brighter green that ran for miles from east to west and marked the Red River valley.

They crossed into Texas on the Highway 39 bridge at Arthur City, where she watched their reflection warp and disjoin and form again in the storefront glass. They turned onto a gravel side road, recrossing the railroad tracks and dropping into the cool and empty shade of the riverbank.

You need to pee? he asked, setting the hand brake.

I don't know.

If you don't know, who does then?

He killed the engine and shouldered his door, slipping the paper sack into his seat pocket as he alighted. She watched as he walked into the rushes and curtsied and fumbled with his trouser front. Then he crossed the little clearing to a downed log and settled himself in the shade, fanning his face with the hat.

You all comin out? he called to the truck, and she opened her door and closed it and moved through the dappling sunlight and the pustular smell of rotting bulrush.

You gettin hungry?

A little.

He shifted where he sat. They's a café in Paris. That's about a half hour's drive from here. Think you can hold out?

I guess.

As she settled on the log beside him, he placed the cowboy hat on her head and leaned back to study the effect. He reached for the sack, folded back the paper, and uncorked the bottle within with his teeth. He took a long drink of the amber liquid and of-fered the bottle to her.

You sure? . . . All right then, suit yourself.

He set the bottle on the ground, crossing his legs and prying his boots off each in turn. He wore no socks and his feet were as a child's feet, small and veined and pale as candle wax.

I got me a notion to wash up, if that's all right with you. Cleanliness bein next to godliness and all.

He stood and unsnapped his shirt, draping it on a low branch. He was lean and hard-muscled, tanned on his neck and forearms, and he smiled at her over his shoulder as he sauntered through the canebrake. At the river's edge he stopped to roll his pantlegs before wading into the water.

She watched him closely, pretending she was not. Watched as he produced a kerchief from his pocket. Watched as he dipped the cloth and wrung it, half-squatting, scrubbing at his face and neck. Watched as he turned to where she sat, his voice echoing across the wide and silent river.

Come on, Bonnie Parker! A little water won't kill you!

She looked from the man to the bottle and back again to the man. To the truck, like a great wounded beetle with its one door open. To the shirt, limp and empty as a snakeskin.

At the river's edge the air was warm and alive with insects seen and unseen, and she watched the threaded grasses streaming in the water beyond the wide shadow of her hat brim. Palmer stood in full sun, hands on hips, the cold water glistening on his chest.

Come on in. It ain't that fast.

She waded out to where he stood, the cold mud oozing between her toes, stepping and pausing, stepping and pausing, her weight braced against the heavy current, while upriver, before the riveted railroad bridge, sunlight danced on the water.

He lifted a hand to her cheek, rubbing a spot there with his thumb, his hand lingering on her face and on her neck as though gentling a skittish yearling. Then he slapped the bandanna across his shoulder, reaching his hands to her shirtfront.

What're you doin?

Just hold still a second.

Quit it!

She twisted away, backing and almost falling.

Hey! Careful of that hat!

She stood with her legs braced, her fear and her excitement veiled by the shadow of the hat brim.

I was only tryin to help. It was kindly gettin close in that truck, if you get my meanin.

Her face burned. She looked to her feet, or to where her knees below the rolled pant cuffs met the sheeting water.

What's the matter now?

She shrugged. I'm cold.

Here.

She accepted the cloth, and after he'd waded past her toward the bank, she bent and submerged it in the river, raising it to her nape, shivering as the water ran in hard, icy fingers down her shirtback.

I'll be over yonder with my eyes closed! his voice faded behind her. Don't you worry about me!

She lifted her sweater and her shirttail, scrubbing at her underarms. She swirled the bandanna and wrung it out and sniffed of it and swirled it again.

Hey! You ain't drowned out there I hope!

She could not see him, but when she'd waded ashore, she found him fully dressed and reclined against a treetrunk with his hands nesting the bottle in his lap.

How was that?

She shrugged.

He rose, brushing at his seat and accepting the wet cloth and retrieving the hat from her head.

I don't know about you, he said, but I could eat a folded tarp.

Back inside the truck cab, he uncorked the bottle and took another drink.

Here.

No thanks.

Go ahead. I won't tell your daddy.

That's all right.

You ain't scared, are you?

She looked at him, and at the bottle. She accepted it, sniffing at the neck and crinkling her nose.

Go on, it won't kill you.

I know it. She looked at him again and closed her eyes and drank.

A spray of bourbon whiskey wet the windscreen. At this Palmer roared, rocking and red-faced, his child's feet stamping the floorboards.

Whoooeee!

'Tain't funny, she gagged, coughing into her sleeve.

Tell you what though, it'll do till funny comes along. Give that here.

He drank again and wiped his mouth on his shirtsleeve. And as he nestled the stoppered bottle inside the valise, she saw through still-watering eyes the hard, blue shape of the pistol.

They sat as bookends in a booth by the window. Fly husks on the faded sill were hard and iridescent in the sunlight, and Lottie watched them and their faint reflections rocking in unison to the slow wash of the ceiling fan. A waitress, herself nearly as desic-cated, filled their mugs and produced napkins and flatware from a sagging apron pocket.

They's a children's menu on the back, she said.

Palmer ignored her, intent on the streetscape. There were more and newer cars than in Hugo, and fewer horses. On the corner opposite the café, a Negro boy yoked in a wooden sandwich board held a newspaper aloft to the passing cars. The headline read MORE RELIEF FOR FARMERS.

Palmer opened his menu, and Lottie did likewise. There were breakfast plates and lunch plates and blue plate specials.

What all can I have?

Whatever you want, sweetheart.

The waitress returned with a pad, and she dug a pencil from behind her ear as Palmer ordered the chicken-fried steak with biscuits and gravy and pinto beans.

Lottie bit her lip, twisting and untwisting the same lock of hair. She ordered pancakes with bacon, and fried chicken with green beans, and hot apple pie with a slice of cheddar cheese.

Expectin company? the woman snorted, jotting the order with eyebrows raised.

Palmer turned to follow her receding back before reaching into his valise and tipping the bottle into his coffee. He stirred it and tinked at the rim and raised the mug as if to Lottie's health.

How much further to Peerless?

He sipped. Thirty or forty miles.

How long will that take?

Maybe a hour, maybe more.

You reckon they's worried about us?

You ask a lot of questions, do you know that?

That's what my daddy says. He says I'm like the queen of Sheba, right there in first Kings.

He set down his cup and leaned forward and thumbed back his hat. Listen, sister. If I wanted a sky pilot for company, I'd of stopped at one of them churches and waved me a dollar bill.

What do you mean?

I mean not everbody was raised up on dried prunes and proverbs.

Don't you never read the good book?

The good book. What's it say in that book of yours about farmers gettin run off their land? What's it say about Jew bankers takin food money from widows and orphans?

Her face was a blank.

You think they's anybody in them churches gives a rat's ass whether you eat or starve? Well, let me tell you somethin I learnt a long time ago, and that's this right here. You want anything in this life, you got to go on out and grab it. You just do what you gotta do, and don't go askin no permission or beggin no forgiveness. And for Pete sake, don't go all the time askin the good Lord for help, cuz if you want my view on the matter, he's done got quit of the helpin business.

She blinked.

You got a problem with that, you let me know right now, and I'll give you a ride straight back to your daddy.

I didn't say nothin.

Okay then.

He leaned back in his seat. He returned his attention to the window, where the newsboy's sign lay jackknifed on the side-walk, the boy himself gone as though vanished in some heavenly rapture peculiar to his race.

Lottie took up her knife and tilted it, examining her reflection in the blade. Palmer watched her with a sidelong glance as the light bar played on her face.

Try that spoon there. You'll be all topsy-turvy.

She set down the knife and took up the spoon, holding it out like a mirror.

Tell me somethin. How long you been hoboin with your pa?

She shrugged. I don't know. Two years.

What about before that?

Before that I lived with Uncle Mack, up to Wilburton.

Uncle Mack.

She nodded. Tilting her head, examining the upside-down girl.

What all happened to him?

I don't know. Got tired of havin me, I guess.

So where's your mama, anyways?

Dead.

Well, shit, there you go. My mama too. Maybe that's how come I knowed right away that you and me was gonna become special friends.

The waitress appeared beside them with heavy plates two to a hand.

More coffee comin, she said, tearing a sheet from her pad and slapping it down at Palmer's elbow.

Lottie ate the pancakes, and the chicken, and they nudged the pie plate back and forth between them. They ate mostly in silence, watching the cars pass on the street, and when she would glance at him and their eyes would meet, she would giggle and cover her mouth with a hand.

When they'd finished eating, Palmer peeled back the check and studied it and told her to go outside and wait in the truck.

She sat with the window rolled watching the fountain in the town square until Palmer appeared from the alley side of the building, hurrying to the truck and climbing in after his valise. He fumbled with the key and jabbed at the starter, grinding the gears and lurching them into traffic as cars swerved and horns sounded. They turned right at the first corner and left at the next, with Palmer all the while watching behind them in the mirror.

In late afternoon they quit the highway for the county road. They passed through miles of wooded fields and blackland farms before swinging onto a gravel track by a cemetery, where a small dog shot through the iron gates and heeled them for almost a mile.

The track then narrowed and darkened as shade trees crowded their passage. They rounded another curve and Palmer braked the truck and tilted his hat, leaning out the window to hawk and spit through their settling dust cloud.

There she is.

Lottie sat up to look. Through a gap in the tree line she made out a long field sloping away to a swaybacked barn. Beyond the barn was a peeling clapboard house flanked by shade trees, one living and one dead, and beyond the trees was a pasture, this with an empty stockpond in which two rawboned horses posed with their heads low and their tails swaying and switching.

Another tree line marked the far boundary of the pasture. She saw no cattle or goats and no pony horses, and she could imagine no swimming hole on the land or in the jagged cut that ran beyond it.

Okay then. Here we go.

He climbed down to free the rusted loopwire that held the

sagging gate upright. The horses lifted their heads as he returned to the truck and slammed the door and drove it forward and alighted again to close the gate behind them.

They parked in the shade of the barn. Swallows flew at the sound of their slamming car doors. Somewhere in the distance, chickens gabbled and clucked. Palmer turned to the house, cupping his mouth with his hands.

Hello! Anybody home?

All was silence.

The barn before them listed precariously. One stall housed a rusted jalopy blinded by missing headlamps; the other, an ancient two-furrow horseplow. Littering the ground and lining the open-stud walls were sacks and barrels, tin cans and fruit jars, and rusting tools of every description. Against the back wall, spotlighted by a gap in the high tin roof, stood a tumbledown tower of hay.

I got to pee bad.

Privy's around back. I'll go on inside.

The outhouse was rank, and so she squatted in the bare dirt behind it. The sun was high and the air warm and still, and the stillness of it hummed in her ears. She listened for the distant sound of voices raised in greeting, but she heard nothing.

The porch sagged where the paint had worn, and her bootheels rang hollow on the steps. She opened the screen door and paused, and there spied Palmer's back framed in an open doorway where he knelt before a woodstove. He pivoted at the sound of the doorspring.

Come on in. Looks like we missed 'em.

The house was cool despite the sun. A small front parlor was sparsely furnished with a cracked leather sofa and a matching wing chair, its brass rivets missing. Lace hung limply over milky windows. Beyond this room was the kitchen, and beyond the kitchen a narrow hallway that ran darkly toward the back.

Where all'd they go?

They's a note, he said without turning.

It lay on the kitchen table beside the valise; grease pencil scrawl on a flattened paper sack.

Clint—Could not wait no longer. Rode out with girls to river. Will camp for the nite. Make yorself to home. H.P.

She stared at the scribbled words until the words vibrated and blurred and she felt a hot streak on her cheek. At this the vague shape of him rose from the stove and crossed to where she stood, and she felt his strong hands on her shoulders.

Come on, Bonnie Parker. Don't go bawlin now. It ain't the end of the world. We can ride with 'em some other time, and that's a promise. Meanwhile, we got the place all to ourselves, and we can have us a swell time. Come on now.

She nodded, leaning away to look at him.

I'm sorry, she said, sniffling. I know it's the Lord's will.

The slap was swift and sharp, the force of it spinning her sideways into the table.

What did I tell you about that nonsense?

She raised a hand to her face. She opened her mouth to speak, but no words came. She turned and ran for the door.

He caught her in the front parlor and pulled her backward, kicking and squirming, and he wrestled her onto the sofa.

Hold on now. I said stop, dammit, and settle down.

His hands gripped her wrists, straitjacketing her in his lap.

I hate you!

You listen to me for one second. Just listen.

She struggled again, and then was still.

I done fed you, and I drove you all the way down here so's you could have a little fun for yourself, and all I ast in return was one little thing. All I ast was for you to quit your mealymouthed holy-rollin for one goddamn day. Now is that so much? Huh? Is it?

He leaned and tried to turn her, but she wouldn't turn.

Come on, Lucile. Where's that other cheek I keep hearin about?

She tried to stand, and he hugged her tighter.

Let go!

Come on, darlin. This ain't no way to be.

She looked away, turning her face to the door and the porch beyond. Don't you never hit me again.

Don't you never give me no cause again. How's that for a square deal?

On the porch the angled sunlight quartered the floorplanks. Houseflies jumbled noisily beyond the screen.

All right.

All right then.

He released his grip, and she slid quietly from his lap.

I got to start us a fire. And then I got to feed and water them nags. Then we can play some dominoes or take us a little walk, all right?

She nodded.

Will you help me with them horses?

Can't they be rid?

Well. These ones ain't exactly saddle broke is the thing. Unless you're some kinda buckaroo cowgirl and me not knowin it.

Not hardly.

Well then, maybe we'd best just feed 'em and leave 'em be. He rose from the sofa. Course if anyone asks, we can always say we grabbed apple and marked 'em up the side. How does that sound?

All right.

All right then. Are we still friends?

She shrugged. I guess.

He lit the woodstove with the paper sack and fanned it with his hat and stood back to consider the result.

All right then. Let's get after it.

The air outside was cooler now, the shadows longer. She trailed behind him as he threw feed to the chickens and pumped water into buckets and carried sack oats and water to the mirrored horses nickering in the pasture. In the side yard she set firewood for him to quarter, and when he'd split the last of it, he squatted and held his arms out like a surgeon while she stacked it and ran ahead and held the door for him to stagger through.

They lingered on the front porch watching the horses, the road, the fallow field. They walked the wire fenceline for a distance as Palmer narrated. He showed her the spot where a wolf took his 4-H heifer, and the spot where he broke his leg roping, and the spot where his best bluetick dog ate a copperhead snake and dropped stone dead at his feet.

At the top of a low rise he stood akimbo, surveying the landscape of his childhood; the joys and sorrows etched upon the weathered barnwood and the hardened turnrows and the dying play of sunlight on the roof shakes.

When I was a kid, he told her, I couldn't wait to get quit of this place. I run away, and I come back, and then I run away again. Finally, when I was sixteen, I run away for good. At least I thought I did.

How come?

He shrugged. I don't know. The old man went and got remarried. I guess I felt like I'd lost my place somehow, and that if I got away and looked somewheres else, I might find it again. Almost like you can't really be home until you know what else is out there, and then you figure out for yourself that whatever it is, it ain't really home. Does that make any sense?

What happened?

Huh?

Your place. Did you ever find it again?

He squatted and plucked a grass stem and held it in his mouth.

I don't know. I don't know if you ever know a thing such as that. Maybe I did, but I just didn't realize it. Or maybe I ain't got there yet. He removed the stem and studied it. Maybe I'll get there tomorrow, or the day after that. Or maybe I won't never get there a'tall.

Or maybe you're there right now.

He looked up at her face, guileless and pink in the low light of sunset.

By God, you may be right.

He stood and placed the hat on her head.

Maybe I am at that.

Palmer backed the sofa onto the porch, and when he went inside again, he returned with four warm bottles of orange Nehi and the last of the bourbon whiskey. He popped the caps on his belt buckle and lined the bottles along the railing, topping them off each in turn with a measure of whiskey.

They sat with their boots on the railing and sipped their drinks and watched the land turn from green to blue, the rising tide of darkness swallowing first the driveway and then the fenceline and then, as the night air cooled, the very steps below their feet.

Now crickets chirped and bullbats swooped and the plow horses shifted and snuffled somewhere in the darkness.

You see that one there? Lottie closed one eye and pointed her empty bottleneck.

Where?

Them three in a row like that?

Okay.

That's Orion. She pointed again. That there's supposed to be his sword.

Don't look like no sword to me. More like his dick maybe.

She giggled, slapping his hand. You're bad.

You know a lot about stars, I guess.

Did you know that they's more stars in the sky than specks of dust on the earth?

Go on.

That's a fact.

Says who?

Everbody. My uncle Mack.

He lolled his head to take in her upturned profile and her parted lips and the dusting of starlight in her eyes. The staggering beauty of her innocence.

What?

Nothin. I was wonderin what you was thinkin is all.

She looked again to the heavens, and for a long while did not speak.

I used to stare at the sky of a night, she finally said, and pretend my mama was up there somewheres, lookin down and watchin over me. All dressed in white, like a angel. But the older I got, the more I come to think that maybe it was always the other way around. Like maybe I was the one was all the time watchin out for her. Watchin and waitin for some sign that ain't never gonna come, and all the time missin what was under my nose.

She turned her face to his.

Only thing is, there ain't never been nothin under my nose to speak of but hard dirt and hoecake.

He reached and took her hand in his.

Until now, he told her.

They ate corn bread and Karo syrup straight from the pan, her head floating in the amber lamplight and the whiskey and the heat from the open firebox. The walls of the little kitchen closed around them and seemed to her to ripple, like a room viewed through antique paneglass.

He took her hand and placed her fingers in his mouth and sucked them each in turn as she held her breath and watched him.

Come over here.

He shifted his weight and lifted her into his lap and kissed her softly at first and then with greater urgency. She closed her eyes and her head swam and she felt the warmth of his mouth and the wet thrill of his tongue between her lips.

You ever had a boyfriend before? he whispered, his breath a hot caramel apple of whiskey and syrup.

She shook her head. No.

He kissed her again.

Could I be your boyfriend tonight?

Chapter Two

THEM ALL'S THE RULES

BY MR. PHARR: How would you describe Mr. Palmer's relationship with your father?

A: I don't know. I thought it was real friendly-like at first. Like maybe Clint wanted somethin, and he thought he could cozy up to Daddy and get it.

BY MR. RYAN: Objection. Rank speculation.

THE COURT: Sustained.

BY MR. PHARR: Was there ever a time when your father and Mr. Palmer entered into business together?

A: Yes, sir. Clint was lookin for a partner in his rooster operation, and he invited us to move there to Roebuck Lake.

Q: When was that?

A: May. Middle of May.

Q: How long did you and your father live with the accused at Roebuck Lake?

A: Around ten days or so.

Q: And then what happened?

A: Then we moved down here to Peerless.

Q: Why? What precipitated the move from Roebuck Lake to Peerless?

BY MR. HARTWELL: Calls for speculation.

THE COURT: I'll allow it.

A: I don't know about precipitated. I know there'd been a patch of trouble, and maybe Clint used that as a excuse to get us all down here into Texas.

They found her father in his bedroll, the fire cold and the old Dutch oven gaping in its bed of ash and coated with some black and glistening residue. He appeared to be fully dressed, and an empty fruit jar lay in the dirt by his feet.

You reckon he's dead? Palmer said, lifting and sniffing the jar mouth.

She bent and touched her father's forehead. He groaned as he rolled, covering his face with an arm.

He ain't dead. He's soused though.

Palmer dropped the jar and crossed to the larder, where he toed through their meager provisions.

This here's your food store?

Yep.

He shook his head, turning and appraising the campsite. The tumbled house. The odd assemblage of pans and mismatched crockery. The worn and orphaned tools.

What all do you do for water?

They's a well just yonder. That's how come we stay here.

She had straightened her father's blankets, and now stood so as to shade his head from the sun. Palmer moved beside her, and together they regarded the sleeping man like belated witnesses to some mishap.

This happen often?

She shrugged.

Where's that rooster I brung?

She turned. He's around here somewheres.

They found the cage on its side in the shade, the gamecock strutting tight circles on a speckled carpet of shit. Lottie righted the cage and fetched some soda crackers and a jar lid of water.

Shouldn't you be goin? she said as she stood again, wiping her hands on her pants.

You tryin to get quit of me?

I didn't say that.

He stepped closer, glancing at the sleeping man. He touched a hand to her face. When will I see you again?

I don't know.

You sore at me?

I ain't sore.

He lifted her chin. Remember what we talked about.

I know, she said, looking away. I ain't stupid.

By the time her father sat upright and ran a trembling hand across his face, the sky had darkened and the wind had risen again and the blankets snapped around him in a pyre of dusty flannel. He willed himself upright, staggering to the well and pumping himself a bucket. He steadied it on the concrete apron and took a breath and submerged his entire head.

He turned dripping and blowing back to their campfire. He walked two steps and sat as though on a chair, but there was no chair and he landed instead on the ground with his legs splayed. She rose to help him, but he stopped her with a hand.

I'm all right. Just stumbled is all.

They sat with their backs to the highway, and he rested his sodden head on his forearm. She thought he might have dozed.

I'm feelin poorly this mornin.

This evenin you mean.

He raised his eyes, blinking and bloodshot, to the western horizon.

Oh, Lordy.

You'll go blind drinkin that moonshine.

He nodded. I know it.

It's a wonder you ain't blind already.

It's a wonder I ain't put a strap to your backside already.

Yes, sir.

They sipped their coffee and ate their biscuits cold, watching the dark clouds drifting and shifting above the treetops, melding into blackness with the gathering dusk.

She told him all about Johnny Rae and the swimming hole, and about the half-broke ponies they'd raced in swirling dust clouds across the Palmer farm. She told him about the corn bread she'd baked and the fried chicken they'd eaten with green beans and the games of forty-two that kept them up laughing and drinking warm Nehis around the kitchen table until past her bedtime.

When she'd finished the telling, she refilled his cup and gathered up his plate and, in so doing, glanced at his face, apricot in the fireglow, and saw that he was weeping.

Dawn found Lottie sleeping. But Dillard Garrett, already risen, had sharpened his ax and his bucksaw before setting out for the Upchurch farm.

By the time Lottie was awake and stretching in her bedroll, her father had finished loading the Model A Ford, and she saw that he'd shaved his face and changed his shirt and had the coffeepot on and warming.

What time is it?

Early to bed and early to rise, he said without turning.

What're you doin?

He was squat on his haunches, chalking a scrapwood board with a blunt of old charcoal. He leaned aside that she might read his writing.

FIRE WOOD.

She lay back in her blankets and groaned.

They finished their coffee standing, their shadows long on the ground, and when they loaded the sign into the Upchurch car, they took care that they not mar the upholstery.

After a short drive in which few words were spoken, the water tower appeared on the horizon and they turned eastward into the low sunrise toward the Kiamichi. They parked by the river's edge and waded with their tools like naiad woodsmen through sumac and creeper knee-deep and fragrant and snatching at their pantlegs. Sunlight shafting through the tree canopy bathed them both in a silvery radiance. At last they came upon a small clearing at whose center a tree stump rose, and there her father set down his tools and turned a slow and appraising circle.

This'll do, he pronounced.

He chose a large hickory snag and hiked himself upward, grunting and scrabbling. Lottie handed up the bucksaw. He spread his feet and commenced to sawing at the thin and uppermost deadwood, which Lottie dragged backpedaling through the understory from where it landed.

He worked his way downward in this fashion, sawing and resting, resting and sawing, the zip-zip of the sawblade echoing in the empty clearing, until an hour had passed and his face was damp and his hair and eyebrows and the ground around them were dusted white as from some dreamscape blizzard in whose passing her bootprints had tracked.

He brushed sawdust from his shoulders as he knelt to drink from the river, and when he'd finished his drinking, he crossed to the stump and sat, wiping his face with his shirttail. He waited for his trembling hands to quiet. When he rose again, he took up the saw and set to bucking the piled branches into lengths, the least of which Lottie gathered and carried to the twine she had laid on the ground in long, parallel strips.

Once the cut wood was sorted and piled, she returned to her father at the stump and set the largest of the remaining pieces on end. He rolled his shoulders and spit into his hands, and he split the rounds each cleanly with a single stroke of the ax. When all were thus cloven she gathered the half-rounds to her body and stacked them with the others, building in the forest marl a half dozen tapering piles.

All of this they did without speaking, like actors in a pantomime, moving in rote to an old and familiar script.

They parked under a towering elm by the railroad crossing. Here they'd set their wares in the shade, leaning the makeshift sign against the foremost of the wood bundles. When an hour had passed and no cars had stopped, her father lifted the sign and braced it atop the car. After another hour a Packard slowed and a woman with tight, blonde curls lowered the passenger window to ask how much. Ten cents a bundle, he told her. The woman turned to her husband, and they conferred in low tones until the woman smiled tightly and rolled up the window and the car drove on.

Lottie napped through the noon hour, and she woke to the sound of a locomotive. They had sold no wood and had eaten no dinner, and the rumble of the passing train cars echoed in the rumbling of her stomach. Her father watched her from the bumper where he sat with his jackknife poised as she propped herself upright, counting the cars that waited, idling at the crossing gate.

Palmer's truck was the last in the line. It trundled over the rails, and stopped, and reversed in a rack of bluish smoke and a low grinding of gears.

Afternoon! he called across the seat.

Her father nodded.

Had any luck?

Her father leaned and spat. Just got here.

Palmer raised a finger and drove the truck forward, crossing the tracks again and turning into the shade. Her father folded his knife and brushed the shavings from his lap. He rose stiffly, both hands moving to the small of his back.

Fixin to be a scorcher, Palmer pronounced, fanning his face as he approached.

Reckon so, her father replied, frowning at Lottie, who stood silent with her eyes downcast.

How much?

How's that?

For the wood. How much?

Well, her father said, scratching at the back of his neck. This here is hickory wood, all cut and dried. I reckon I'd take fifteen cents a bundle. They's about forty pounds apiece.

Fifteen cents.

Her father spat. Course, seein as how you brung us that

rooster and whatnot, I'd sell you the whole lot for . . . heck, call it seventy-five cents.

Palmer nodded, a hand to his chin. A man making his own calculation.

Tell you what. I got roosters in back and errands I got to run. If you ain't sold it all by three o'clock, how about you haul whatever's left down to Roebuck Lake. You know where that's at?

Down south somewheres.

That's right. I got me a little cabin there. You ask anybody where it's at. You haul it down there, and I'll pay you twenty cents a bundle, cash money, delivered and stacked. How does that sound?

How far you say it was?

No more'n seven or eight miles from where you're standin.

After three.

And I'll tell you what else. I'll throw in a chicken supper for your trouble. Palmer turned to Lottie and winked. You ask me, you couldn't beat a deal like that with a stick.

The lake, when they found it, was a shimmering oxbow overhung by thick stands of winged elm and blue beech whose shadows formed a dark brow over the sun's mirrored eye. There was a hobo camp of Negroes and Indians where the gravel road emerged into a small clearing. Her father set the brake and stepped down to crouch amid the filthy men and the scorched grass and the glitter of broken bottles.

The cabins, when they found them, formed a tight crescent along a stretch of open shoreline. They were squat buildings of log and clay mud chinking, six in number, their stovepipes poked like pea shoots through patchwork roofing tin. Scattered before them were outhouses, chicken coops, a small hog pen, tethered goats, clotheslines bowed with washing, and a motley assortment of sagging tents and boxing-plank shanties, the whole of it littered with logs and boulders and the shells of rusted motorcars through which brambles and saplings grew.

Men like farmers in overalls, and men like miners in stiff dungarees and suspenders, and men like the shadows of men in soiled rags gathered in groups of threes and fives and smoked and nodded and followed the Ford's arrival with wary circumspection. There were women as well, shapeless crones who swept or tended washing, and a lone camp dog lazing in the tree shade, perking its ears at the newcomers' approach.

At the center of their squalid metropolis, a low log parapet girded a circular earthen pit.

I don't see any kids, she whispered to her father.

Me neither.

Look! Yonder's his truck.

It sat in shade between the last of the cabins and the largest of the chicken coops, the latter a teetering rick of pinewood crates. They drove to the far end of the camp and parked beside a derelict Overland jalopy. The bird smell as they alighted was overwhelming.

Clint?

Lottie pinched her nose and hailed the open doorway while her father lingered at the coop to stare openmouthed at the tower of caged roosters that squawked and fluttered behind the grid of wood and wire, their pink heads bobbing like some vast anemone netted and swaying in a tidal current.

Palmer stepped shirtless onto the stoop, his face lathered for shaving, a cigarette dangling from his lips. He rubbed his belly and squinted, gesturing with a razor as he spoke.

You can stack that wood back of the coop! Come on in when you're done! He turned into the doorway and signaled with his head that Lottie follow.

The cabin was a dank and squalid cloister with a table at its center and a bed against the back wall. In one corner was a woodstove fashioned from a sheet-iron boiler, and in the corner opposite was an old chifforobe. The room's only window was a salvaged automobile windscreen that had been rough-bucked and chinked at eye level beside the door. Wooden pegs between door and window held Palmer's hat and some old and mismatched tack leather.

A railroad lantern was on a sideboard, and a zinc bucket, and Palmer returned to these and dipped his razor, the cigarette bobbing as he spoke.

I was afraid for a while you wasn't comin.

We brung the wood.

How much?

A dollar's worth.

Shit.

You got a dollar I hope.

He paused to look at her, and at the open doorway behind her. He pinched out the smoke and spoke in a low voice.

Just between you and me, darlin, I ain't got a plugged nickel. But don't go worryin your pa none, cuz we's a cockfightin tonight, and I'll have it soon enough.

He replaced the smoke and lifted his chin to the razor.

Yes, sir, he said, scraping as he did. A dollar and then some. You just stick around and watch.

There was no sun save the pink memory of sun above the tree-tops. Crickets and bullfrogs struck up their eternal chorus, and the cabin was soon awash in their soothing nightsound. Then lanterns appeared out of the darkness, flowing and converging on the cockpit, where pikes were set and lanterns hung and a halo formed above the parapet.

Muffled voices and drunken laughter burbled in the gloaming, and there appeared the red tracers of cigarettes. Then motor sounds, and rocking headlamps, and the hollow slamming of car doors. Shouted greetings and the pop and tinkle of breaking glass. Black shapes of men gathering like shadow puppets in the ring of golden lamplight.

Dillard Garrett sat and smoked and watched the scene unfold, until Palmer at last emerged from the cabin, holding something aloft.

Didn't know if you was a temperance man, he said, but this right here might be good for what ails you.

That chicken supper would go a long ways to curin what ails me, Garrett said, accepting the bottle and studying its label.

I wouldn't worry about that. They'll be chicken aplenty tonight.

The men at the pit grew silent, and a lone voice spoke from across the distance. Then a tumult rose and subsided, and there was silence again in which they heard the awful shrieking of the birds.

We gettin in on this?

Palmer took the bottle and smiled. Don't worry, cousin. Once these country boys've drunk a little corn and smelled a little blood, then they'll be ready for us. Right now they's just pinchin nickels and watchin out for their old ladies.

They aligned themselves on the stoop three abreast, the bottle moving back and forth between the men with Lottie bracketed by the warmth of their bodies and the medicine smell of the whiskey. Across the clearing, the action at the pit took on a rhythm of commotion and silence and frenzy and silence that grew familiar as the fire reddened and the bottle emptied and the stars above them formed in the night sky.

Showtime, Palmer announced, flinging the empty bottle into the grass.

He carried the railroad lantern from cabin to coop, returning with a cage under each arm and the lamp bail clamped in his teeth, his face underlit and eerily spectral. He spit as Lottie took the lantern, and he passed a cage off to her father.

These two should be bird aplenty for this bunch. Come on.

Lottie led their procession to the cockpit with the lantern raised, and her appearance in their midst was to the sporting men as miraculous as a child Venus risen from the waters of the lake. The men parted and fell silent until Palmer stepped lastly into the lamplight. Then catcalls, some of them friendly, sounded from around the circle.

Howdy, boys! Palmer crowed, raising on his toes. Brung over some culls we all was gonna have for supper! Thought we'd save us the trouble of wringin necks!

An old Mexican in a leather apron stood at the center of the circle, his legs bowed and his shirtsleeves rolled, his flickering shadow a compass rose on ground already feathered and bloody.

Palmer set his cage on the log. I got five dollars says this little bird right here can outfuck and outfight any prairie chicken in this camp!

The crowd murmured. The referee scanned the lamplit faces, returning again to Palmer's and beckoning him forward with a hand. Palmer vaulted the logs and lifted the cage and set it carefully at the center of the circle.

Bullshit! called a voice from the darkness.

Heads turned, and Palmer shaded his eyes.

Is that you, Junior Wells? I hope you brung a cock bigger'n what's in your pants, son.

A plow-ground farmboy stepped through the rain of laughter and into the ring, his straw hat bent and torn, his overalls filled to bursting. He lumbered forward and unsnapped his bib and coaxed forth a lean and lacquered gamecock.

I got a dollar says you're fulla shit, Palmer.

Let's see it, son.

The boy pried a bill from his pocket and surrendered it to the Mexican. Palmer patted his trousers and his shirtfront, then half-turned and called behind him.

Hey, Bonnie? Do me a favor and run get my billfold off the table! You hurry up now!

Heads turned again as Lottie perked and straightened, excusing herself and shouldering her way through the crowd, beyond the lamplight where, alone in the darkness, she stalked the shifting circus of light and shadow until, stumbling onto a low boulder, she boosted herself upward.

The referee called the men together. Palmer squatted and opened the cage, and when he rose again he held his bird like a dowser, outstretched before him with both hands. The boy did likewise, and as the birds grew closer, they swelled and coiled, lunging and squawking like the arcing of twin electrodes.

After the third such presentation, the old man pronounced the odds at even money. He pulled a pad from his apron and licked his pencil and nodded to acknowledge the chorus of shouted wagers.

Lottie watched as Palmer passed the trembling bird to her father. When he returned again to center, he and the farmboy presented their gaffs for the referee's inspection. The old man held them up to the lamplight, squinting like a pawnbroker.

Her father held the bird, inverted now and strangely quiescent, while Palmer fitted the cockspurs. The audience grew still. Then Palmer nodded into the crowd and was handed a fruit jar, from which he took a mouthful.

Palmer carried his bird again to center and hoisted it aloft, as if to offer some final advice or whispered benediction, but instead loosed into its face an aerosol blast of spittle and moonshine. The enraged cock squawked and flapped and nearly tore loose from his grasp.

The old Mexican spoke some final instructions as both handlers squatted. There were shouts from the crowd, and whistles, and a shrill clamor that built and swelled until it swallowed even the frenzied keening of the birds. The old man leaned with one foot forward, nodded left and right, and then dropped his open hand.

The gamecocks met like windblown newsprint, clapping and rising and tumbling downward in the grasp of a phantom whirlwind, feathers flying and blood arcing in crimson pinwheels. The crowd, red-mouthed and savage, was a sea of corded necks and pumping fists. Then, as suddenly as it had begun, the fight was over, with one bird strutting in drunken triumph over the twitching body of its rival.

The crowd howled as the farmboy cursed and turned a circle, lifting a bloodied boot to stomp the head of the fallen. This last affront reanimated the carcass, which rose anew and staggered crazily until it fell again, jerking and scrabbling in a circular parody of its master.

Foul! the boy bellowed, his face darkly flushed. Foul! Y'all saw it! You cheatin son of a bitch!

The boy bent to his boot, and when he rose again, Lottie caught a slender glinting of steel.

The old Mexican backed to the logs and there was swallowed whole by the sporting men, who, at the sight of the knife, had begun overflowing the ramparts. They surged forward to close an inner circle around man and boy, their shadows forming a jagged iris at the center of the pit.

Palmer, to Lottie's surprise, did not retreat. Instead he crouched, crabwalking slowly to clockwise, until, with a feint of his head, he drew the razor neatly from his pocket. At this the crowd whooped and the circle tightened and the farmboy froze in his tracks.

They stood that way, a lamplit David and Goliath sculpted from the shapes and shards of the surrounding rabble. Further words were spoken, but Lottie could not hear them. Then the farmboy, his eyes still locked on Palmer, bent and groped for his bird, lifting it by the legs and slicing the cockspurs free.

The boy spoke a final threat, or epithet, gesturing with his knife. Then he turned and pushed through the crowd, which parted and quieted until, like a thing unplugged, it drifted slowly apart.

Thirty. Forty. Forty-five. They's four dollars and fifty cents here. Lottie spoke with a note of wonder in her voice.

Palmer set plates on the table, heaped and steaming, and the scent of fresh-grilled chicken filled the little cabin. He disappeared through the open doorway, returning again with his shirttail wrapped on the handle of a coffeepot.

Give your pa that dollar, he instructed, setting the pot on the table. That's for the wood, plus ten percent of the rest is thirty-five cents.

Garrett turned from the sideboard. What's that for?

Bein my second.

Second my ass. I didn't do spit.

Second gets ten percent. Palmer licked his fingers. Them all's the rules, cousin. I didn't make 'em.

Lottie was the last to carry her plate to the washbucket. At this they all moved onto the stoop, where the men reclined to belch and pick their teeth, their faces intermittently bathed in the sweep of departing headlamps.

A gentle night breeze rose off the lake, and the smell of fire-smoke drifted from the neighboring shacks. The sound of crickets. The long, pale smudge of the Milky Way. A lone figure, the old Mexican, lingering yet in the cockpit with his head bowed, his shoulders rolling as he swept.

So what do you think?

Think about what?

Palmer gestured. All of this here.

Her father surveyed the emptied clearing. The laboring man, the glowing cabins, the last of the departing taillights.

Seems like a good place to get yourself shanked.

Shit. Palmer leaned and spat. Let me ask you somethin.

Wear yourself out.

How long'd it take you to cut and bundle all that wood today?

I don't know. Hour maybe.

More like three would be my guess. Plus all day to sell it.

Your point bein?

Workin from can to can't, and all for what? A dollar twenty? Them's nigger wages, son.

Honest wages you mean.

The smaller man chuckled. Honest. Tell me another.

I take it you got a better idea.

Palmer struck a match off the porch post and lit another smoke.

You see them gamecocks yonder? He shook the match and pitched it toward the fire. I got thirty birds out there, give or take, plus I got a gal who sells me cockerels at a dollar a head. The water's free, and the feed sets me back around two bits a week for the lot. Now you think about that for a minute.

I'm listenin.

Palmer tipped his head and blew a stream of smoke. Here's my proposition. They's a dozen cockpits within a day's drive of where we're settin, and if I wasn't stuck feedin and workin and doctorin these ones here, I could take maybe three or four birds a day on the road, and I could make maybe five to ten dollars a day average.

If you win, you mean.

Average is what I'm sayin.

Garrett's ash tip glowed and faded. I'm still listenin.

I had me a notion that you and Lottie here might like to mind the roost. Say for a dollar a day, guaranteed. Plus I'd pay you ten percent of the take, plus all the chicken suppers you could eat. You could even train your own birds, startin with that one you already got. And if that ain't enough, you could cut wood or grow truck or do whatever else you take a notion to do on the side. Palmer gestured toward the coop. And that old Willys yonder? It's yours to keep, you get it runnin. He leaned again and spat. I don't claim to be no Rockefeller, but that seems to me a damn sight better'n bustin ass in a tree all day like a goddamn monkey.

Lottie watched her father. He stared into the darkness, his foot tapping, the cigarette growing cold between his fingers.

When the truck arrived at the appointed hour, man and girl were waiting with their camp packed and their prayers said, and any qualms that her father might have felt he masked in a stiff rectitude born of Scripture and self-delusion.

I ain't so sure about this.

He turned to face his daughter. How's that?

What makes you think we can trust him?

What makes you think we can't? He kept his word once, didn't he?

You mean about the wood?

I mean about him takin you to Texas and bringin you back all safe and sound.

She did not answer. She watched the truck as it swung wide on the blacktop, backing toward them in a churning dust cloud.

And besides, her father added, hefting his bedroll. I done prayed on it, and there ain't no more to be said.

They pitched their army surplus tents upwind of the coop. They unloaded the truck and gathered rocks for a firepit and strung a new clothesline. They dug a latrine. They folded their clothes and stowed their tools and sorted their kitchen, and then they rolled their pantlegs to fill earthenware jugs from the lake's grassy shallows, the men from the camp standing and smoking and watching, and none of them offering to help.

After a familiar order was at last imposed on their new surroundings, Lottie sat on the stoop and blew the hair from her face. At the neighboring cabin, a droop-eyed hag in a flour-sack dress labored at her laundry, the clothespins moving rapidly from apron to mouth to sagging line. She paused long enough to scowl in Lottie's direction, her face gaunt and brown against her washing, and she mouthed a silent word.

Whore.

They ate their supper in the cabin, the men taking whiskey with their coffee and talking all the night of roosters.

At bedtime Lottie took her father's arm and helped him down the stoop to his tent, where she untied his shoes and stripped his dirty socks and set them all outside to air. Then she gathered up her bedroll and kicked pebbles in the darkness to make her pallet outside by the firepit.

She lay in her boots and studied the stars, blanketed by the murmur of distant voices and the rustling sounds of the birds in their cages and the courtship song of the crickets. The moon when it rose was cold and white and its reflection on the lake was as a crescent chalked on blackboard. One by one she watched as the houselamps darkened and the cookfires faded, until at last the only lights in camp were the aureate glow of the cabin's window and its trapezoid effigy cocked beyond the dark andirons of her boots.

Merciful Jesus, she whispered to the moon. What have I got us into now?

Then a shape appeared in the window, its dark form lifting her to an elbow. The featureless shadow centered in the lamplight, patient and watching, like something trapped in amber.

A minute passed, or an hour.

And then, as suddenly as it had appeared, the shadow moved off, and the windscreen brightened.

And then all was darkness.

Toward evening of the day following, Lottie prowled the lakefront sedges, running and skipping and tossing feed to the ducks while the ragged camp dog yapped and coiled, charging at her heels. Some hundred yards distant, broom in hand like a lunatic charwoman, her father worked the day's final rooster in the run he'd built behind the Palmer cabin using scrap boards and wood stakes and rusted chicken wire.

Blackbirds rose at the sound of Palmer's horn. There were shouts, and a whoop, and when she looked to the run where her father had been, the cock alone stood beside the abandoned broom.

She found them in the cabin, both men grinning, each holding a glass of amber liquid. On the table between them a pile of greasy bills lay paperweighted by the open whiskey bottle. Palmer was sunburned and sweaty, his jeans filthy and blood-spattered, and he thumbed his hat and leered drunkenly toward the doorway in which girl and dog had appeared.

There she is. Fetch her a glass, Dil.

Now hold on.

Oh, Jesus, don't be such a old lady. Palmer reached to the sideboard and clapped a beveled tumbler beside the bottle, pouring out a thin finger of whiskey.

Here's to grabbin what's yours. Palmer grinned, raising his glass. And the devil take the hindmost.

They clicked glasses and drank, Lottie bracing to stifle the choke and burn. Her father's eyes watching, his look both reproving and surprised.

Run and fetch that bird back to his cage, he snapped. Then go clean out the back of the truck.

There'd been wild talk of driving to town, and of pink champagne and fish eggs, but the inertia of the whiskey had soon taken hold and reduced their ambitions to naught. And so the men sat in the cabin, drinking themselves torpid, while Lottie counted and recounted the day's winnings.

A windstorm arrived with the night. It swept off the lake, flattening the grasses and flagging the trees and sending camp trash cartwheeling through the clearing. It grounded the birds and silenced the crickets, and it buckshot the grill of Palmer's truck. Inside the cabin it whistled in the chinking and moaned in the stovepipe, and when Lottie ventured outside for the coffeepot, she heard the mad flapping of their tents beyond the guttered firelight.

The men had been drinking for several hours by the time Palmer rose from the table and bent to the curtained space below the sideboard. Where the hell is it? he muttered, striking his head as he straightened. Shit!

What's all the commotion? her father demanded, rousing from his stupor.

I been waylaid by my own larder. Palmer rubbed his head as he set a tin on the table. Here you go, Bonnie. I been savin these for just such a occasion.

Bonnie? Who's Bonnie?

Palmer grinned recklessly. Why, Dil, she's a first-class, natural-born cock handler is all she is.

Who is?

Look, Daddy, shortbreads! They're your favorites!

She opened the lid and spread the crinkling paper for her father's inspection.

I'll be damned.

Have one, Daddy.

Tell you what, her father said. These here would go right nice with just a whisker more of that store-bought.

By midnight he was unconscious, and man and girl shared a glance across the table.

You'd best give me a hand with him, Palmer said as he stood.

They scraped back his chair, and as Lottie held her father upright, Palmer squatted and barred his arms across the sleeping man's chest.

Grab his feet, honey.

They carried him, shuffling, to the doorway, then down the stoop and into the maelstrom, the stars at distant anchor their only witness. They sat him down and loosened his tentfly, and they eased him like some prostrate catechumen into a canvas baptismal.

Outside her own tent, with its grommets whistling and its canvas snapping, Palmer lifted Lottie like a new bride.

You can't sleep out here in this! he shouted as he turned her crossways to the wind and, staggering, bore her back to the cabin, and onto the stoop, and thence over the threshold.

Chapter Three

DAMN FOOLS AND SOLDIERS

BY MR. PHARR: When you said there'd been a patch of trouble, what did you mean exactly?

A: Daddy and Clint had a fight. Not a fight, really. They had words, I guess you could say.

Q: What about?

A: I reckon Daddy thought Clint had got fresh with me.

Q: Had he?

A: No, sir.

Q: And as a result of this misunderstanding, did your father threaten the accused?

A: Probably.

BY MR. HARTWELL: Speculation.

BY MR. PHARR: I'll rephrase. Did you hear any threats made by either man as a result of this misunderstanding between your father and the accused?

A: No, sir. I wasn't there when it happened.

Q: When what happened?

BY MR. HARTWELL: If she wasn't there when it happened, then whatever it was that allegedly happened, counsel knows full well he's eliciting hearsay or speculation from the witness.

THE COURT: Henry?

BY MR. PHARR: Not necessarily, Your Honor. For example, the accused might have told her that he'd had words with her father.

THE COURT: Ask her that.

BY MR. PHARR: Did Mr. Palmer ever tell you that he'd had words with your father, or that either man had threatened the other?

A: Yes, sir. Clint said that Daddy had gone to the sheriff, and that he'd had to trace Daddy down and get him drunk so's to calm him down a little.

She woke with a start.

She lay in her clothes on the hard wooden floor with Palmer in the bed above her, his breathing slow and measured. The cabin was dim as yet, a gray light from the windscreen shining through the empty bottle whose shadow fell like an accusing finger across their jumbled boots.

Floorplanks creaked as she rose and tiptoed barefoot to the window. There she pressed one cheek to the cold glass and then the other, a hoarfrost butterfly clouding her vision of the outside world in waiting.

Hinges squealed as she stepped onto the stoop and thence to the corner, from where she saw her father's brogans as they had left them, paired and empty before his still-fastened tent-flap.

Water splashed behind her, and she wheeled to the sound. From the porch of the next cabin, the hag-woman shook her pail, her droop eye glowing dull and malignant in the low light of sunrise. She leaned and spat, and wiped her mouth, and turned back to her doorway.

Lottie returned from the lake with her old clothes in a bundle. By now four men were at the rusted Overland, arranged like surgeons on tiptoes, leaning over the patient and reaching with blackened arms to point and poke and stanch some oily hemorrhage. Her father drew a clean rag from his pocket.

She set the clothes with the others to be washed and with her fingers ran the wet knots from her hair. Of all the cabins, Palmer's alone remained dark and still despite the hour. She gathered her hair and tied it back, then she set the soap and the scrub brush in her pail.

I'm doin the washin! she called to her father's back, and he raised his rag in reply as, from the fender opposite, a face lifted into sunlight and grinned, and she saw in the grinning a fleeting flash of gold.

The day was bright and still, and the only sounds where she stood on the bank were the echoing calls of the ducks and the plash and splatter of her own enterprise. She dunked and scrubbed and dunked again each of the garments, wringing them out to hang on the sagging lakeside branches until she herself was tented and moved within them like a bedouin.

Her jeans lay neatly folded with her boots nearby and her legs were bare and blotched by the serial ablutions of warming sun and frigid water. The hymn she hummed was the only tune she really knew, the fragmented score to a fading memory of a whitewashed church and hard oak pews and the talcum hand of a mother whose golden cross hung now slapping lightly at the hollow of her own throat. *When I survey the wondrous cross on which the Prince of glory died, my richest gain I count but loss, and pour contempt on all my pride.*

And so she never heard the footsteps.

The hand that grabbed her was calloused and hard, and it yanked her backward and spun her roughly to the ground.

Daddy, don't! Daddy!

But the eyes she saw through the pulsing of her blood were not her father's eyes, or the voice her father's voice.

You dirty little mink, the man breathed softly, his face streaked and flushed. He fumbled at the knot that was his belt buckle, and as his pants fell away, his long, pink cock bobbed free.

I'll scream, she whispered, backing in the dirt. I swear I will.

The gold tooth glinted. Go ahead. I'll bet your daddy'd like to hear all about you and that half-pint convict ruttin like spring goats behind his back. You go ahead and call him over here so's I can tell him all about it.

He dropped to his knees grabbing at her ankles. She kicked and tried to rise, but he bulldogged her and dragged her twisting onto her stomach, tearing the thin, white panties loose from her clawing fingers.

Don't. Please.

Don't, please, he sneered, spreading her legs.

She tried to scream but gagged instead on a bitter loam of earth and snot as he gripped her neck and pressed her face into the dirt.

The report of the pistol cracked like a whip, echoing across the lake. The rough hands fell away, and Lottie scrambled and twisted, and only then saw Palmer holding a level bead on the man's back.

You want a new asshole, or you want I should plug the one you already got?

The man lifted both hands slowly. Hold on, neighbor. I didn't mean no harm. We was just havin a little fun is all. Ain't that right, miss?

The crash of footfalls in the woods halted the arc of the pistol Palmer had raised over the kneeling man's head. He glanced over his shoulder, then to Lottie, where she lay wet and dirty and cowering.

You'd best put them drawers back on, he said calmly.

The men, when they arrived, were three in number, her father at the lead. They drew up short in comic unison. Then her father made a wounded sound that was part shout and part whimper, and he threw himself flailing onto the kneeling man's back, his fists windmilling into flesh and bone and earth.

Oww! Shit! Help! The man curled himself tightly, warding off blows with his arms.

The other men watched as her father pounded the man head and ribs and head again until both his fists were bloody and both his arms were too tired to lift. When he slumped to all fours, spent by his efforts, the groaning man rose to a like position, and any discernible difference between victor and vanquished was lost in the shared gasping of breath and the pooling of blood and tears.

Fucking. Bastard.

I didn't. It was him. The man gestured with his bloodied face. Ask the wife. She saw them. Ask her.

When Garrett stood again, Palmer backed a step, reaiming his pistol. I ain't the one with my pants round my ankles.

Garrett, still heaving, looked first to the gun and then to the other men. He unbuckled his belt and drew it from its loops and doubled it in his bloody fist. He brushed past the others and raised the belt high and brought it down with a crack across the cowering girl's legs.

No, Daddy! No!

Again, again, again. Lottie kicked and cried, gouging tracks in the dirt as she backed, balling herself under a tree. Her father stepped forward and raised the belt again.

All the men jumped at the second crack of the pistol.

That's enough, Palmer said evenly. Put it down.

Garrett lowered his arm.

Lucile, you grab your pants and get. Go to the cabin and lock the door.

Lottie scrambled to her feet and ran careening past the leering men and the raking branches and the patchwork curtain of clothes. She gathered up her pants and boots and she kept on running, her heart pounding and her ears ringing, past the chicken coop, past the tents and the truck, past the old car, all the time listening for the sound of the third gunshot that never came.

Inside the cabin, sprawled on the bed, she finally wept.

Her tears came at first in great gulps of pain and anger, but soon softened to a torrent of bitter shame, until, at last, clutching at the blankets, she convulsed soundlessly at the injustice of a world in which she herself was but a thing adrift, like some speck of flotsam on the windblown lake that rose or sank at the whim of forces beyond human sense or reckoning.

The first sounds she heard were angry voices rising from the woods. Next came the slam of a car door and the sound of an engine sputtering and catching and of gears rasping as the old Overland flivver limped from camp like a man on tender feet. Then, at last, a hard rap at the door.

She looked to the windscreen, where Palmer's face was cupped to the glass.

Figures he'd get that thing runnin now, he said without preamble, brushing past her in the doorway. He crossed to the sideboard and wrapped the gun in a dish towel and carried it to the chifforobe, where he knelt and with his pocketknife levered up a floorboard.

Where's he goin? she asked, smearing her face with a sleeve.

To find him a shotgun, would be my guess.

Palmer stood and looked about. He swept some coins from the table. He crossed to the door and lifted his hat from the peg.

Where are you goin?

I got a notion he's headed for the sheriff, Palmer said, setting his hat. Has he got any gas in that thing?

I think so.

Shit.

He paused, his fingers drumming the doorframe.

Okay, here's what's what. You lock this door and don't let nobody inside, understand? I'll try and find him and talk some sense to him. And if the law comes by, you ain't never seen no gun, you got that?

She nodded. He studied her face before turning, then stopped again on the threshold.

Just remember one thing, he told her. Only damn fools and soldiers stick their necks out for nothin.

★   ★   ★

She had paced at first, and then, when she'd tired of pacing, she'd lain in bed and cried again, and when she'd finally slept, it was a fitful sleep of terrors vaguely imagined.

When she woke, it was to blades of moted sunlight slicing through the crumbled chinking of the cabin. She'd sat up blinking, taking in the half-light. Then she stood and paced again, until, tired of pacing, she busied herself by making the bed and sweeping the floor, taking care to avoid the windscreen or any shadow she might make upon it.

Now she sat at last in full darkness and ate the stale shortbreads with the last of the tepid house water, listening to the sounds of the men as they gathered at the cockpit.

When she'd tilted the tin and shaken the last crumbs into her mouth, she fumbled for the washbucket below the sideboard and set it on the floor. She lowered her pants and squatted and, in the ringing darkness, felt her leg welts tighten, tracing their swollen outlines with her fingertips.

You didn't have no cause, she whispered to the darkness.

She leaned at the window and watched the backlit men at the cockpit shifting and swaying like pagan supplicants at some red and heretic mass. As though in the blood of the contest, some greater truth might be divined. As though truth itself were the thing exalted, and blood but its base and corporeal attendant.

She didn't realize she had dozed again until she was startled awake by a crashing sound at the door. Palmer cursed and stumbled heavily into the room, the bucket clanging against the chairleg where she sat.

Holy shit!

Are you all right?

Light the goddamn lamp.

He hung unsteadily by the doorway as she felt for the matchbox and lifted the blackened chimney, and the walls when they appeared out of darkness were to her in her lingering somnolence as the ribs of the whale, and she inside was as Jonah cast out and saved and waiting to learn her fate.

Where is he?

Palmer removed his hat and tossed it toward the pegs, from which it caromed and wobbled, circling back to where he stood. He stepped over the hat and lifted a chair and straddled it backward, his chin resting on his arms and his arms resting on the hard ladderback.

It went just like I thought, he told her. He run straight to the sheriff, and he made 'em call down to the sheriff at Sulphur Springs. What all did you tell him, anyways?

Nothin, I swear.

Palmer leaned and spat on the floorboards. That stiff-necked son of a bitch done shat in every nest I got.

What happened?

Nothin happened. I told Cross he was a crazy drunk is all. Then I tracked him into town and by God got him drunk. I told him he was all wrong about you and me, and that ol' dead-eye was a born troublemaker who could spin a yarn longer'n a whore's life story, which is the God's own truth.

Did he believe you?

He smiled wetly. Did he believe me? Come here, darlin.

He tilted in his seat and kissed her lightly on the forehead.

What matters now is that we be careful till I get this sorted.

Sorted how?

He stood and turned the chair and carried his hat to the pegs.

You'd better scat. Your pa's in his tent, and you'd best be in yours when he wakes up.

But—

But nothin. Go on.

He held the door and waited. Outside, a pale fluorescence bathed the empty clearing.

Lottie rose, righting the pail as she passed and pausing beside him where he stood in the open doorway. The outside air was cool and fresh, and a lock on Palmer's forehead twitched in the gentle night breeze.

Thank you, she told him. If you hadn't of come along—

Forget it. He brushed her cheek with his fingers. Oh, but there is one thing. You get a chance tomorrow, could you take a mop to this place? I think a cat done pissed itself in here while we was out.

Lottie's tent sagged under the twin burdens of morning dew and a cold, gnawing dread. The risen sun burnished the thin scrim of canvas that shielded her, like the cloak of Elijah, from the judging eyes of the camp. Inside, her body rigid, she lay breathing the mildewed canvas and listening to the morning calls of roosters and the murmur of distant voices. Then a shadow passed across the tent wall, and she heard the clack of stacking kindling.

When she crawled forth into daylight, she found her father hunched before the cookfire. Beyond his crouching form, the camp was awake and in motion. He lifted his head.

Coffee? He lifted a cup for her approval.

She smoothed her hair and joined him on the log, feeling the prying eyes on her back.

Yes, sir. Thank you.

They sat looking into the half-distance, at the Overland jalopy and at the slumbering lake beyond it, barred yet in the muted blues and grays of morning light and shadow.

I was thinkin we'd take us a little walk this mornin, her father said. Just you and me. He passed her the cup by the rim. Careful, she's hot.

She glanced toward Palmer's cabin. It alone remained dark.

I hear they's a trail runs clear around the lake. I never been to the other side, have you?

No, sir.

Well, there you go then. I'd call that a plan.

They followed the narrow path through alternations of dark forest and bright clearings, catching and losing sight of the lake. Her father carried his Bible with him, first in his hand and then, farther along, snugged in the belt of his trousers.

There were bees in the meadows, and butterflies, and the fragrant scents of mallow and sweet gum adrift on the morning air. At a glade on the northern shoreline her father stopped and stooped to gather stones, which he flung sidearm onto the water, watching their skip and splash with a stern demeanor alien to the endeavor.

Lottie sat, watching as he paused and weighted the stones in his hand.

I'm gonna ask you just the one time.

Sir?

He turned to face her.

Did you lay with that man?

She looked away.

I ast you a question.

No, sir.

Do you swear it?

Yes, sir.

Say it.

I swear. I ain't never done such a thing in my life.

He turned again to the lake. He tossed another stone and watched its coruscating ripples spread and intersect. He wiped his hands on his jeans and took a seat in the grass beside her.

Let's you and me pray together.

He rolled onto his knees, and she followed his example. He drew the Bible from his waistband and opened it to a page that he'd flagged. He set the book on the ground beside him. Then he unlooped his belt and doubled it and set it beside the book.

They were face-to-face then in the open meadow under the open sky and fully revealed to God in his terrible omnipotence. Her father's eyes closed, his hands paired before him. Lottie posed in like fashion, save that her eyes were asquint, and that she was watching him carefully. And that she had already started to tremble.

Thus sayeth the Lord God, he began, glancing askance at the page. Because you poured out your lust and revealed your nakedness in your harlotry with your lovers and abominable idols, and because you sacrificed the lifeblood of your children to them, I will now gather together all your lovers whom you tried to please, whether you loved them or loved them not; I will gather them against you from all sides and expose you naked for them to see. I will inflict on you the sentence of adulteresses; I will wreak fury and jealousy upon you. I will hand you over to them to tear down your platform and demolish your dais; they shall strip you of your garments and take away your splendid ornaments, leaving you stark naked. They shall lead an assembly against you to stone you and hack you with their swords. They shall burn your apartments with fire and inflict punishments on you while many women look on. Thus I will put an end to your harlotry.

He licked his lips and closed his eyes again. Dear Lord, he continued, protect this innocent child from the wickedness of men that she not be made to suffer the punishments of the flesh that are your commandment. And please, Lord, give me the strength to do thine will should she fail to heed the word of God and stray from the path of the righteous, amen.

He eased back onto his heels. His eyes opened.

You got anythin you'd like to add?

No, sir.

You sure about that?

Yes, sir.

He nodded. He looked to the water for a long time, then back again to the girl.

Lucile, I know you had your period already. You talked to Miz Upchurch about that.

Her face flushed.

You need to understand that once a girl gets to a certain age, then boys commence to take notice. Men too. Thinking revelry a delight, they are stain and defilement as they share your feasts in a spirit of seduction. Constantly on the lookout for a woman, theirs is a never-ending search for sin. He sniffed. That there's from Peter, Second Epistle.

Yes, sir.

Now a woman who couples with a man such as that commits the sin of adultery. You understand that, don't you?

She nodded.

I'm talkin to you.

Yes, sir.

Good, he said. That's real good. He gathered up his things. I'm glad we had this little talk.

What about that man?

What about him?

Ain't you gonna do nothin?

What do you expect me to do?

I don't know. Call the law.

The law? Let me tell you the law. Men are men, and any girl runs around half-naked like a goddamn whore gets exactly what she deserves. That there is God's law.

Palmer was late in returning that evening, and after supper the two men sat outside for a long time, their faces coppered by the fire, their voices quieting whenever Lottie passed. Come bedtime her father read aloud to her from Psalms, and as she lay awake, she watched his solitary fireshadow on the canvas tent wall as he sat and smoked and stared off at the cabin, smoking and staring until shadow and darkness became one.

The next day at breakfast, her father wiped his mouth and stood up from the fire and announced it was time to pack.

Pack for what?

Pack for Texas.

Texas?

That's right, he said, bending and scraping the last of his plate onto hers.

What all's in Texas?

Work, for one thing. Me and Clint, we got ourselves what you might call a business opportunity. Anyways, the question ain't what's in Texas, but what's not. He nodded toward the ragged men in the distance, laughing and passing a jar. This lot here for instance.

What about the roosters?

I got my share of burdens in this life, Lucile, but Clint Palmer's roosters ain't one of 'em.

They spent the morning disassembling their tents and bundling their tools and clothes and loading it all back into the truck. A few men from the camp drifted over to shake her father's hand. Palmer, once he'd emerged from his cabin, led one of the men to the coop with a hand on his shoulder.

When the truck was fully loaded, Palmer reappeared from the cabin with a canvas bedroll and his valise, both of which he tossed through the passenger window.

Go slow, her father told him. And keep an eye out behind.

Palmer locked the cabin door and pocketed the key, pausing on the stoop for a final look at the camp and its people and the shaded lake beyond. The truck started with a bluish cloud and a stannic rasping of gears. Father and daughter followed in the Overland, which shuddered and backfired a parting shot at the ramshackle habitants of Roebuck Lake, Oklahoma.

Men raised a hand, or a jar, and the barking camp dog scurried from truck to car. On her porch, the droop-eyed sibyl leaned on her broom, nodding at their passing.

They arrived in Peerless with the dusk to dry lightning and the low rumble of distant thunder. They parked before a two-story house, where a man in a straw hat rose heavily from the porch swing.

Introductions were made. The man, whose name was Steen, wore suspenders and spectator shoes. He mopped his face with an oversize kerchief and led them all on a tour of the empty rental, upstairs and down, noting radiators and closets and demonstrating the workings of the furnace and the electric icebox.

There were three bedrooms in all, and each smelled more strongly of paint. When at last they'd returned to the entry, Steen tousled Lottie's hair and surrendered the housekeys to Palmer, receiving in return some folded bills that Steen counted out twice before smiling and doffing his hat.

Home sweet home, Palmer said as the door closed. He moved to the empty living room, where the floor was dark and polished, the baseboards newly gleaming. There was a ceiling fan with a pull chain, and fireplace tools in an iron caddy, and a neat pinewood bundle on the freshly swept hearth.

Lottie turned a circle, her mouth agape.

Is this all for us?

Get used to it, sister. Palmer removed his hat and set it on her head. This here is just the beginning.

Lottie woke to the ticking of the radiator.

She rose from her bedroll and crossed to the window, the hardwood cold and creaking underfoot. The view was onto an elm tree, with a grass lawn beyond it freckled with spring flowers, the greens and yellows dazzling in the clear light of morning. A fence divided the lawn from another lawn beyond, which climbed to a white clapboard house on whose porch two men stood in close conversation. The smaller man, she realized, was Palmer.

There were sounds from the kitchen, and when she'd descended the stairs on stocking feet, she found her father at the breakfast counter lifting groceries from a box. The lights were on and the stove was lit, and the familiar odors of woodsmoke and coffee masked the lingering paint smell.

There you are. Thought we was gonna have to send a posse.

She rubbed her eyeball with a fist.

Are you hungry?

Yes, sir.

Palmer's voice echoed in the front room. Hey! Hows about a hand out here?

Lottie found him straddling the threshold with a stool under each arm, the screen door propped with a foot.

Take one, he told her, and when she reached for the stool, he kissed her quickly on the lips.

Don't! She glanced toward the kitchen. He's like to kill us both.

Palmer stood the stools by the kitchen counter and went to rummage the cookware, returning with their iron skillet.

Ever had huevos rancheros?

Way what?

Never mind. He rubbed his hands together. Sit yourself down and watch a Texan at work.

He greased the cold skillet with his fingers, then cracked a half dozen farm eggs into the pan.

My whole time I was away, he said over the rising sizzle, this right here is what I missed the most.

Was you in the army?

Honey, I was the scourge of Fort Leavenworth. He winked at her father behind her. They wanted me so bad, they wouldn't let me go.

He chose a jar from the box and opened it and poured a thick crimson liquid into the scramble. The pan hissed and sputtered, the pungent aromas of onion and fried tomatoes filling the room.

What all did he say? her father asked over the top of Lottie's head.

No problema.

What did who say?

Oscar's his name, Palmer said without turning.

Me and Clint, we got some things that need doin. Might take us all day. Man lives next door says he'll keep a eye on you till we get back.

I don't need no babysitter.

That's good, Palmer said over the sound of his cooking, cuz Oscar ain't no babysitter. He's a artist, for your information, and he'll pay you two bits cash money if you'll help him with a sign needs paintin.

He will?

Humming now, Palmer lifted and shook the pan, spooning the runny eggs onto plates. Tell me if this don't beat your hoecake.

Lottie wrinkled her nose, probing the plate with her fork. What all will you be doin while I'm next door?

Don't you worry about us, darlin. Palmer carried the skillet to the sink. Your daddy and me, we'll be out in the great state of Texas, makin our fortunes.

Oscar Akard wore white cotton overalls and paint-spattered shoes, one of which he'd wrapped with electrical tape that had come unstuck and trailed behind him like a fuse. Lean and unshaven, he was a tall man with deep-set eyes and an Adam's apple that moved like a trombone slide whenever he spoke, which to Lottie's reckoning wasn't very often.

Man and girl stood on the shade side of the house, where paint-speckled sawhorses braced a huge rectangle of sheet metal screwed to a thin wooden backing. The face of the sign shone a high-gloss white, and a trio of open paint cans weighted the canvas drop cloth on which they stood.

You ever painted before?

No, sir.

Are you prone to clumsiness?

Not so's I ever noticed.

The man regarded the whiteness before him in the way that the God of Genesis must have studied the void, a hand to his chin, his head tilting this way and that.

He snapped his fingers. We'll start with black. Thinnest brush.

Lottie bent to the turpentine can, inspecting each of the brush heads in turn. She showed him her selection, and he nodded. She handed the brush to him along with the hinged wooden implement he called his maulstick. Then she proffered the paint can, as he had shown her, held in her palm by the bottom.

Here we go. Keep close but don't get underfoot.

He dipped the brush tip, and with one hand holding the maulstick he crossed his wrists and etched a pinstripe border. The line he drew was thin and even and straight as a string pulled taut.

Stay with me now.

He stork-walked the stick and dipped again, extending his line to the bottom of the sign and rounding it off at the corner.

Hmmm, he said to himself.

Lottie followed like a mendicant as the tall man dipped and dabbed, shuffled and dipped, until at last he'd circumnavigated the sign and closed the loop in a smooth and flawless junction. He raised the brush and backed a step to better attend his handiwork.

I'd say you sure know what you're doin, Lottie said after a pause.

He glanced at the girl. It ain't brain surgery, but I thank you all the same.

I couldn't do such as that in a hundred years.

How do you know?

Sir?

He gestured with the brush. If you've never tried it, how do you know you can't?

I just do, that's all.

The man nodded. It's not your fault, he said, wiping the brush tip on his bib. It's a curse of the female psyche.

Sir?

He bent to the turpentine. I don't claim to have studied the question, but it seems to me that if you show something new to a boy and a girl both, it's the boy that wants to take it apart and put it back together again, and it's the girl that wants to sit and watch him do it. Now why do you suppose that is?

I don't rightly know.

He straightened again and stood beside her. Neither do I.

They studied the sign together, as though in its newly bordered symmetry some answer might be found.

Maybe it weren't broke in the first place?

He eyed her again.

How old did you say you were?

Thirteen.

Thirteen. I believe I've got shoes older than that.

I'd say that's the truth, she replied, and he followed her eyes to the end of his pantleg.

Lucile, is it?

Yes, sir.

That fella left with Clint Palmer, he's your pa?

Yes, sir.

He harrumphed.

They's gone out to the Palmer place on business. I been there once myself to meet his sister and her daughter Johnny Rae, only we missed 'em when they was out ridin and campin somewheres by some river. So we done chores instead and rode them horses out there that wasn't saddle-broke yet.

The man said nothing.

Sir?

The man looked to the sign and back again.

Lucile, let me tell you something. A word to the wise, as it were. I've known Clint Palmer and his kin for longer than I'd care to recall, and I can tell you two things you'd best keep in mind. The first is, Clint's sister Gennie was my wife, and his other sister, Ruby, lives clear out to Little Rock, and ain't neither one of 'em got a daughter named Johnny Rae. The second thing is, that boy Clint is crazier than a shithouse mouse, you'll pardon my French. Not that your daddy's business is any of my business, but if you want some friendly advice from a old paint dabber, I'd say you'd best stick close to your pa, and whatever you do, you'd best watch your backside around that half-pint son of a bitch.

At five o'clock Lottie returned to the still and empty house. She washed her hands at the kitchen tap and dried them on her pants.

She sorted through the tumbled clothes pile, and with arms and chin she carried those that were hers upstairs to the room in which she'd slept. There she found that her bedroll had been tidied, and that a square shape now bulged from under her blanket.

The package was wrapped in newsprint and tied with a new pink satin ribbon. She crossed to the door and closed it, then sat with the gift in her lap, smoothing the hair behind her ears. She loosened the bow and examined the ribbon and folded it and laid it carefully beside her.

Inside the paper was the dented shortbread tin, and inside the tin was another sheet of newsprint, balled and nearly weightless. She hefted it and felt within the paper something small and hard between her fingers that she somehow knew, even before she'd unwrapped it and studied it and held it to the light, was a gold human tooth.

Chapter Four

YOU MIGHT RUN BY HIM

THE COURT: Your witness, counsel.

BY MR. HARTWELL: Miss Garrett, isn't it true that you left Texas with Mr. Palmer of your own accord?

A: Sir?

Q: He didn't force you to go with him, did he? He didn't, say, drag you into the car by your hair or put a gun to your head?

A: He told me we was—

BY MR. HARTWELL: Move to strike, Your Honor.

THE COURT: Miss Garrett, just answer counsel's questions yes or no.

A: I'm sorry. What was the question?

Q: You understood the questions all right when Mr. Pharr was asking them.

BY MR. PHARR: Objection.

THE COURT: That's enough, L.D. Just ask your question.

BY MR. HARTWELL: When you left Peerless with Clint Palmer in May of last year, you did so voluntarily and with no physical coercion on his part. Isn't that true?

Lottie had dozed where she lay, and now she scrambled to her feet at the sound of the closing door. The downstairs voices were loud and querulous, and she knew before she saw them that both men had been drinking.

Lottie? her father's voice rang in the stairwell.

Coming!

She pulled the chain stub in the little bathroom and examined herself by the glare of the swinging bulb, touching her hair and straightening the long, pink ribbon that trailed at the back of her neck.

She found them in the kitchen, her father at the sink with the water running and Palmer at the counter, grinning and leaning on an elbow. Her father had his knife in one hand and the darkly velvet ears of a jackrabbit in the other.

Palmer's eyes crinkled at the sight of the ribbon. He bared his teeth like a beaver.

Hope you're partial to hare, he said.

Her father turned. There you are. Did you get lunch?

Yessir. Mr. Akard made us deviled eggs.

Did he pay you that quarter he promised?

She reached into her pocket and produced the coin for inspection. Her father grunted and returned his attention to the sink.

Texaco Motor Oil, she told them, easing onto a barstool. Drain, Fill and Listen. That's the sign we done.

Why, that's downright poetical, ain't it, Dil? And sound advice to boot.

I got to color in the Texaco star. Mr. Akard said I got po-tential.

You hear that, Dil? This girl's got po-tential.

Her father either ignored this or missed it over the hiss and scrape of the skinning.

What all did you do today? she asked them both.

Her father snorted. Palmer cocked his hat as he straightened.

Groundwork is what we done. He tapped his forehead with a finger. Plan-makin before risk-takin. Measure twice and cut once, my daddy always says. Ain't that right, Dil?

Her father half-turned at the sink. Your old man never cut nothin in his life, less it was the cheese. And what I'm wonderin now is how come we give up a moneymakin deal to throw in with that windy old coon.

Palmer shook his head. Piss and vinegar. That's ol' H.P.

Hot air and horse flop is more like it.

Believe me, cousin. When the chips are down, he'll do to ride the river with.

River my ass.

Law me alive. Ain't you all of a sudden the doubtin Thomas.

Her father turned again, pointing the bloody knifeblade. I'll thank you not to blaspheme in front of my daughter.

The mirth drained from the smaller man's face. And I'll thank you to watch where you're pointin that pig-sticker, friend.

After the plates were dried and stowed, Palmer crossed to the sink and lifted the curtain.

Moon's up, he announced. We's already late.

Where we goin?

Not we, darlin. Just me and your pa.

She looked to her father and back again. How come I'm always the one gets left?

Don't worry your pretty head. We'll be back quicker'n you can say Jack Robinson.

Back from where? Why can't I come?

You keep it up and you'll find out why, her father said as he shrugged into his mackinaw.

She followed them to the door, where her father worked and reworked the latch.

Now listen to me. Don't open this door for nobody till we get back, understand?

That's right, Palmer said. There's been reports of some desperate characters newly arrived in the neighborhood.

Yes, sir, she told her father.

All right then. Her father held the door for Palmer, who winked as he crossed over the threshold. When the door had closed behind them, she heard a key in the lock.

Lottie woke at dawn. She rose and stretched and padded to the bathroom, the warmth of her footprints evanescing on the cold wooden floorboards. She peed and washed her face and straightened her ribbon in the mirror. On her way back to her bedroll, she paused again at the window.

The Akard house was still as yet, its windows clad in the golden glow of sunrise. Songbirds clustered in the elm tree, jostling and flitting, and a rooster cawed somewhere close at hand. She smiled at the sound.

She dressed quickly and hurried down the stairs, expecting voices and the sounds and smells of breakfast, but found herself alone in the empty kitchen.

She listened for movement elsewhere in the house.

She filled the coffeepot and fed crumpled newsprint and pine tinder into the stovebox. She tried to light the match as Palmer did, but the match tip chipped beneath her nail and she yelped as it flared, sucking at her thumb.

She remounted the stairs, and she crept to her father's bedroom, rapping lightly at the door.

Daddy?

The cut-glass knob was cold to her touch. The door creaked as it opened, revealing her father's bedding rolled and bundled in a corner. Beside the bedroll was his Bible, and beside the Bible were his folded clothes and his few scattered toiletries.

She listened. The radiator ticked.

Returning downstairs, she paused outside Palmer's door, which she opened without knocking. Inside she found his empty bedroll splayed upon the floor.

Only then, as she passed the hallway bathroom for the second time, did she notice the leather valise where it rested on the toilet seat. She stopped, holding her breath and listening.

Inside the satchel were Palmer's shaving things, his brush and razor and a soap bar in a lidded tin. There was a screwdriver and a pliers, a small scissors and a nail file, a toothbrush and a hair comb, two decks of playing cards, a tin of Dr. Wernet's dental powder, a box of Colt Firearms Company .45 ammunition, and an oval tin of Dixie Peach pomade. She removed these items each in turn and examined them and placed them in a neat row along the sink.

There was no pistol.

Beneath the things that she'd removed, flat and contoured to the satchel bottom, were papers. State of Texas Department of Highways Motor Vehicle Registration. Certificate of Live Birth, frayed and yellowed. United States Army Notice of Induction to

Military Service. Enlistment Record and Report of Separation (Dishonorable Discharge). Her lips moved with the words as she paged through each of the documents.

She was careful to replace the papers as she'd found them, followed by the tools and the toiletries, then the shaving kit. Lastly she reached for the ammunition, spying as she did her face in the medicine cabinet.

What the hell?

She shrieked at Palmer's reflection, the box exploding where it landed, man and girl jigging in tandem at the clattering of cartridges.

I'm sorry! I'm sorry!

She fell to her knees, sweeping and gathering the hard brass cylinders in handfuls from around his boots, until his boots stepped back and pivoted and strode on down the hallway.

She sat for a long time on the cold, hard tile, until the sound of frying eggs lifted her slowly, cautiously, to her feet. She edged down the hallway to the kitchen, where cups and plates and forks were neatly paired on the laminate counter.

Coffee's gettin cold, he said quietly as she eased onto a stool. How do you like your scramble?

I don't care.

He lifted the skillet and shook it and spooned the steaming eggs onto the plates.

Your pa and me bunked at the old man's place. Palmer replaced the skillet and refilled his coffee, joining her on the other side of the counter. In case you was wonderin.

He ate without appetite, his fork moving the eggs like pewter soldiers on a paper battlefield. He was red-eyed and unshaven, and he appeared not to have slept. His fork stopped.

What?

I wasn't snoopin, she told him.

He returned to his food, reaching a hand and placing it on her knee.

It reeked of gasoline.

H. P. Palmer was a superannuated facsimile of his son, cord-thin and clear-eyed, his aquiline face fissured and deeply tanned. But as the scion's hair was dark and full, so the forebear's stood scarce and whitish, capturing the sunlight and wreathing his leathery pate in a gossamer halo.

Lottie watched both men from the parlor window. They stood at a distance in the field half-furrowed, their conversation animated, their heads turning toward the house and then, in unison, toward the sound of an approaching motorcar.

The older Buick trundled past the listing barn and out into the field, slicing like an errant plowshare through the newly ordered furrows.

The driver, when he alighted, although backlit by a sun stained umber in the settling car dust, was clearly not her father. Now the three men stood together.

A barn cat, gaunt and mottled, buttered itself on her pantleg.

What about you, pussy? Lottie lifted the purring animal. Have you seen my pa anywheres about?

Out beyond the window, the conference had ended. The old man placed a hand on the shoulder of the new arrival, then glanced toward the house as he leaned and spat. He returned to the team still hitched and slumbering in its traces. Palmer removed something from his pocket and handed it to the other man, then he started toward the house.

At the sound of the doorspring, the cat jumped free. Palmer hawed and kicked, but the cat dodged and threaded the opening behind him.

Who all's that? Lottie asked him.

He joined her at the window. Oh, that's just Buddy. Him and me is gonna help the old man for a spell. Then after supper all of us is gonna take a little drive.

Drive to where?

Heck, if I told you that, then it wouldn't be no surprise.

What about my pa?

The Buick was moving again, cutting a loop back toward the barn.

I wouldn't worry none about your pa. You and me'll see him soon enough.

I been to Wilburton, the old man said. He pushed his plate aside and with the bread knife carved a slice from the twisted plug he'd drawn from a shirtfront pocket. He worked the chaw with a focused effort, then he reached for a can on the sideboard.

Helped run cattle from Panola to Fort Smith, back in '85 or thereabouts. He leaned and spat, lifting his watery eyes across the table to where the girl sat watching. Before these here bread-snappers was born.

Here it comes, Buddy said.

Course, there was grass in them days. Not like today. The old man set the can on the table and leaned back on his chairlegs, hoisting his galluses with his thumbs. Yes, sir. Stirrup-high grass clear out to the Arkansas, and that's a fact. And not so many damn fences.

Palmer and Buddy shared a look across the table as the old man repositioned his chaw.

They was Indians too, he continued, his eyes drifting to the kitchen window and beyond the darkness there to the open prairies of his youth. And not the fall-down drunks and idlers you see hereabouts today. I'm talkin prideful Indians on horseback, workin cattle and makin a livin with their hands. He shook his head sadly. No, sir, not like these 'uns nowadays.

By gosh, that explains it, Buddy said.

The old man's eyes narrowed. Explains what?

How it come you got yourself scalped like that.

Palmer lurched forward, squirting coffee through his nose. Buddy roared as Palmer sputtered and coughed, and both men banged the table with their palms, rattling plates and jumping silver.

The old man rose, imperious.

You see, miss? This here is the thanks I get for raisin these two niggers like they was my own.

They rode in the Buick three abreast, with Palmer driving and Buddy shotgun and Lottie angled on the seat between them, her feet paired primly on the one side of the gearshift. Buddy Virgil resembled his stepbrother only in profile, the contours of which Lottie considered in stolen glances by the light of passing cars. Younger certainly, and taller. But clearly not as handsome.

Buddy, for his part, was oblivious to her appraisal, his head nodding with the bounce of the roadway and his gaze shifting at intervals to the porch lights passing like revenants on the old country road.

Up ahead, floating eyes shone small in the roadway, and Palmer swerved the car to meet them, laughing at the thump-thump under the Buick's wheels.

I ever tell you about the time I house-sat for old man Law-rence? Buddy leaned forward to address Palmer. Had him a tom-cat, big as a damn raccoon. I was to let him in the house at night and feed him and then let him out again in the mornin. Well, it was about the third day I come home and found the cat all squashed in the road out front of the house. Only it was just his back half got squashed; up front he was still alive and squalin and pawin at the road.

That's pitiful.

Pitiful is what it was. So I look around and find me a big ol' rock, see? Figure if I can catch him clean at the neck, I'll put 'im out of his misery. And that's what I done, bam! Only the dumb-ass cat starts a'twitchin and a'scrabblin all over the road, and with me chasin after him with the damn rock. Well, sir, after five or six good thumps, that cat is finally still. Only now I'm all heavin and spattered, and I got this bloody rock raised up over my head with both hands to give it one more go. And just then, I look up and see a bunch of pickaninnies comin my way, maybe five of 'em afoot, and not a one more'n four feet tall.

Shit.

So these little niggers, they all freeze and bunch together like spooked calves, and I'm standin there with that bloody rock. And then the biggest of 'em, he can't be but ten years old, he sidles up to me with eyes like chicken eggs and he says, What's the matter with you, mista? Don't you like cats or somethin?

Shit, Palmer said, his shoulders shaking.

And the damnedest thing was, that old tomcat showed up about a hour later without a mark on him. Turns out I'd been whompin on someone else's cat.

I'm about to piss my pants.

It was the goddamnedest thing. Hey, comin up quick.

The lane where they turned was narrow and rutted, and in the bouncing arc of the Buick's headlamps Lottie saw a house set small and dark against the greater darkness beyond.

Give me a runnin start, Buddy said, shouldering his door as they stopped. Then come in with both guns blazin.

Gravel crunched, and his legs flared brightly as he circled the idling car.

What is this place?

Friend of Buddy's, Palmer said as he shook a cigarette from the pack and tapped it on the dashboard.

Lights appeared in the house windows.

What are we doin here?

In the pop of the match she saw Palmer's reflection material-ize and dissolve again in the windscreen.

Makin some arrangements. He shook the match and pitched it through the window. About a rooster.

He looked to the house as he smoked, his fingers drumming the open windowframe.

What rooster?

Just give it a rest.

They watched the house in silence, until the door opened to a furtive gesture. Palmer killed the engine.

Okay, let's go.

The moon had not yet risen, and she followed his bobbing ash glow up the darkened lawn.

The door was ajar when they reached it, and Palmer's rapping entrance halted the conversation between Buddy and a woman in a bathrobe. She too was smoking, with her wrist cocked in a theatrical pose. She was pale and fleshy, and her head was wrapped in a kind of Gypsy scarf from which coppery ringlets spilled. She studied Lottie through the curling smoke, then turned her face to Palmer.

What all did I do to deserve this?

Nice to see you too, Lonnie. What's it been?

The woman ignored the question. She crooked a finger at Buddy and led him down the hallway.

The room where they waited smelled of perfume and cigarettes. Magazines were piled in stacks on the floor, *Movie Mirror* and *Photoplay*, and a sofa slumped behind a low table on which an ashtray had been set. A new Philco radio gleamed like a cathedral in miniature, and these and the floorlamp by which she viewed them were the room's only furnishings.

From down the hallway came voices, low and angry, then silence.

Don't seem like we was expected, Lottie whispered, to which Palmer turned and crossed to the window and there stood gazing past his own reflection, silent and ruminative, as though looking through the light to view some inner, darker self.

Lonnie Kincaide set aside her magazine.

What now?

The girl, curled on the bed beside her, only shrugged.

C'mon, kid. Don't go all weepy on me. They said they'd be back in a jiffy.

Lottie was startled by the hand that reached to stroke her hair. She rolled to face the older woman.

Is Buddy your beau?

The woman arched her eyebrows. My beau? She reached to the nightstand and tapped out a cigarette. Sometimes, I guess. Not regular-like. Ain't nothin regular about these Texas boys. But I guess you could say he's my beau. Yeah, sure, why not?

Does he got a sister, him or Clint?

Clint's got two sisters, Ruby and Gennie. Why?

Does either one of 'em got a daughter?

The woman frowned. I don't know about no daughter. Why?

Lottie pressed herself into a sitting position.

Has Buddy ever lied to you?

The woman made a short, snorting sound. Let me tell you somethin about men, honey. If you see a man whose mouth is movin, and if he ain't eatin or chewin snoose, then he's probably lyin.

She shook a matchbox and lit a cigarette and blew a stream of smoke.

Why, you got yourself a boyfriend at school or somethin?

Lottie shrugged. I don't know.

You don't know.

Lottie studied her fingernails. How do you know when you're old enough to even have a boyfriend?

The woman smoked and considered. Well, that there is a good question. When I was your age, I believed that the right man when he finally come along was gonna change everything. Not like in a fairy tale or nothin, but more like, I don't know. Like I was some kinda candle, just waitin for a light. To have some purpose in life, you know what I mean? And then I got married, and I got cheated on, and I got separated. And then one day, maybe ten years and twenty pounds later, I sat down and took stock of my life, and I realized that havin a steady man ain't the be-all or the end-all it's cracked up to be, not by a long shot. And I reckon that was it.

That was what?

That's when I realized I was finally old enough to have a boyfriend.

Lottie looked at the woman. Her head was reclined on the pillow and she was studying the patterns of the smoke curling upward toward the ceiling.

That don't make no sense.

The woman laughed. This boyfriend of yours, he's been less than truthful, is that it?

Lottie shrugged again.

Well, the woman sighed. Don't be too hard on him, honey. Lyin is in the nature of man and boy alike. I think it has somethin to do with their testicles. She held her thumb and finger apart. Hell, I went for years thinkin this here was six inches, till I started datin me a carpenter.

Lottie was sleeping when the sound of voices lifted her upright in bed.

Out in the front room, a hatless Clint Palmer sat cross-legged on the floor, his hair lank and disheveled and his blue eyes shining like antifreeze in the angled lamplight. On the sofa opposite, Lonnie Kincaide's head rested on Buddy's shoulder as an orchestra played softly on the glowing radio. Cigarettes burned in the ashtray, and beside the ashtray stood three mismatched glasses and a nearly empty bottle.

I told you you'd wake her, Lonnie said.

Palmer looked at Lottie standing in the doorway in a way that made her glance down and examine herself.

Tell her what you said.

Shut up, said Buddy.

Buddy says you look like Claudette Colbert.

Lonnie straightened and swatted Buddy's shoulder.

I did not. Her kid sister is what I said.

Well, Bonnie Parker, what do you think about that?

I don't know.

Why, honey, Lonnie said as she reached for a smoke. You know Claudette Colbert, don't you? The movie actress? *It Happened One Night*?

Lottie shrugged.

Oh, honey. Ain't you never been to the picture show before?

Course she's been! What kind of ignorant question is that? Palmer rose unsteadily, lurching and jostling the table.

You don't have to yell. All's I meant was—

You think you're somethin special, don't you? You and your fancy magazines and your big-city airs. Palmer stood like a man in a rowboat. Hell, you think you're better'n her, is that it?

I didn't say that.

But that's what you think, ain't it?

Now you listen to me, Clint Palmer. I don't have to take—

Palmer kicked at the magazines and sent them sprawling. Piss on you. This little girl right here is pretty as a red wagon, and she's worth ten of your big-city swells and movie stars.

He noticed the bottle then and snatched it up, holding it to the light and drinking it dry as the others watched in openmouthed silence. Then he slammed it on the table, clipping one of the glasses and shattering glass and bottle both in a fountain of flying shards.

Fuck!

His hand was bleeding. He held it limp with his elbow raised as Lonnie Kincaide rushed from the room. Whether in anger or ministration, none was really certain. The room had fallen silent but for the muted strains of the orchestra.

Come on, Palmer said, grabbing his hat. The old man'll be up waitin.

The moon was up now, and the two men swayed and stumbled down the lawn beneath it, cursing and laughing. When they all had reached the Buick, Lottie stopped short in the gravel.

The backseat brimmed with pans and tools, clothes and bedrolls. Lottie bent to better see. The leather satchel was there, and her father's Bible, and the shortbread tin that held her trove of treasures.

At first she said nothing while Palmer and Buddy busied themselves wrapping the wounded hand. Only once they'd reassembled and the car was started and Palmer's bandaged hand lay draped on the seatback behind her head did Lottie finally speak.

What're we doin now?

Some of us is drivin, Palmer said.

Drivin where?

She felt Buddy's glance across the seat, but Palmer responded neither to question nor to glance, and they rode back to the Palmer homestead in a long and vitreous silence.

Do you know you're gonna see your father? the old man asked from where he stood with his foot propped on the running board, his shaggy goat's head centered in the open windowframe.

No, why?

I thought I'd better tell you. You might run by him.

The wormwood face flexed like a balling fist as the old man leaned and spat. That's what I heard, anyways.

The screen door slammed. Palmer and Buddy, their figures

backlit by the yellow porchlight, hauled a saddle and bridle and other paraphernalia from the house. These they loaded into the backseat alongside a gasoline can and an army-surplus canteen and a box of borrowed groceries.

You could open a mercantile, Buddy said as the last items were passed off and positioned. Lottie watched as the siblings stood and faced each other for an awkward moment before embracing, Palmer's hat levering back and nearly falling from his head.

As Palmer circled the car, the old man stepped away from the driver's window to lay a bony hand on his son's shoulder. He steered Palmer out of earshot, where they stood close-quartered in the darkness with their backs to the car, their conference finally ending with a shared nodding of heads and a long stream of tobacco.

She noticed they did not embrace.

As the Buick bounced through the open gate, Palmer turned and honked once and raised a hand to the receding porchlight.

New Mexico, he said before she could put the question. Your pa went on ahead. We'll catch up with him in Santa Fe.

Fenceposts and the shadows of fenceposts ran like railroad tracks at the edge of their headlamps.

But what about his car?

Honey, that rattletrap wouldn't make it out of Hopkins County. Palmer reached for the pack on the dashboard and tapped out a cigarette. He went and borrowed himself a new one.

Borrowed from who?

You're wearin me out, do you know that?

He cupped the match in his bandaged hand and blew into the windscreen.

I guess you could say he borrowed it from whoever it was owned it before he borrowed it.

They entered Paris with the sunrise. The streets were empty and the fountain dry and the storefronts dark and shuttered.

On the main thoroughfare, a lone truck slowed at the traffic signal, and a man in the truckbed heaved a heavy bundle to the sidewalk. The Negro boy was there, catlike in the shadows, and he knelt to slice the twine and fit the morning's headline onto the sandwich board tepeed beside him on the sidewalk.

Wait a goddamn minute, Palmer said, braking and backing the car in the empty street and angling it until the newsboy raised a hand to his eyes.

Yes, suh, big news today! the boy enthused, palming the coin that Palmer proffered and sliding the folded paper through the window.

Palmer spread the broadsheet on the steering wheel, snapping it taut. The headline was huge and black and it filled the front page in capital letters screaming CLYDE BARROW, BONNIE PARKER KILLED IN HAIL OF BULLETS.

They drove all day, pausing only to nap in the car at Denton, and they arrived with the dusk in Ardmore where Palmer cruised the darkened streets in search of a rooming house where he claimed once to have stayed.

He emerged from the main house whistling, his shadow long in the dim porchlight. He gathered up his satchel from the car and took her hand and shushed her around the back and up a wooden staircase to a single room above a garage where he closed and latched the heavy door behind them.

There was but one bed in the room with a single lamp beside it, and he switched on the light to reveal under sloping eaves a small and windowless space.

They had just the one room, Palmer said, ducking to stow his satchel under the nightstand.

I could sleep out in the car.

Don't be silly. He patted the musty bedspread. Come and sit.

She perched beside him on the bed, the walls around them bathed in a jaundiced light from the burlap-covered lampshade.

I ain't sleepin here with you, she told him as he bent to work his boots.

I don't see as you got a whole lot of options.

She stood and started toward the door, but he grabbed her shirt collar and pulled her backward to the bed.

You're hurting me!

Shhhh. You don't want the law pokin his nose up here. Not with your daddy on the lam like he is. He held her collar and stroked her, in the manner of a man calming a dog he held by a chain. Not with me the only one knows where to find him.

She turned away as he undressed, his shadow huge on the wall before her, and then she felt him pull back the bedspread.

Come on, darlin. I won't bite.

She didn't move. He gripped her arm and turned her.

Look at me and I'll prove it. Watch this.

He reached a hand into his mouth, extracting his upper teeth with gums attached. He set them on the little nightstand.

Thee? I couldn't bite you if I wanted.

Again she tried to rise, but he wrapped his arms around her, this time working the buttons on her shirtfront.

Stop it! She fought to shrug him off, but he only hugged her tighter, kissing her wetly on the neck.

I'll scream, she said.

No, you won't. You'll take your goddamn clothes off and get in bed.

She had already started to cry. He stripped her shirt, then eased her onto her back where he stood naked before her and removed her boots and dungarees.

She lay on her side now, balled and quietly sobbing. He snuggled in behind her, his body pressed against hers and his breath hot on her neck, whispering to her that everything would be all right. That she needed to relax. That she'd thank him in the morning. Whispering to her and telling her that this was the way it was between them. Telling her that, in the world of men, this was the way it had ever been, and the way it would ever be.

PART TWO

Chapter Five

WEST OF HERE

Q: Didn't you?

A: No.

Q: With your schoolgirl charms and your feminine wiles?

BY MR. PHARR: Objection.

THE COURT: Counsel will ask a question.

BY MR. HARTWELL: Mr. Palmer followed you over hell's half acre looking for your father, isn't that true? Trying to help you?

A: Help himself.

Q: You led him by the nose.

A: I done what he told me.

Q: A virtual captive, is that what you were? A prisoner?

A: That's right.

Q: And when you tried to escape all those times, what happened?

THE COURT: The witness will answer.

A: It weren't like that. He told me—

BY MR. HARTWELL: Move to strike.

THE COURT: The witness will answer counsel's questions.

BY MR. HARTWELL: Surely you had many opportunities to

escape from the clutches of this villainous blackguard holding you hostage?

A: It weren't like that.

Q: I daresay not. You stayed with him for an entire year?

A: About a year.

Q: Through town after town?

A: Yes.

Q: State after state?

A: Yes.

Q: You shared his bed the whole time?

A: Yes.

Q: While the two of you searched high and low for your
father?

A: Yes.

Q: Who was, as far as you knew, alive and well and on the
lam?

A: Yes.

They mostly traveled by night.

Oklahoma City, Shamrock, Amarillo. Long and flat horizons.
Vast plains shrouded in dust clouds that billowed and raged and
swallowed the Buick, dimming their headlamps and forcing them
to the side of the road. Then, clear nights with cow towns and
Okie campfires twinkling like starlight to the farthest edge of
nothing.

Vega, Tucumcari, Santa Rosa. Dark canyons and low mesas.
Quirts of dry lightning on the distant mountains. Hours of darkness broken by cities that rose up in bright lights and traffic and
gave way again to the dark.

They swapped their license plate in McLean, and they slept in hobo camps or in motor courts, or on the ground beside the Buick. When Palmer talked to her at all, it was not of the past, but of the future; of pinto horses and grazing cattle and rolling wildflower meadows. Of a log cabin hard by a river, backset by snow-peaked mountains. Of a place where they would be law unto themselves, free and unbound by convention or disapprobation and answerable to no authority.

Their future, he told her. Together.

For their new lives he chose new identities. Clint became Jimmy, and Lottie became Johnny Rae. Palmer became Montgomery. To strangers she was his niece, or sometimes his daughter. Alone together, she was his wife.

They attended a square dance in Adrian, and a cockfight in San Jon, and outside the farming town of Milagro, drinking applejack cider with a Panhandle farm family, he bobbed Lottie's hair with sheep shears.

Johnny Rae Montgomery! he said, laughing drunkenly, twirling her in the firelight.

Their provisions lasted until Moriarty, and their cash until Albuquerque, where Palmer learned of a roadhouse card game from which he'd returned at dawn without his belt buckle.

And so it was that Jimmy and Johnny Rae Palmer, or Clint and Lottie Montgomery, or some amalgam thereof, arrived in La Villa Real de la Santa Fé de San Francisco de Asis, the capital city of New Mexico and of the northern territories of Mexico and New Spain before it, broke and filthy and nearly starving.

Palmer popped the shortbread tin and handed her the ribbon and shook the gold tooth and the thin gold cross and chain into his palm, spreading them with his thumb.

I'll be a minute, he told her. Why don't you stretch your legs. He opened the door and slid from under the wheel. Mind who you talk to.

The town square by which they'd parked was green and treed with ancient elms and bustling with activity. Men in suits and hats and jet-haired women in Sunday finery, some with mantillas and old-fashioned parasols, strolled or sat on benches or picnicked on the shaded grass. A stone obelisk stood at the center of the plaza with a trellised bandstand beyond from which came the rhythmic strum and bleat of ranchera music. On the far sidewalk, in the shade of a broad portal, Indian women sat crosslegged against a mud wall hawking jewelry and beadwork and other crafts.

Lottie followed the covered sidewalk. In the storefront windows were dry goods and millinery, sundries and curios and brightly patterned blankets. A barbershop and a bakery restaurant. And at the far end of the street, a massive stone cathedral, stark and aureate in the late-morning sun.

She saw him then, on the block ahead, tall and lean in his jeans and mackinaw, adding his shuffling gait to the variegated crush of parishioners drifting slowly toward the cathedral. She surged forward, elbowing her way past shoppers and strollers, then into the street, where a car swerved and honked.

The church bells tolled. She glimpsed him again, then lost him as the crowd filled the street, jostling and murmuring, converging on the wide stone steps that led to the elevated *cercado*.

Daddy! she called above the heads on the stairway. Several turned, and a way was made for her to push through, ducking and dodging, until she saw him again passing under the cathedral's towering archway.

Daddy! Wait!

She grabbed, breathless, at his coat sleeve.

The man pulled free, his black eyes flashing. Several of the parishioners had paused to watch, and a bottleneck quickly formed.

¿Qué quiere, joven? the man demanded, his dark brows knitting. *¿Estas pérdida?*

She turned and fled, across the lawn and down the stairs and back into the roiling crowd.

Palmer sat on the fender with one foot on the wheel hub, his neck stretched and craning. He'd been smoking, and when he caught sight of her approaching, he flicked his butt to the gutter and circled the front of the car.

Let's go, damn it.

The car was already moving as Lottie fell in beside him.

You come this close to gettin left. Where the hell'd you go?

Walkin, she said, nodding. To the church yonder.

You and your goddamn church.

The roads around the plaza were traffic-choked, and he muttered and honked and edged his way onto a side street. The block they circled was taken up by a single building; a multitiered confection of stepped walls and staggered roofs that appeared to have risen in stages from the red clay mud on which it stood, and to have melted over time and a thousand rains into the very earth of its origin.

An awning spanned the sidewalk, from the entrance doors to an idling Harvey tour bus, whose passengers leaned from the windows to haggle with the Indian women holding pottery and silver jewelry aloft as in oblation to some multilimbed deity.

Palmer parked at the curbstone. He turned to Lottie and studied her in the manner of a man estimating whether a wardrobe might fit through a doorway.

What?

Man at the pawnshop says they's a card game upstairs. I might be a hour, or I might be longer.

I'm hungry.

Palmer leaned and straightened and counted the bills from his pocket.

All right, he said. Come on.

The lobby of the La Fonda hotel was the largest room Lottie had ever seen or had ever imagined seeing, its plastered walls and dark vigas framing a vast salon in which couches and chairs were grouped in threes and fours on a floor of polished stone. Herringboned *latillas* and intricately carved and painted ceiling corbels. Rugs of dazzling color and geometry. Sconces and chandeliers of amber glass and hammered tin and riveted iron.

For all the tumult on the sidewalk, the lobby was cool and hushed, and their footfalls on the flagstones echoed of Spanish armor and Tewa moccasins, of Mexican huaraches and the bootheels and rowel spurs of untold generations of soldiers and ranchers and farmers who'd passed this way before them.

They found their way to a cantina off the main lobby. There a man in a vest and shirtsleeves stood polishing bar glasses, and there sloe-eyed girls in peasant blouses arranged a plankwood table with the fruits and *pastelerías*, the tamales and posole, of a Sunday-morning buffet.

Palmer slapped a coin on the copper bartop and ordered a Nehi.

This here is as good a place to wait as any, he told her. Once the church lets out, you can sneak yourself some grub. He took a swig from the bottle that the barman set before her. Anybody asks, you tell 'em you're waitin on your pa, who's gettin his hair cut, understand?

Palmer stood and straightened his pockets. The barman watched his retreating back and then took up again his sodden towel.

The cantina grew crowded as the day wore on. Men alone in ones and twos, then couples, and soon entire families streamed in from the lobby, their faces flushed and their conversations animated. They spoke in Spanish, or in English, or in some local conflation of the two. First the tables filled, then the barstools, and soon Lottie found herself surrounded by men who sat or stood in dark wool suits and some with hats and silver bolo ties smoking cigarettes or slender *puros*.

Bills and coins of silver crossed the bartop. The men smelled of bay rum, or of tobacco. They ordered cervezas or tequila or soft drinks for the children who clung to their pantlegs and gazed up at Lottie with dark and questioning eyes.

Although she'd finished her Nehi long ago, the barman had left the bottle unclaimed, and once, when she'd turned to watch the musicians arriving in their black, fitted suits with buckled silver edging, he'd replaced it with a full bottle.

The music when it started was a lively pulsing of guitar and fiddle with sudden bursts of brassy horns. On the worn parquet square before the bandstand, couples, some quite elderly, moved and swayed or shuffled and spun with clicking heels and swirling skirts to the shouts and claps of their fellows.

Waitresses moved among the patrons with painted clay pitchers and fresh plates for the buffet. A young Indian girl with braided hair displayed a fabric board on which earrings and pendants of silver and turquoise were fastened, petitioning each of the diners and then each of the bar patrons in turn, and when she came in her circuit to Lottie on her barstool, she passed without a glance.

When at last Lottie left for the women's toilet, she returned to find her bottle missing and her seat taken. She stood in the archway of the cantina and regarded the buffet and the women in their dark skirts and embroidered blouses tending and replenishing it. The surrounding tables were all yet occupied and other townsfolk late arriving stood vigil in the corners and aisles and out in the hallway, chatting and waiting to eat.

She passed through the lobby, the music fading behind her. Outside the hotel, the shadows had lengthened and the plaza had all but emptied. She walked a slow circuit, past the open storefronts and the lingering strollers, past the last of the Indian women banded where they sat in bars of light and shadow.

Before the empty bandstand was a bench, and beside the bench an iron trash can rimmed with pigeons that scattered, fluttering, at her approach. She found there among the papers and wrappers and other refuse of the day a stiff tortilla smeared with cold frijoles that she carried to the bench and ate quickly, tossing the papery crumbles to the pigeons that circled her with bobbing heads, harrying one another for her scatterings.

When she'd finished eating, she closed her eyes to listen. To the cooing of the pigeons and the flit and trill of smaller birds. To the dolorous tolling of the church bells. To the cars and buses rumbling in the street. And when she opened them again, she saw white clouds banked in towering drifts over the stunted towers of the cathedral.

Down the path by which she sat, an old man bent and lifted a guitar and placed some copper coins in its open and battered case, as though rewarding himself for this small labor. He plucked strings and twisted pegs on the headstock, his ear lowered to the tuning, and when he straightened again, he nodded gravely in her direction and played a showy flourish.

Lottie smiled, and the man smiled in return.

Pigeons flew as she stood. The man sat with his legs crossed and his eyes closed, his music haunting and tragic, his fingers on the fretboard the languid remembrance of a lover's caress. Lottie stood for a long time listening, and when she turned and started again toward the hotel, the music stopped.

Joven, the man said. *Espérate.*

He bent to the guitar case and picked out a penny and pressed it into her hand. Go with God, he told her in English, and then he settled back and closed his eyes and resumed his mournful song.

The cantina was all but empty. The buffet table had been cleared and the bandstand stood vacant under colored lights and the few patrons who remained amid the wash pails and the bustling charwomen were hunched and smoking at the bar. The new bartender wore a thick mustache and glanced at Lottie in the archway and dismissed her with a toss of his wrist.

She roamed the hotel hallways like a shadow, and like a shadow left no impression on what or whom she passed. The shopwindows all were darkened now, the fireplaces lit. In the courtyard off the lobby, a woman sat cross-legged on the rim of a tiled fountain, her foot tapping, her cigarette glowing and fading and glowing again in the slanting half-light as laughter echoed down from an upstairs window.

Lottie sat in an alcove by a telephone. The telephone was tall and black and sat in its tiled *nicho* like some Bakelite icon wanting only for a votive. She lifted the handle and listened, but nobody was talking.

People passed by in the hallway. Some were couples arm in arm, and some were men in low conversation. Two women wearing aprons, giggling. A Mexican boy sweeping.

She dozed. Then a man appeared and startled her awake, frowning and gesturing toward the telephone, and she rose and hurried past the man and past the reception desk and past the empty cantina, entering again into the women's toilet, where she vomited into the sink.

The plaza lay in darkness. She breathed the cool night air and smelled the piñon woodsmoke, pausing in vain to listen for the old man's guitar.

She was very much alone.

She retraced her afternoon promenade, the docked hair and gangling gait of Johnny Rae Montgomery trailing her by lamplight in the black and empty storefronts. Moving like the hour, or like the declination of solstice, and the stone obelisk in the center of the plaza some ancient nodus by which to chart the course of her movement.

In the back of the Buick she found a saddle blanket, and in the front she lay curled beneath the steering wheel, her eyes closed and her hand splayed at her cold and naked throat.

And there she wept.

When Palmer emerged blinking into the new sunlight, his face was freshly shaved and his barbered hair was parted and slicked with pomade. He brushed his hat as he scanned the curbline, his eyes lighting on Lottie where she sat upright and rigid in the front seat of the Buick.

Where've you been? he asked as he slid behind the wheel. I been lookin all over.

She turned her face to the street.

Don't you start with me. I told you I'd be a while.

He turned the ignition and released the brake and wheeled the Buick sharply into the street. They'd circled the block, past the stone cathedral and the little park beside it, and they were heading west along the river before either spoke again.

I'm hungry, she said quietly.

Well, what do you know. She can talk after all.

The café huddled in the shade of an ancient church with buttressed walls and a leaning bell tower whose shadow threw a long and crooked cross onto the cobblestones before it. Lottie ordered doughnuts and coffee while Palmer sat smoking and watching the morning strollers pass through the rippling cruciform, ceremonial in their transit, as communicants might walk in some ritual passage from shadow into sunlight.

He spoke without facing her. He told her of the men he'd met in the game, and of their advice to him that the land he sought and the life he'd described lay three hundred miles due north, in the mining town of Durango.

Silver is crashed and the mines is shut and they's givin away land for a song, he said, his eyes shifting in the plate glass. Horses everywhere, turned out to forage and free for the takin. Plus the bank's been run, so the whole town's full of men got their life savings buried in coffee cans and nothin to do but drink and play at cards all day and wait for the mines to reopen.

Sounds like you'd fit right in.

He gave her a look.

I thought you said we was gonna meet him here.

Palmer stubbed his cigarette. Oh, yeah. He patted his pockets, palming out the pack. That's the other reason we need to head north. Word is that's where your daddy's gone.

She turned away.

Now what?

She shook her head.

He tapped out a cigarette, watching her. Come on, let's have it.

You don't act like you want to find him, that's all.

Ah, hell. He lit the smoke and leaned back in his chair and picked tobacco from his lip. Guess I didn't realize you was so partial to Bible-thumpin and belt-whippins.

She didn't answer.

Well?

He's my daddy, that's all.

Palmer stood from his seat and probed his pocket and sprinkled some coins on the table.

Tell you what. I ain't your daddy, but I ain't your goddamn enemy neither. Now you got yourself a choice to make. Either you stay here where you think he's at, or you come with me to where I know he's at. I'll leave that to you.

He leveled his hat as he pushed through the door and passed in the window before her.

She sat. She watched the cobblestone street and the tilted roodshadow and the figures passing beneath it. A woman adorned in turquoise. A young priest from the chapel. A trio of stooped crones in black *mantónes*, so alien to her in their language and dress.

She thought about Palmer. Of the night just passed, and of

those without number yet to come. And she thought of her father, alone and hunted and on the run.

She stood and crossed to the door.

They drove through the pueblo towns of Tesuque and Nambé, through a rolling landscape of cedars and piñons and mud hovels and dark and ragged children tending goat strings in the weedy roadside barrancas. They crossed the Rio Grande outside Española, New Mexico, and there the pavement ended and the roadway forked and they stopped to provision at a roadside bodega, its walls of brown mud and its portal stippled by the gnarled and ancient cottonwoods whose seed chaff fell like pixie snow on the Buick where she waited.

By noon they'd crossed the Rio Chama, climbing steeply into a landscape of sandstone bluffs and low mesas where ravens flew and pronghorn antelope rose up and scattered before their rattling dust cloud, and thence into the land-grant village of Abiquiu.

From there the roadway parted a breathtaking tableau of tumbled boulders and red-rock cliffs that glowed in the high desert sun like slag metal in a forge, all of it revealed under a blue sky limned to the east by the darker blue tumescence of the Sangre de Cristo Mountains, which Palmer told her meant the Blood of Christ and marked the start of the fabled Rockies.

After three more hours of dust and jarring roadway they'd forded the Canjilon and the Cebolla Rivers, where the gravel resumed and the landscape flattened, and by nightfall they'd crossed and recrossed the Old Spanish Trail and glimpsed in the broad valley below them, like the council fires of some nomadic people, the lights of Tierra Amarilla.

They parked the smoking Buick in the last light of sunset with the jagged dogteeth of the San Juan Mountains glowing pink on the near horizon, their rocky peaks etched with the threads and arrowheads of a late-winter snow.

They stood down and stretched, and Palmer spat, and together they reconnoitered their surroundings. The car sat on a low promontory with an irrigation ditch gurgling and sucking below the grade. Barbed-wire fencelines framed the road course and ran to infinity in both directions.

I reckon this is as good a spot as any, Palmer said.

They built a cookfire of gathered sticks and ate their beans and bacon wrapped in charred tortillas. Palmer sat cross-legged, his face to the mountains, or to the memory of mountains cloaked now in darkness beyond the firelight, and the stars when they emerged in the clear night sky left shadows on the ground around them.

Lottie rinsed their cookpans in the acequia and stowed them in the car while Palmer lugged and spread their bedrolls. He stripped off his jeans and shirt and folded them for a pillow, and she did likewise, and together they lay like truants, drinking in the nighttime sky.

She woke to a slamming of car doors and the twin shadows of men silhouetted in the roadway. She kneed the dozing Palmer, who rolled and clacked his mouth and settled back to sleep.

Well, shit. Would you look at this.

The men descended the embankment in a welter of dust and pebbles as Lottie rose to her elbows with her blanket at her chin.

The men loomed over her, their hat brims eclipsing the sun. They wore matching boots and khaki pants with blue piping. The shorter man placed a hand on his hip as he stubbed Palmer with his toe.

Hey! Wake up, Nancy.

Palmer rolled and shaded his eyes. He sat upright.

The man backed a step. Get up, he ordered. Nice and easy.

Palmer rose from his bedroll, his blanket sliding away. He wore a yellowed T-shirt and nothing else and he stood pale and dangling with his hands raised in mock surrender.

You too, said the taller man.

Lottie rose with her blanket pressed to her chest, until the man stepped forward and snatched it away.

Ah, hell, he said, half-turning toward the mountains. We thought you was a boy. He held the blanket out to her at arm's length.

They were lawmen in khaki shirts with epaulets and pleated pockets. They wore patches on their shoulders and sidearms high on their hips in flapped leather holsters. The shorter man wore a leather strap across his chest in a vaguely military fashion.

How old are you? the shorter man demanded. His hair was gray and close-cropped in the shadow of his hat brim.

Now hold on, Sheriff, Palmer began, but the man cut him off.

Lottie gripped the blanket with both hands. She looked from the man to Palmer.

Sixteen.

The man jerked his thumb, and the deputy turned and started toward the cars.

Put your pants on, you.

Glad you boys come along when you did, Sheriff. Palmer spoke rapidly as he hopped into his dungarees. The missus and me was just gettin some shut-eye. We come all the way—

Shut it.

Above them, the deputy drew a clipboard from the front seat

of the police car. He tilted his hat and circled to the rear of the Buick.

You get your clothes on, miss. He turned and nodded to Palmer. You come with me.

The man waited while Palmer tugged at his boots and shrugged into his shirt. He placed a hand on Palmer's arm and guided him up the embankment, with Palmer turning to look at Lottie where she stood.

Lottie dressed quickly and carried both bedrolls to the Buick. The police car was angled on the gravel before it, blocking their escape. The black Ford coupe had white doors on which RIO ARRIBA had been stenciled in arching letters over a large gilt star.

The men stood talking at the rear of the Buick. You all must be Mormons, she heard the deputy say as he handed off the clipboard. My great-aunt—

Lester, the sheriff said. Lottie watched him as he flipped pages and glanced from his list to the license plate, the deputy eyeing the sheriff and Palmer eyeing the deputy's holstered gun. Then the sheriff handed off the clipboard and stood with fists on hips, waiting for Lottie to join them.

I don't suppose you've got a driver's license? he asked her. Or some other ID?

About what?

The man looked up the roadway. He sighed.

Look, Sheriff, it ain't like we's tramps or nothin. We come up from Texas on our way to the rodeo in Durango. I was noddin off come nightfall, and I thought it'd be safer to park here than to keep on goin, that's all.

Hot damn, I knew you was a cowboy, the deputy said, grinning. Ain't that what I said when I seen the saddle? My uncle Jim Thomas was a pickup man up at—

What events you ride? the sheriff interrupted.

Saddle bronc mostly. Some bareback.

The sheriff nodded. He was looking at the girl with the dirty face and the thin and dirty clothes who stood biting her lip as if hoping for a wind that might lift her up and carry her eastward into the Brazos.

I allowed maybe you was a calf roper.

What's that supposed to mean?

It means we got laws in this county about vagrancy, the sheriff told Palmer, still eyeing the girl. Bein from Texas ain't no defense I ever heard of. He leaned and spat in the roadway. You go on and get in your car, and consider yourselves warned. Come on, Lester. Let's get.

The sheriff stayed and watched as they circled their car, and he kept on watching as the doors slammed and the dust jumped and the engine sputtered and caught. Only then did he step up to the Buick and nudge his hat and lean his face into the doorframe.

Mister, it's thirty-five miles straight ahead to the state line. Make sure you don't get lost.

You see 'em? Palmer shouted over the engine sound as they threaded the Chama valley with the Buick yawing on the gravel washboard, bouncing and pinging and trailing great billows of dust.

The enveloping landscape was a patchwork of pine forest and rolling grassland, green against darker green through which creekbeds ran and cattle moved in slow and beaded strings. They bore west onto State Road 17 near the village of Chama, New

Mexico, where they crossed the Continental Divide and glimpsed the distant La Platas, lilac dark and snow-veined in their upper rincons. Then north again at Lumberton, through brakes of scrub and cedar framed by low and rolling hills.

It was coming noon when they crossed the state line, then the Navajo and Blanco Rivers. There they met Highway 450, and they followed it westward into the resort town of Pagosa Springs, Colorado.

The main street was a western-town set of wooden falsefronts and covered sidewalks, of Victorian homes and sandstone emporiums before which flags fluttered and cars and trucks were angled. They stopped for gasoline, and then for lunch at a small café on whose rear deck they sat at a painted table to watch the San Juan River tumble and eddy in a sulfurous haze that enveloped the near-naked bathers who waded and basked on the gravel bars amid huge and steaming boulders.

You done good back there, Palmer told her. It ain't me I'm worried about so much as your pa. They probly got a warrant out by now. We got to be careful who we talk to.

What's a Mormon? she asked him.

A Mormon is kindly like a Catholic, only from Utah.

Where's Utah?

West of here. The Utes is Indians, and the Mormons is white settlers.

How come that deputy thought we was Mormons?

I don't rightly know. We must look Utah somehows, and I guess he figured we wasn't Indians.

Below them, boys were running and splashing. Palmer rose and crossed to the railing and called down to them. The boys stopped and looked up, and one of them waved. Then they were off again, sleek river otters in cutoff denims chasing and roughhousing in the vaporous shallows.

Damn, that looks like fun, he said, returning to his seat.

They ate sandwiches with lemonade, and Palmer ordered a beer. When they'd finished their dinners, they climbed down to the riverbank and Palmer rolled his pantlegs and waded into the steaming shoals while Lottie held his boots.

He talked to the boys. He fished coins from his pocket and tossed them, and the boys ran jostling and diving to claim them. When the coins were gone, he splashed at the boys and they at him, and he ran laughing and dripping back to where she waited on the gravel bank.

We'd best be movin on, he told her.

The high country through which they next passed was to Lottie like a veil uplifted to expose the glowing face of God.

Verdant grasslands joined with towering ponderosa pine and blue spruce interwoven with stands of quaking aspen. Ice-melt streams coursed and crashed on granite cobbles. Blue escarpments glowed with sunlit snow. Elk and mule deer grazed in tall bluegrass flecked with iris and lupine and mountain columbine. They rode with windows lowered, all the world's colors passing in a slow parade across the dusty glass of their windscreen.

They drove through Nutria and Grandview, across the Piedra and the Florida Rivers, and below the granite tower of Chimney Rock. The sun hung high before them, and they followed it for miles, topping out at last on a precipice high above the wide and mighty Animas, swift and boulder-studded in the canyon below.

There she is, Palmer told her. The river of souls.

They traced the river northward, descending on a cliff face

that switched back and deposited them at last amid smokestacks and warehouses, and then onto the ordered street grid of Durango, Colorado.

Lottie straightened. The main street when they found it was a canyon of corniced buildings of red brick and quoining sandstone built by Easterners as though in effigy of some grander place.

There was scarcely any traffic. Some parked cars, a few pedestrians. A single rider on horseback. They turned south onto the main street and drove its empty length until the pavement ended at the Denver and Rio Grande Railroad depot, where the train cars, massive and inert, sat slumbering on their tracks.

Even there, all was eerily quiet. As though the city, once alive and vibrant, now held its sooted breath.

They parked the Buick in the railyard plaza where the clip-clop of the shod horse was the only sound they heard. The rider when he reached them touched his hat brim and continued on until horse and rider and sound all vanished together around a corner.

What day is this? Palmer asked her.

Day of the week or day of the month?

Either one.

I don't know.

They started up the sidewalk. The storefronts they passed were mostly dark and mostly vacant. In one, a sign read CLOSED UNTIL SILVER = A DOLLAR, the paper curled and yellowed, the writing all but faded. It was a grim procession of padlocked doors and empty windows, or of sun-bleached displays of notions and dry goods rimed with spidery dust.

How will we find him?

What?

My pa. How are we gonna find him?

Across the way a door swung open and the syncopated bars of a ragtime piano spilled into the street. An older couple exited, laughing and touching, buoyed aloft by the music. The word SALOON was gold-leafed on the corner windowpane, and beyond the glass were tables and booths and people moving among them.

I reckon there's as good a place as any to start.

The hotel was Victorian in its appointments, and the desk clerk, a young and bespectacled man, looked up from his newspaper and nodded. The barroom, which they entered off the lobby, had velvet wallpaper in scarlet and gold and oak tables and an oaken bar with a brass footrail. A high and empty balcony. A bartender in sleeve garters and center-parted hair. And in the corner by the picture window, a player piano.

The scene was a Western Germelshausen born of nostalgia and reminiscence and peopled by merchants and miners and teamsters unwittingly confederate in its reenactment. It was a sepia-toned daguerreotype, hand-painted and newly animate.

They found a booth by the window. A waitress, herself theatrically costumed in a flapper's red bustier and feathered headpiece, came and took their order. Two men watched from a nearby table, and one of them raised a glass.

Welcome, stranger. To your health and good fortune.

The accent was old-country Irish. The man wore a tweed suit that shone at the elbows, and a silk necktie, and a pearl-headed stickpin. He downed his drink and clapped the glass as the piano segued from one jaunty tune to the next.

A stranger it is, am I right? And a genuine cowboy at that?

The man beside him appeared to be a miner, or maybe a hod carrier, dark and simian.

Palmer removed his hat and set it on the table. Who is it wants to know?

The waitress returned with two soda pops, and as she set them down, the Irishman scraped back his chair and carried his glass and his bottle to their booth. The big man followed, squeezing unbidden onto the bench alongside Lottie.

Make yourself to home, Palmer told him.

The smaller man, still standing, fished into his pocket and proffered a printed card between two fingers.

McGuirk's the name, and real estate's my game. Residential or commercial, ranch or farm. He nodded to Lottie as he slid into the booth.

Palmer studied the card. Must be a burden in your business, you bein so shy and all.

The Irishman smiled. You see there, Monk? Did I not just say, now here's a man of rare intellect and humor? But I'm afraid you have me at a disadvantage, friend. Mister . . . ?

Montgomery.

Montgomery. And who might this lovely creature be? Not your daughter, of course, for I see no family resemblance.

This here is Johnny Rae.

Johnny Rae. The man placed a hand to his heart. She walks in beauty like the night, of cloudless climes and starry skies, and all that's best of dark and bright, meet in her aspect and her eyes. He nodded again. Pleased to make your acquaintance.

The big man had uncorked the bottle, and now he measured out two shots, sliding one across the table. The Irishman lifted his glass.

The formalities observed, to business. You and your young friend will be needin a place to tenant whilst in our fair metropolis, and a stroke of luck it is that you've happened upon the finest land agent in all La Plata County. *Sláinte.*

The strangers clicked glasses. The big man's fist was huge and hairy, the beveled tumbler a thimble within it. All noticed, at the apex of his motion, the third finger missing at the knuckle.

I don't reckon as the house would appreciate you shillin off their business.

Ah, yes. Well. The Strater is a fine establishment, Mr. Montgomery, make no mistake. But my guess is that a couple of sojourners like yourselves, Mormons to my eye, subscribe to the biblical injunction against ostentation and profligacy.

Lottie leaned across the table. We was lookin for a man named Dillard Garrett. He's from Oklahoma. Have you seen him anywheres about?

Lottie flinched at the clap of Palmer's bottle on the tabletop. The Irishman noticed both.

And what sort of man would I be lookin for, miss?

He's tall and kinda skinny. He's got reddish hair and he wears old shoes and dungarees and a tan jacket. And he sometimes limps a little.

The piano shifted again, to the "Mississippi Rag." At the bar, someone began to clap.

Monk?

The big man frowned and shook his head.

I'm afraid we can be of no help in regard to your Mr. Garrett. But in the matter of accommodations—

The barroom quieted. All in the booth turned toward the bar, while all at the bar had turned toward the lobby door, where two deputy sheriffs with holstered sidearms stood in close conversation. Palmer pressed his weight into the seatback, and the Irishman noted this as well.

The waitress spoke with the deputies, and the deputies conferred again before touching their hats and leaving. Barroom conversations resumed, and the man who'd been clapping began clapping anew.

Tell you what, Palmer said as they all shifted in their seats. My grubstake's a little thin right now, but if you could put me onto a cockfight, you might have yourself a cash customer.

The odd companions exchanged a glance.

Well, pilgrim, the Irishman said, we've got dogfights, and we've got bare-knuckle fistfights. I've even heard tell of a bear-bait once, but I can't attest to it. But cockfighting? He shook his head ruefully. Alien, it is, to the local culture.

Well then, how's about a little stud poker?

Ahh. The Irishman brightened as he reached for the bottle. Mr. Montgomery, you'll be pleased to know that more silver has changed hands in this town over a deck of cards than over all the assay scales combined.

They took a room, at the Irishman's suggestion, in a side street boardinghouse, paying the week's rent in advance, no board and no bath. Now they sat on their yellowed mattress surrounded by the whole of their worldly estate and resumed the quarrel that had begun on the sidewalk outside the hotel.

You'd think you'd of learned, that's all.

All I did was ast one question.

All I did was ast one question, he mimicked in singsong. You keep your big mouth shut around strangers, you hear me?

She turned to the window. I want to go home.

And what home would that be? Last I seen you was livin by the side of the road.

He stood and stepped over his saddle to study his face in the dresser mirror. You'll put us all in the calaboose, do you know that?

What do you mean?

I mean your daddy's hot, darlin. He's in Dutch. Johnny Law finds him now, he'll be in jail for life. And so will you.

Why me? I didn't do nothin.

Palmer examined his teeth. You're not very smart, do you know that.

What're you talkin about?

I'm talkin about accessory. I'm talkin about aid'n and abettin. You ever heard of them?

No.

He turned around to face her. You got a lot to learn, sister. Like, when the law wants you, the law finds a way to get you.

He crossed to the bed and resumed his seat beside her.

Look. I'm sure we'll get word from your pa soon enough. But in the meantime, you mind what I say, understand?

They sat for a long time, listening to another couple, another altercation, rising up through the floorboards. As time passed, the room around them darkened.

I'm goin now, he told her, rising to a chorus of bedsprings. He found his hat and his satchel, and he set them on the edge of the dresser.

Goin where?

Goin to work. He removed his pistol from the satchel and dropped the cylinder and eyed the movement as it spun. He flipped it closed and replaced the gun and gathered up his hat.

Don't lose no more belt buckles.

He froze in the doorway. And then he slammed the door behind him.

They fell, day by day, into the semblance of a routine. Each evening Palmer left at nightfall. Each morning he returned before
sunrise. Each day he slept until noon.

Some days he was gay when he awoke, and solicitous, and would
tease her and coax her back to bed. On these occasions they would
sleep late and take the air and eat an early supper at the hotel.

Other days his mood was dark, and Lottie was made to feel like
a houseguest who had overstayed her visit. On these occasions
they ate not at all, or else in brooding silence at the drugstore,
where Palmer smoked and watched the street with furtive eyes,
pretending to read his newspaper.

On their sixth day in the boardinghouse Palmer woke and
stretched and rose from the bed and crossed to the dresser. Here,
he told her, opening a drawer. I brung you a present.

The dress he gave her was old and blue and faded in color.
Frayed at the hem and yellowed at the lace collar. She held it
up to her chin. It's too short, she said.

Try it on.

She turned her back and stripped out of her jeans and worked
the dress over her head.

See? She stepped toward the mirror where he stood, turning to
examine herself.

Go sit on the bed. Like that, only with your legs crossed.

I ain't barely covered.

Get your hands out of your lap. There, just like that. Now take
them drawers off.

What?

You heard me. Take your drawers off and sit just like that.

I ain't gonna do that.

She flinched at his hand. Take off your goddamn drawers.

She rocked and scooted and peeled her dirty panties and dropped them to the floor.

Now cross your legs again.

He studied her from several angles, pacing as he spoke.

They's a big game on Monday, and you're comin out with me. You're gonna sit behind me, just like that. Give them Injuns a peek at some nice white coochie. Sweet as apple pie. Keep their minds off their cards.

I am not.

You are too.

You're crazy.

I am crazy, he said, returning to the mirror. Crazy like a goddamn fox.

On their seventh day in the boardinghouse Lottie woke to an empty bed. She dressed and sat watching the street from their window, marking the cars as they passed and listening to the sounds in the hallway. She paced and sat, and lay as if to sleep, and rose to pace again. She stood before the mirror with the dress held to her chin.

In the afternoon she was dozing when the click of the door latch startled her awake. But it wasn't Palmer's shape that she saw in the filtered half-light, but the great plaid bulk of the man-ape from the saloon. He stood in the doorway, ignoring Lottie where she lay, reading the room around her. Then he turned abruptly and left, the door closing quietly behind him.

She took some coins from the dresser, and she left by the back stairs. Dark clouds were gathering to the north, and the afternoon breeze carried with it the leaden promise of rain. She sat at the soda fountain with her back to her breakfast plate and watched the street grow darker. Cars passed, and a few pedestrians with fists clutched at their collars.

The train schedule was framed in a glass box, like a thing of great value on display. There was a 3:05 to Denver, and she counted out her remaining coins as the ticket vendor watched.

Can I help you, miss?

I'm all right.

Children ride for half fare.

That's okay.

The man leaned down to peer below the cage. Are you waiting on somebody? The train from Salt Lake's due in twenty minutes.

Lottie reexamined the schedule. Is there a train goes to Wilburton?

Wilburton? What city's that near?

I don't know. Red Oak, I reckon.

The man vanished within the booth, and when he appeared again, he was leafing through a large gazetteer.

Red Oak. I don't see any Red Oak. Or any Wilburton, for that matter. Is that up near Fort Collins? Miss?

But the girl was already gone, past the hotel and the drugstore and halfway to the boardinghouse when the rain began to fall. She shielded her eyes and quickened her pace. Then at the sight of the Buick idling at curbside, she broke into a run.

The car boiled in a cauldron of its own exhaust, the front seat empty, the dark shapes of saddle and bedrolls crowding the back. She crossed the lawn and mounted the front steps of the boardinghouse and only then saw Palmer, his collar upturned, circling from the rear.

There you are! Let's go, dammit! This here's the last!

The sky had opened, and the rain was cold and slanting. Palmer slammed the driver's door and shook out his hat and set it on the satchel as Lottie fell in wet and breathless beside him.

Looks like a gully washer! he shouted over the flat slapping of raindrops on the windscreen. Then as he turned to face her, she caught her breath.

His lip had been split, wide and purple, and the swelling at his temple had closed his left eye to a slit.

What happened to you?

Palmer smiled thinly, then winced. He started the wipers and worked the gearshift and leaned to the inside as to make out the street behind them. They backed and clutched and swung a blind U-turn southward in parallel with the main street.

There had been trouble, he explained, shaking a cigarette from the pack. New players to the game. Boilermakers laid off from the smelter who'd drunk too much and won too little and had made Palmer out for a sharp. Monk, the Irishman's partner, had been summoned by the house. The players were ejected, but had lain outside in wait.

Did they get your money?

Palmer's smile was lopsided. He bent into his match. My, but you've grown downright practical. No, darlin, all's they got was a close-up look at my pistol.

Then what happened to your face?

Oh, that, he said, leaning toward the mirror. The sheriff must of got wind somehow, cuz them deputies was waitin for me at the hotel.

They done that?

Nope. This here is a souvenir from some of the local boys was in the cell they put me in, after tellin 'em some lie or other.

What lie?

It don't matter. What matters is, I'm out on a twenty-dollar bond and due at the courthouse on Wednesday.

They bypassed the downtown, meeting the main road from behind the depot and following it out to the river. Water streaked the windscreen, and Palmer's head moved like a boxer's in time with the beat of the wiper, and soon they were climbing into a fogbank.

What're we gonna do?

Get as far from here as we can in two days' drivin, that's what.

What about the bail money?

That'll be McGuirk's problem, come Wednesday.

They topped out above the fog, and there the day brightened and the rain softened to a light and drizzling mist. Lottie caught sight of the Animas, brown and newly turbid, coursing in the valley below them. Along its far bank, train cars snaked eastward under the white pennant of a locomotive.

What about my pa?

I got word on that last night. Man said they's a letter waitin on you at the post office in Bayfield.

What man?

Just a man in the game.

Where's Bayfield?

He nodded. It's up ahead. We passed it comin in.

The drive took under an hour, through rain-slicked grasslands spotted with cattle steaming in the afternoon sun. They re-crossed the Florida, angry and swollen, and then the Pine, and they parked the Buick at last on the puddled main street of a tidy Western hamlet.

Come on, he told her, palming his hat crown. Let me do the talkin.

The building stood on a street corner, its flagpole barren, its stone-faced entrance angled to the covered sidewalk. Inside were wooden cubbies, and a wide oak table, and behind the counter a storklike man in what appeared to be a printer's apron.

Afternoon, he greeted them, his smile wilting at the sight of Palmer's face. Had us some rain.

General delivery for Lucile Garrett.

The man waited as if expecting more, then retreated to the back. There was sheet glass on the countertop, and beneath it postage stamps in golds and greens pressed like leaves in a child's scrapbook. Palmer bent and tilted his head, studying his own reflection.

Here you go, miss. The man eyed Palmer warily as he handed her the letter.

The postmark read DURANGO, COLO. She tore at the envelope, extracting a folded sheet etched with the Strater Hotel logo. The letter bore no date. Her lips moved as she read the words to herself.

Dearest Lottie,

Missed you in Durango. Must head to Missouri now, but will see you in Utah come Christmas or New Years. Stay with Clint Palmer, as he will take care of you. Do as he says, and give him no trouble.

Love,
Dillard Garrett

Is everything all right, miss?

Give it here, Palmer said, taking the sheet and folding it into his pocket.

They stood outside on the covered sidewalk in view of the mud-spattered Buick. Here, Palmer said, handing her the letter, and she read it again.

Tear it up.

What?

I said tear it up.

How come?

On account of your daddy bein hot, stupid. And if someone was to get hold of it, they'd know where to find him, that's how come.

He nodded, and she tore the folded paper into smaller and smaller pieces, dropping them like storybook bread crumbs as they made their way to the car, the breeze behind her catching them and herding them off the sidewalk and into the muddy street.

Chapter Six

SOMETHING ABOUT A HORSE

BY MR. HARTWELL: Your father was a notorious bootlegger?

A: I don't know.

Q: He made applejack?

A: Not that I ever seen.

Q: You saw him drink moonshine?

BY MR. PHARR: Your Honor, the deceased is not on trial here.

BY MR. HARTWELL: Deceased? What deceased?

THE COURT: That's enough. The objection is sustained.

BY MR. HARTWELL: Your father had enemies?

A: No, sir.

Q: Men were after him?

A: I don't know.

Q: Then why did you think he was on the run?

A: I don't know. Clint said he stole a car.

Q: And you believed him when he told you that?

A: I didn't have no reason not to.

The mountain was exactly as Palmer had described it, in the shape of a sleeping Indian.

It rose in black silhouette against the blood horizon, stark and unmistakable in its human aspect. Recumbent body. Folded arms. Long and trailing hair.

There it is! she cried, leaning forward and pointing.

They had skirted Durango to the south, crossing the Animas and rejoining the main roadway where it rose up through Hesperus and then the Mancos valley, the Buick straining and smoking in search of the corridor of which Palmer had been told that ran through a warren of canyons and mesas and would carry them through to Utah.

They filled the Buick and their spare gasoline can in Cortez, where a uniformed attendant cleaned the glass and checked the oil and cautioned that the car was low and leaking badly. Parts could be ordered, the man told them as he wiped his hands with a rag, but a proper repair would take two weeks to complete.

The road past the Indian's head led them under cover of darkness into a wide canyon of saltbush and sage that curved with the streambed of its origin, through a blue landscape of ancient cottonwoods and pocket hayfields. Stone houses appeared at intervals, dark watchtowers set against the purple bruise of nightfall. No cars were on the road, and no riders, and none but the glowing eyes of mule deer bore witness to their passing.

Farther on, the canyon narrowed, and boulders and giant walls of slickrock scrolled past the edges of their headlamps.

The sound, when the engine finally seized, was terrible. The Buick bucked and the headlamps flickered and died, and they ground to a shrill halt in darkness so complete that neither could read the other's face.

Shit!

What happened?

What do you think happened?

The driver's door squeaked, then slammed with a bang. Lottie smelled the oilsmoke and heard the crunch of Palmer's footsteps circling the car.

Shit, he said again.

When the door reopened, she heard him take up his valise and rummage its contents.

We ain't passed a car all night, he told her, so I don't suppose you'll get hit. But I was you, I'd get off this road just the same.

What are you gonna do?

The gun clicked and ratcheted and clicked again.

You might like to grab your bedroll and get some shut-eye. I could be a while.

She opened her door and stood her foot on the running board. The night air smelled of burning tires. There was no moon and there were no stars, and when Palmer spoke again, his voice was disembodied in the void.

If you do see a car, don't flag it down.

His footsteps faded in the roadway.

Wait! she called. What if they stop? What if they's Indians?

The footsteps halted. Hell, the voice replied. If they's Injuns, ask if they got any firewater.

The sound to which she woke was the slamming of a car door in the roadway. She sat up in her bedroll, a vague premonition of sunrise lighting the eastern mountains.

Clint?

A horse snuffled. She rose and tiptoed to a boulder and, from that vantage, saw the slender shape of a man wreathed in the breath frost of a scrawny broomtail bay.

You ain't exactly quiet, you know.

Palmer wore his pistol in his waistband and his bridle slung over a shoulder. He turned the horse and led it from the Buick by a neck strap that she realized was his belt.

How's about a hand over here.

The horse was wild-eyed, and it sidled at her appearance in the roadway. Palmer talked to it and leaned on the belt strap and dropped the bridle to his free hand.

He looked like a broke horse, but now I ain't so sure. Here.

He handed her the bridle. The horse balked at the exchange, and Palmer shushed it and turned it and walked it in a circle.

Fetch me a shirt from the car.

The rattle of the shirt snaps spooked the horse anew. Palmer stroked its neck and whispered to it as he slipped the shirt over its head, covering its eyes, bunching the fabric at the jaw.

The horse quieted. As Palmer released the belt strap, she handed him the bridle.

You'd best stand over there.

As he raised the bridle, the steel bit clacked at the horse's teeth, issuant and yellowed, and the horse jerked away. He tried again, and again the horse jerked and backed a step.

Come over here, he told her. Take your finger and stick it right in there.

The horse's cheek was silken and whiskered, its breath hot against her hand. She ran her finger to where Palmer had indicated, at the high corner of its mouth.

What if he bites?

He ain't got no teeth there. Go ahead.

She slipped her finger between the bony gums, and the mouth loosened, and the bit slipped into place. Palmer lifted the head-stall over the horse's ears, and with an easy dexterity buckled the throatlatch with the fingers of his free hand.

There you go, big fella. Like the man said, you got nothin to fear but fear itself.

He worked his shirt from under the bridle, and when he yanked it free, the liquid eyes blinked and the long head dipped and nodded placidly.

Here. Palmer passed her the reins as he walked to the car and removed his saddle and leaned it against the wheel hub. He then emptied out the backseat, dragging all that was theirs to the side of the road.

What're we doin?

I'll tell you what we ain't doin, and that's waitin no two weeks to get this thing fixed. It'll be hot by then anyways. Hell, it's probly hot already.

He squatted and spread his bedroll and placed within it the skillet and the tin dishes, the cups and the utensils, and a mixed assortment of food and clothing. She watched him in silence beside the breathing horse.

Anythin else? he asked her.

The Bible.

He hung his head. Then he added the book to their swag pile and rolled it tightly and cinched it off at the ends.

Palmer next took up the gas can. She watched as he opened the car doors each in turn and rolled down the windows and closed the doors again. When he circled the car a second time, splashing gasoline through the windows, the horse rolled its eyes and tried to back.

The sun had by then risen, and the vapors from the open

windows shimmered over the curving roofline. Palmer spun and flung the can clattering into the rocks. He wiped his hands and hoisted his saddle and lugged it to where she waited.

Go on and fetch your bedroll. Hurry up.

The saddle was already in place when Lottie returned, with Palmer's soogan tied behind it and the canteen hanging by its canvas strap from the saddle horn. Tied to one side of the saddle was the calfskin valise, while to the other he was fastening the blackened coffeepot.

The horse stood perfectly still.

Bring it here, he said. He handed her the reins and he lifted her bedroll, wedging it tightly behind the cantle, forming with his larger soogan a kind of crude pillion.

Okay. Now let's see what we got ourselves into.

He looped the reins and stood square to the horse, and with one hand gripping the saddle horn he kneed the horse roughly in the ribs. The horse wheezed as it lurched sideways, and Palmer tightened up the cinch.

Watch out now.

He tried his weight in the stirrup. The horse backed a step as he swung his leg, then it jigged sideways, bucking and crow-hopping with the satchel flapping and the coffeepot clanging until Palmer had turned it and steadied it and brought it to a halt. Now the horse stood backlit by the sunrise, blowing and trembling.

You ever rid before? he called to her, and she nodded. He trotted the horse forward in a neat figure-eight. He stopped it and backed it three steps and walked it to a rock.

Take a hand, cowgirl.

He dropped his foot from the stirrup. She gripped his offered hand and stepped into the empty stirrup and swung her leg wide over the bedrolls. She hugged his waist with both arms as she scooted forward and settled into her seat.

Ready? he called, and she nodded against his shoulder. He turned the horse and walked it through their scattered remnants and into the roadway.

Good-bye, car, Lottie whispered as Palmer pressed his hat crown with his free hand and drew a match from his shirt pocket and popped it with his thumbnail.

Hang on!

At the *whoomp* of the fireball, the horse flattened its ears and bolted. Palmer whooped and Lottie shrieked, and in the galloping clatter of hoofbeats she turned to watch as flames rose black and orange in a tall and twisting column, the smoke and flame blotting out the sun and all the world that lay behind them.

Three days later the riders appeared before sunset on the main street of Monticello, Utah. The bay horse exhausted, impervious to the weary urgings of Palmer's bootheels. Its coat streaked and salt-rimed, its sunburned riders of a piece. The camel shadow of horse and riders aslant before them on the cracked macadam.

They had provisioned that first day at the Ismay trading post, where Palmer had bartered while Lottie secreted the horse in a rocky side-draw. That evening, encamped on the willow brakes of the San Juan River, Palmer had snubbed the horse to a tree-trunk and altered its brand with a glowing length of fence wire.

The next day they'd followed the river westward, through a high desert landscape of mud cliffs and telescopic mesas, past faceted red-rock escarpments pocked with the arching eyebrows of ancient rockfalls, and thence into the Mormon settlement of

Bluff. They'd had their supper on the ground by the old Bluff Fort, and by nightfall they were south of Blanding, camped on the open sage plain with the Sleeping Ute to the east and the dark promise of Blue Mountain looming silently to the north. The dry nightwind ragging their campfire, tousling their stiff and salted hair. The moon a scythe, the stars the scattered chaff of its reaping.

In Blanding proper, on their third morning in the saddle, they'd eaten breakfast in a café and grazed the horse on the ball field of an old Mormon schoolhouse, the muffled hymnsong of the children within like some ballad sung in celebration of their passing. By afternooon they'd climbed the northward pass into rimrock and ponderosa and there glimpsed the notched and frosted summits of the Manti-La Sals.

Lottie held the horse, bedraggled and footsore, while Palmer mounted the steps of the Monticello courthouse. He rattled the doors and cupped his face to the plate glass.

What're we doin?

Thought I'd check out the grazin allotments. Figure who to talk to.

He returned to where she waited, and he took the reins from her and led the wasted horse afoot.

Now what?

I don't know about you, but I could stand me a hot bath and a soft bed.

Three women on a park bench besieged by children were chatting and laughing, and the women stopped laughing and the children stopped playing when they saw the strangers approach.

They joined their fellow lodgers for breakfast. There was an English couple en route to Phoenix, and a roughneck up from

Mexican Hat. A young Mormon family from Salt Lake in town to visit kin, and an earnest missionary, younger still, working his way south to Mexico.

The women talked of the food, and the weather, and the sere beauty of the country, while the men spoke of Wall Street, and of Baer versus Carnera, and of sundry world affairs. They all talked, even the children, of Dillinger's latest exploits.

Lottie, who knew nothing of bulls or bears or King Leopold, followed their conversation with darting eyes. None asked her age, or her views, or her relationship with the wiry man who laughed easily and tousled the children's hair and seemed so at peace with the world.

The horse had been stabled out back with the dairy cows, and now it lifted its head and nickered at Lottie's appearance. It had been curried and brushed, but not by her, and a yellow salve had been applied to the suppurating blister on its flank.

Look at you, she cooed, entering the stall and offering her hand to the whiskered lips, the suction-cup nostrils. The horse nosed at her shirtfront, and as she bent to whisper her secret, its ears flattened and pricked again at the sound of the barn door opening.

Girl and horse both turned to the figure of the old hotelier, backlit in silhouette.

You been ridin double on that horse?

Yes, sir.

For how long?

She started to answer, but did not.

Never mind, the man said, and the door slid closed behind him.

★ ★ ★

After an hour spent among the maps and the dusty ledgers, they left the stone courthouse and walked back to the hotel, which was, in truth, little more than a bungalow in a block of lesser bungalows set in the tidy village street grid. They found their room door locked, and the kitchen empty, and in the barn out back they found their clothes and bedrolls piled in the straw.

Palmer set down his satchel. So much for your Christian charity.

What happened?

I guess you might say the room and board come to more'n I expected.

You mean we's busted again?

Palmer toed through his bedroll. Flat as a flitter.

The horse lifted its dripping muzzle from a bucket.

What're we gonna do?

Well. It's like old H.P. used to say. When all your tolerable prospects is exhausted, you could always try workin' for wages.

He rode out at the noon hour, horse and rider fully outfitted, and in his absence Lottie roamed the streets and wandered the little downtown area at whose center the courthouse stood. Men touched their hats at her approach, and women turned and eyed her departure with maternal solicitude.

By dusk she had thrice circumnavigated the town, and now she sat on the cold curbstone across from the hotel and watched the shadows of the boarders within moving as a Punch-and-Judy in the lit upper windows. A woman stopped in passing to ask if she was all right.

I'm just waitin, Lottie told her.

Have you a place to sleep?

I got me a bedroll. It's in the barn just yonder.

The woman squatted beside her. She had a kind and weathered face. She said she was a volunteer with the Red Cross, and that she had a spare bedroom in her home nearby for just such emergencies, but Lottie assured her that there was no emergency, and that her father would soon return, and that she would be all right.

When night finally fell and the hotel windows all had darkened, Lottie hugged herself and rose and squinted north and south into the empty street. Another hour passed. Then, as by the errant force of her entreaty, there materialized in the darkness not a horseman in the road but a phantom afoot on the sidewalk, a sepulchral wraith bearing before it in outstretched arms some limp and boneless cohort.

Lottie backed as she rose.

Here, the woman said, draping the housecoat over her shoulders. I think we've had quite enough of this foolishness.

The widow Redd watched over her spectacles as Lottie rolled and snipped the cotton bandage and applied with great solemnity the barbed metal clips. She proffered the finished bundle for the woman's inspection.

That's fine, dear. Just like that.

A clamor erupted in the kitchen, and the woman set aside her work and started to rise but called instead for an explanation, the timbre of her voice summoning out of bedlam first silence and then the docile quiescence of children preparing the evening meal.

I don't know who it was that said many hands make for light work, the woman sighed, settling back into her seat. But I know it wasn't a mother.

Lottie smiled. Yes, ma'am.

Do you have any brothers or sisters?

No, ma'am. I was firstborn, and my mama died when I was three.

I'm so sorry. But perhaps that explains it.

Ma'am?

Your father's intolerable behavior. One must never underestimate the civilizing effect that a woman can have on a man raised among horses and livestock. Mark my words, a grown man without a wife is like a gander without a goose. Only half as tidy and twice as noisy.

Lottie giggled. Yes, ma'am.

Another outburst from the kitchen arose and subsided.

You sure was lucky, havin six healthy young 'uns.

The woman's eyes twinkled. Six still at home. Ten all together.

Each resumed her respective office, Lottie rolling and cutting and the woman stripping muslin from the bolt on the floor beside her, each listening to the low babble and purl of the kitchen voices.

Ma'am?

Yes, Johnny Rae?

What's it like? Havin babies, I mean.

The woman peered over her glasses. She removed them and set them on the table.

My dear, the miracle of childbirth is the Lord's special gift to all womankind. In a lifetime of lesser achievements, the arrival of my firstborn was my proudest and happiest moment on earth. I know that makes me sound like some dotty old dowager, but someday, the good Lord willing, you'll know exactly what I mean.

But don't it hurt?

Hurt? Pshaw. Pain is corporeal and fleeting and is a woman's lot in life. But the joy of motherhood? She closed her eyes and touched a hand to her breast. The joy of motherhood is a thing that lives in the soul and lasts a thousand lifetimes.

Palmer appeared in the doorway on Lottie's third morning in the warmly chaotic household of her widowed benefactress; a bloodshot and dirty Harlequin in calfskin gloves and a sagging red kerchief, the bay horse grazing hungrily on the lawn behind him.

Beggin your pardon, ma'am, he said, removing his hat, but I believe you got somethin belongs to me.

They rode out that same afternoon, doubled as before, with food in their bedrolls and the great blue horizon beckoning in all directions. Palmer smoking and scouting the country and Lottie slumped behind him, turning to glimpse over her shoulder the receding Monticello skyline.

He'd hired on with a cow outfit up on the Blue, he told her, until trouble, his old trail partner, had found him out again. Allegations were made over some missing liquor, and he, being the new man, had fallen under suspicion. A small misunderstanding that might easily have been resolved but for the mulish intransigence of the foreman, leaving wages unpaid and scores, therefore, unsettled.

They followed the dirt road south until they'd cleared sight of the town and come to an old wagon track that crosscut through the stunted cedars heavy with mistletoe. Here Palmer pulled rein and turned the horse and drew his foot from the stirrup.

Hop down, he told her.

What for?

On account I said so is what for.

She dismounted and stood on the dusty selvage. She looked up at Palmer in the saddle, and at the rising of the cedar forest, and at the darker blue pleating of the mountain beyond.

Now what?

Untie that coffeepot.

She worked the saddle strings while Palmer leaned and opened his valise, arching his back and snugging the revolver into his waistband. He lifted the canteen and drank from it, the water dribbling onto his filthy shirtfront. He wiped at his mouth and doffed his hat and slung the canteen strap over his shoulder in the manner of a Mexican bandolier.

You just keep out of sight, he told her. And be ready to ride.

You could just let it be.

What?

Is it worth gettin yourself shot over two days' wages?

The horse stamped. Palmer looked at her and looked at the mountain and leaned and spat in the dust.

Darlin, he said, I thought you might of knowed me better by now.

She started at the sound of the hoofbeats. There were two sets by her reckoning, moving at a trot. She stood and took up the coffeepot just as Palmer appeared in the roadway before her.

He sat astride the bay horse, but now with a catchrope dallied to his saddle horn and a sleek buckskin filly side-wheeling in the cross-trail behind him. The new dun horse was groomed and saddled, her stirrups pinioned to the horn. She wore no bridle, but Palmer, or someone before him, had knotted the woven catch-rope into a mecate.

Get on, he said, wiping his face with a shirtsleeve. She's green, but she'll pony.

Where'd she come from?

He twisted in his saddle and sighted the tree line above them.

Can you just this one time do what you're told?

She took down the stirrups and slid her whole hand under the latigo.

No time for that. Let's go.

Resting the coffeepot on the pommel, she stepped into the stirrup and hopped once and swung herself into the saddle. The saddle was huge and the stirrups were overlong and she reached them only on tiptoes.

Anyone come past here while I was gone?

I don't think so. I fell asleep.

Gripping the horn, she leaned and rocked until the saddle again was centered. Palmer, meanwhile, had uncoiled the catchrope and held it in his gloved fist.

You ready to ride?

She shifted forward and regripped the horn with her free hand. I'm ready.

He touched his heels to the bay horse, and they moved off in tandem, the bay loping and the buckskin trotting easily behind. He some cowboy Quixote in his gaudy kerchief and bandolier, and she his loyal Panza, her head bobbing, her kettle held aloft as though awaiting some signal to serve him.

They quartered the sun across the southern horizon, traversing the high plain and dropping down over the pass. Palmer turning to mark her, or the road behind her. They saw no cars and no other riders.

We get you a proper bridle and we could see us some of this country, he called to her. It don't take much money to live on the hoof.

On the outskirts of Blanding they picked their way into a side wash that grew into a narrow canyon. They followed the canyon westward, Palmer leaning or standing in the stirrups to read the silted washbottom.

The canyon forked and forked again, the air cooling as the walls rose higher around them leaving sunlight stranded on their upper palisades. The footing was soft and crusted in places where water once had run. After a while the horses perked and quickened, and they heard the lilting trickle of a spring.

They entered a massive chamber of red-rock walls draped in trailing moss where seepwater bled from the cool sandstone to pool in greenish puddles. The floor of the chamber was hardened sand, with a ring of firestones at its center.

They stood down from their horses and unsaddled them and left them loose to drink. Lottie was tired and sunburned, and she slumped with her back to a rock slab while Palmer knelt with the horses, wetting his kerchief and dabbing his banded forehead.

Need to get you a hat.

Lottie nodded, her eyes still closed.

How do you like that claybank?

She didn't respond.

I'm talkin to you.

Ain't they gonna come lookin for her?

Palmer rose and crossed to his soogan. He squatted and felt

within it, removing a stoppered whiskey bottle. The new horse lifted its head.

Don't worry about that, Palmer told her, uncorking the bottle and drinking and wiping his face on a shirtsleeve. I run the whole remuda. By the time they finish countin noses, we'll be long gone.

Lottie was silent. Palmer rose again and crossed to stand above her.

What is it?

Nothin.

Like hell nothin. You gonna sull up now cuz I pinched you a nice ridin horse?

I ain't sulled.

The hell you ain't. He drank again and turned and studied the horses where they stood with their heads lowered. Don't think I don't know what you're doin.

I ain't doin nothin.

Yes, you are. You're settin there all high and holy and you're passin judgments on me.

Am not.

He walked to where the new horse was standing and set down the bottle and gripped her roughly by the mane, lifting her head and leading her in a circle to where Lottie had risen and stood now with her heart in her throat.

You don't want this horse, is that it?

She didn't respond. Palmer drew the pistol from his waistband and cocked it and took aim at the horse's head.

Don't!

The gun fired and Lottie screamed, the echoes of girl and gunshot overlapping in their lithic refuge. The horse reared and galloped down-canyon, showering Palmer in sand where he stood with the pistol raised to skyward and the gunsmoke curling in the half-light above him.

Lottie began to sob. Palmer grabbed her by the shirtfront and yanked her forward and spun her roughly to the ground, the shirt cloth tearing in his fist. He kicked her once, twice, where she lay curled.

Damn you! Damn you to hell! Look what you made me go and do!

The morning was late in coming, and when Lottie finally woke, it was to Palmer bent over a cookfire with sunbeams angling from over the rimrock bathing him in a gauzy radiance. Nearby, both horses stood as bookends with their muzzles in the spring pool, the buckskin lifting its dripping head and nickering as Lottie stirred.

Her ribs ached and her head was light as she stood upright and moved but two steps from her bedroll before kneeling to retch, and to retch again.

Palmer was beside her as she spat and wiped her mouth. He lifted her gently by an elbow.

Easy now. Coffee's just about ready, and I got biscuits in the chute.

She could not straighten. He cupped her shoulder and walked her weak-kneed to the fire, where the saddles lay angled in the sand like jetsam left by a tide long receded.

Here we go. You need a blanket? How about that coffee?

He moved nimbly, fetching her blanket and her cup and pouring her coffee. Solicitous in his every aspect. He poked at the embers and unstacked the plates and reached for the iron skillet.

Whooee! Here. Hold this.

He passed her a plate and wrapped a glove onto the panhandle and parsed out the blackened biscuits. She nibbled and swallowed, and he hung as on tenterhooks on her verdict.

How's that? Good?

She nodded. He filled his own cup and sat and watched her as she ate in small bites, avoiding his eyes. Behind her, the bay horse moved across the sandy wash, sniffing at her empty bedroll.

I seen some cow track on the way in, he told her.

She looked at him without speaking.

Got me to thinkin, maybe I could catch on with a outfit right hereabouts. We could set us some roots, maybe find us a piece of ground. From what I seen of the cowboyin in these parts, I'd be top hand in no time. Then your pa, he could come to us instead of us chasin him all over creation.

What about the horse?

Palmer looked to the dun horse mirrored in the spring pool.

Tell you what, you let me worry about her. He set down his plate, reaching across to stroke her dirty cheek. I'm sure sorry about last night.

She looked away, and he rose on to his knees to face her.

Listen, Lucile. I been in some hard places in my life, and I seen some things no man ought to of seen. I know that don't excuse what I done, but a dog that's been kicked too much, well, he's liable to bite and scratch when he ought to be a'lickin and a'waggin his tail. And that's me right there in a nutshell.

He took hold of her hands.

I been thinkin about this all night, and I figured that you, you're like the little girl what finds that dog and takes him in and gives him a good home. Only it takes a while for that dog to understand that things is different this time, and that he don't have to snap and bite all the time to protect himself. That the little girl is lookin out for him, and that she won't do nothin to hurt him. And that's what I got to learn, I know that, and you've got to have a little patience with me is all. I guess that's the long way around to what I'm tryin to say.

Tears were in his eyes by the end, and she at the sight of them reached out to wipe his face, and in so doing became the very girl of his story.

They rode into Blanding side by side on the main street like thin and ragged heralds of some coming apocalypse, Palmer dirty and unshaven and Lottie hunched forward over her pommel and a town cur yapping and bristling in their wake.

They rode past the schoolhouse and the stakehouse, and they reined in before the lone café, where Palmer dismounted and tied the bay horse to a lamp standard. He reached up and eased the wincing girl from her saddle.

Wait here, he told her, passing her the knotted catchrope.

She watched through the plate glass as Palmer spoke with the counterman. The portly Dane listened with growing interest as Palmer spoke at length and then stepped aside to gesture streetward. At last the man untied his apron and circled the counter.

They stood at the window side by side, the big man nodding at the smaller man's narration. Then he said something and turned, and Palmer flashed Lottie a thumbs-up and moved to the door.

They ate chicken-fried steaks with mashed potatoes and flour gravy, and they drank cold root beers from the bottle through white paper straws. They sat by the window with an angled view of the horses, Palmer rising from his seat cushion whenever a stroller paused too long to regard them.

They had the café to themselves, the counterman washing dishes somewhere in back. When he finally returned, wiping his hands on his dirty apronfront, Palmer stood and followed him outside.

Lottie watched as they circled the buckskin, Palmer pointing and extolling as the counterman inspected the saddle and lifted the horse's pasterns each in turn, cupping her hooves and bending to examine her shoeing. He looked inside her mouth. He stood by while Palmer led her into the street and trotted her up and back. Then he spat on his hand, and Palmer did likewise, and the two men shook.

Palmer resumed his seat while the big man moved to stand behind the counter.

What? Lottie whispered as Palmer touched a finger to his lips.

The man when he returned placed one shoe on the empty chair seat and payed out the bills on the tabletop.

Five, ten, fifteen, twenty, twenty-five, thirty. He produced a pencil and drew a crude map on the back of his checkpad and placed it atop the banknotes.

You tell Mary Jane I'm the one that sent you.

Palmer lifted the stack and squared it and folded it into his shirt pocket.

Much obliged, cousin.

I assume you've got some kind of paper on that horse?

Palmer looked at Lottie. Well, he said, we did, of course. Only thing is, it got burnt up in that fire I was tellin you about.

The man nodded gravely. He turned to Lottie, resting a thick, pink hand on her shoulder.

I'm terribly sorry for your loss, miss. My mother passed on this year as well.

The rental when they found it was more shed than guesthouse, the floorplanks cupped and gapped and the open stud walls nested with skeins of feathery dust. The window glazing rattling in its sashes as the door swung closed behind them.

Lord knows, it isn't much, the woman said, snatching at a strand of floating cobweb. We don't rent it in the winter, of course. But there's a flush toilet and a tub through here, and a closet.

There was a bedstead as well, bare springs under thin cotton ticking, plus a sink and a small eating table. The woman drew a line in the dust with her finger.

I wasn't expecting to show it so soon. I'll send one of the girls down to sweep it out this afternoon. She glanced at Lottie and smiled. And bring some clean linens, of course.

Palmer turned to the window, which looked onto the back lawn and the main house beyond.

The woman spoke to his back. Are you by any chance kin to Lawrence Palmer? He's our county sheriff, you know.

Palmer turned. The woman was broad and potato-faced, with large hands and clear, unblinking eyes. Her age was sixty, or eighty. She wore a white cotton apron over her housedress, and her steel-gray hair was upswept and tightly bound.

Could be, ma'am. My granddaddy and my uncle, they was both Texas Rangers. He winked at Lottie. We Palmers got a long history with the law.

Why then, you'll have to meet my Will. The woman beamed, turning toward the door. He was county sheriff as well.

Palmer soon lapsed into a familiar pattern of gambling and drinking and sleeping past noon, of midnight suppers and afternoon breakfasts, and so was a stranger to Lottie's routine of rising with the sun and retching into the rusted toilet before heading outside to her chores.

The scrawny bay, which Palmer called Shithead or Shitface, but which Lottie had named Henry, became her chief confidant and confessor. He greeted her each morning, nickering at her approach, and he listened patiently to her ramblings as she busied herself currying and brushing his new summer coat and combing his mane and tail and picking the red-earth packing from his feet. Then, before filling his water and gathering his morning hay, she always stood before him, and Henry always stepped close to her and pressed his great oblong face into her shirtfront. Standing perfectly still. Breathing softly, as though smelling somehow her unborn child and remembering in the smell of it some other, former life.

As June bled into the withering heat of July, the slow dissipation of Jimmy Palmer was increasingly noted and remarked upon, both in the household of their tenancy and in the Blanding community in genreal. Incidents large and small grew both in frequency and amplitude, culminating in the Pioneer Day raid on a floating pitch game for which the locals fingered Palmer, who vowed to recoup his resulting court fine by any means necessary.

And so their landlady's offers to commend the Texas cowboy to her husband, who was off tending cattle on his summer range, waned and abated, and then ceased altogether. As did the social invitations once extended, and the pleasantries once passed, and eventually, even the rudimentary courtesies of that small and close-knit Mormon township.

On a Saturday evening in late July a knock sounded, and the door to the guesthouse swung wide, and Lottie looked up from her sewing to find their landlady in the doorway with her hair down and her housedress gathered tightly at her throat. Her eyes moving from the dirty-clothes pile to the dirty horse tack to the dirty dishes piled in the dirty sink, settling at last on the dirty girl, who sat thin and alone amid the manly squalor in a forlorn parody of adulthood.

Johnny Rae, she said, when Jimmy comes home, *if* Jimmy comes home, you tell him that Mr. Larsen was by to see him.

Ma'am?

Mr. Larsen. From the café. She turned again to the door. Something about a horse.

They saddled Henry in the moonlight and were gone before dawn, Palmer loose in the saddle, railing at the state of a world in which a man couldn't even get some proper shut-eye before running from the law.

The sun when it rose was hot and angry, and Lottie rode with her head on Palmer's shoulder in a bid to share his hat shade. They rode through scrub plains flecked with cattle and twisted cedars, and then, farther south, into the verdant geometry of ir-rigated farmland.

Maybe we could try our hand at farmin, Lottie suggested, rousing Palmer from his torpor.

I ain't cut out to be no sodbuster.

How come?

A tractor chugged and belched in the distant field, and Palmer leaned and spat in reply. You mean hitch old Shitface to a plow? I reckon that'd teach him how good he's had it.

The horse whinnied and quickened.

You ever worked a farm before?

We growed some cotton at Uncle Mack's.

Palmer grunted. My daddy growed oats. I never seen the point to it myself. He'd work like a nigger to raise feed for the horses, just so's they could pull the plow to plant the goddamn feed. Now where's the sense in that?

If we growed truck, we'd never go hungry.

The horse clopped and Palmer's hat rocked in languid sway with the movement. A hot breeze rose up from the west, carrying with it the loamy smell of the newly riven earth.

A goddamn sodbuster. Palmer shook his head sadly. My daddy would shit a anvil.

They camped outside Bluff in the shade of the Navajo Twins, whose paired ocher spires blotted the white glare of sunrise. A communal well was nearby, and Lottie brewed coffee while Palmer stood shirtless by the cookfire, scraping the last of the soap lather from his throat. He rinsed the straight razor in his coffee mug and closed his eyes and splashed the soapy lees onto his face, blowing and shaking his head.

Did I miss anywheres?

Wait. There is somethin peculiar, she said. Didn't you used to have two ears?

He smiled the smile of an artist pleased with his canvas, proud of his creation.

You sure you'll be all right?

I ain't afraid.

That's my girl. He fastened his shirt. Anybody asks, you tell 'em your husband's a two-fisted desperado with a quick draw and a quicker temper, you got that?

She looked away.

What's the matter?

It ain't nothin. Get on with yourself.

The land he'd found lay south and west of what town remained of the old Bluff City in those years of exodus and drought. There was a pioneer cabin, and a field choked over with knapweed and cheatgrass and spindly cholla. The scar of an irrigation ditch adjoined the land from the west, and they walked it together, to a wooden sluice gate on a larger ditch where willows grew and where water ran in a thin, silent ribbon through the green and whispering grass.

Can we just take it?

Palmer, squinting, looked up-ditch and down.

Shit, he said. Course we can. That's what it's here for, ain't it?

The cabin walls were cottonwood timbers daubed with the red clay mud of the region. Palmer repaired the door hinges and patched the broken window glass with siding salvaged from the outhouse. There was no barn or shelter for the horse, so he strung a picket line between the cabin and the largest of the cottonwoods, and in two days' time the horse had grazed a clear path through the field.

On the third day, they plowed. Or performed a parody of

plowing, with a device of Palmer's assembly that combined a rusted shovel blade, the wheels of an old ore cart, and the angled roof joist of the outhouse.

Bluebirds rose and darted as the horse strained against its rope traces with Palmer, shirtless and already sweating, standing his weight on the spade pedal.

Hyah! Keep him movin, he called to Lottie, who walked at the horse's hindquarters with a willow switch. Hyah! That's it. Shit, wait!

The blade had detached where the joist had tipped, and it stood impaled like a shark's fin at the head of the furrow. Palmer bent and tugged, stumbling backward as the blade dislodged.

He mopped his brow with a bare forearm and stooped to the task of repair. The horse quivering, stamping the flies from its forelegs.

Shit! Palmer cut himself on the bale wire, and he stood now sucking his finger. All right, let's give it another go. Get in front this time, and keep to a steady pace.

Lottie gripped Henry's cheekpiece as Palmer stepped up and nodded and she walked the horse forward. Twenty feet later, the blade detached again.

Wait, goddamnit!

Palmer stood glowering at the buried spade head. He kicked it, and the blade clanged, and he hopped a little circle, his maledictions ebbing only at the sound of a car horn.

Who's that?

I don't know. You wait here.

He limped to where his shirt hung, then crossed to the back door. She heard the screen door bang in front, and the sound of voices raised in greeting.

She walked the horse forward, to a point where she could see Palmer with his foot on the running board of a black Ford coupe, fanning himself with his hat. There was laughter, and another toot of the horn, and then the passenger door opened.

The car was already moving as the door closed behind him. And though his voice called out to her, his words were lost in the engine sound and the spinning of tires as the car carved a wide circle through the weeds.

The horse stamped.

Well, she told him, I reckon that's enough plowin for one day.

Three weeks later Lottie sat in the castle tower of her cabin, behind the shark moat of her unplowed field, searching the horizon for the handsome prince whose steed stood hobbled in the weedy yard out back.

She sat with one hand on her belly and both feet propped bare and dirty on the peeling porch railing. With her washing luff on the line. With her face blank and wondering, as the leaf must wonder at the wind, in which direction her future lay.

The boys from Blanding appeared at the house like coyotes each dusk, lean and red-eyed in their loud jalopy, their teeth flashing white from behind the dusty windows. Palmer rising and gripping his satchel. To work, he told her, since gambling was the pretext for these nocturnal forays, as for the roof unmended, and the wood uncut, and the field so conspicuously unplowed.

She rode Henry on some days, slipping out the back while Palmer slept, leading the bay horse down into the trees and following the irrigation ditch and the red willows that marked it like the drag-trail of something wounded. Past the old fort, whose cabins lay in ruin against the rocky palisade. Past the stone houses that stood as monuments to a pioneer spirit twice lost, to antiquity and modernity. Then to the post office, where no letter from her father, or any other letter, ever waited.

Some days they rode bareback in Cottonwood Wash, or down to the cool San Juan, walking doves out of the long grass and avoiding any farms or cars or other horsemen who might intrude upon their solitude.

On one such morning in middle August, as she and Henry recrossed the ditch and rode up into the tree shade, the sound of slamming car doors stopped them in their tracks. Men were afoot around the cabin; several men whose dark shapes hunched and scuttled, and all of them had rifles.

She lay whispering on the horse's neck. Quiet boy. Nice and quiet. Then she silently dismounted.

Voices called, and a dog barked. Sounds echoed from inside the cabin; crash and bang. Then doors slammed again, and engines started, and the cars moved off in a slow and dusty caravan.

She waited in the shadows for her heart to quiet. Then she led the horse forward, into the clearing, and left him with the reins trailing as she hurried to the door.

Their bedrolls had been tossed, and their clothes lay scattered at sixes and sevens. Palmer's satchel was open and his papers were strewn on the table. The front door was ajar and creaking, and when it banged open behind her, she screamed.

Palmer was barefoot and shirtless, the pistol grip peeking from his waistband. He scratched at his belly as he surveyed the wreckage. He bent and lifted his hat and punched the shape back into the crown.

You'd best gather your things, he told her. This farm life is wearin me out.

Chapter Seven

IT AIN'T EVEN AMERICA

THE COURT: Back on the record. All jurors are present and the defendant is present. Miss Garrett is on the stand.

BY MR. HARTWELL: You understand that you're still under oath?

A: Yes, sir.

Q: We were talking before the break about your father's letter and about your travels in Utah. It occurred to me over lunch that perhaps there was another reason you stayed with Mr. Palmer all that time, other than searching for your missing father, and that maybe, just maybe—

BY MR. PHARR: Your Honor, is there a question anywhere in our future?

THE COURT: Yes, a question, by all means.

BY MR. HARTWELL: My question for the witness is this. We know you had many opportunities to leave Mr. Palmer if you wanted to. We know you were pregnant with his child. You must have known that the chances of finding your father would be better if you stayed in larger towns or cities. And yet you rode off into the wild with the man you now claim was your captor—

BY MR. PHARR: Same objection.

Q: Isn't it true, Miss Garrett, that you stayed with the man whom you now claim to be both your captor and your father's murderer for the simple reason that you loved him? Miss Garrett?

THE COURT: The witness will please answer.

BY MR. HARTWELL: We're waiting.

BY MR. PHARR: Are you all right, Lucile?

THE COURT: The court will stand in a brief recess.

They'd avoided the roadway, or any sight of the roadway, steering southward by the blistering sun through a maze of boulder-studded canyons and red-sand washes, and at dusk they'd camped in the long shadow of Lime Mesa.

They'd made no fire and left no traces, and in the morning they'd rode out before sunrise and rejoined the San Juan River, following it westward over a rolling and eerily volcanic landscape until it met the road again some ten miles distant at a bridge.

A trading post stood by the roadside. The squat mud building had a rusted truck out front, and above it loomed the rock formation giving name to the windswept patch of desolation known as Mexican Hat.

Henry would not cross the bridge, stamping and rolling his eyes at the whitewashed wooden towers, and no amount of urging or cussing or quirting on Palmer's part would move him. So they dismounted, and Palmer blindfolded the horse, and they led it high-stepping on the creosote planking until midspan, where they stopped with the wind in their hair to lean and watch the green-brown water slide quietly through the canyon below them.

Has he got any last words?

They both turned to the voice. The old man cackled and his

feet shuffled in a sort of hillbilly jig. He was a gaunt and weathered leprechaun with a mottled face and hair the color of corn silk. In his waffled union shirt, yellowed at the underarms, and in the peeled braces that dangled to his knees, he gave the appearance of some mad marionette escaped from its handler.

Ain't you gonna offer him a cigarette at least?

The man's face caved as he laughed, and Lottie could see that he had no teeth.

Palmer drew the pack from his pocket and shook out a smoke. It ain't as dire as that. He lit the cigarette and offered it to the old man. I expect this here is the first bridge he ever crossed.

Much obliged, the man said. Philip Morris, I'll be damned.

Palmer nodded to the other side. Would that be Arizona yonder?

No, sir, not Arizona. And not Utah nor Colorado nor New Mexico neither.

What do you mean?

The man puffed and studied the cigarette, as though preparing to render some judgment.

Navajo reservation is what I mean. Paiute land before that. Injuns claim it ain't even America.

The blinded horse, smelling the cigarette, lifted its nose.

Would I find a man name of Goulding if I stick to this road?

The old man eyed him closely. Could be.

Fella in Bluff told me that Harry Goulding had some sheep might need tending.

The man smoked, his slitted eyes drifting to the end of the bridge.

It's a good thirty mile, he finally said. Give or take. No water to speak of. Hard country on horseback. He nodded at Lottie. Specially for a woman in the family way.

Palmer's head snapped to the girl, who stood with her eyes averted.

I was you, the old man continued, I'd backtrack to the post and get myself another canteen. Maybe better two. There's a spot further down you can water the horse.

Palmer shook out two more cigarettes. He handed one to the man and he bent to light the other, cupping the match flame in his palm.

Don't worry, mister. Them Navvies is plenty strange, but they're friendly enough.

Palmer pitched the match into the river. Do I look worried to you?

No, I wouldn't say worried exactly. The old man sniffed at the gifted cigarette and tucked it behind his ear. More like scared shitless is how I'd describe it.

They rode until dusk, through a vast red barrens and thence into a panoramic dreamscape of stone buttes rising massive and iodide from the desert floor below them. The buttes appeared as ships, or as the petrified stumps of some mythic forest felled by storybook giants, their shadows stretching for unbroken miles in the last, low light of sunset.

Holy shit.

These were the first words Palmer had spoken since they'd left the old man on the bridge, and now he reined the horse and turned his profile west toward the glass-blown sunset. He paused for a moment, drinking in the view, then put the horse forward again.

They made a dry camp, watering Henry from Palmer's hat and leaving him to browse among the stunted saltbush. While Lottie gathered the scarce kindling of their surroundings, Palmer hauled the saddle and dropped it heavily in the dust and prized from his soogan the canned beans and tortillas from the trading post.

Not until an hour more had passed, after the food had been warmed and eaten and the embers had dimmed in a feeble parody of the sun descended, did Palmer light a cigarette and finally speak.

So when was you plannin on tellin me?

She looked away, into the night.

Don't suppose you might know who the father is?

Lottie stood and walked from the firelight. She sought out the horse hobbled nearby and rested a hand on its haunch, on its neck, and it lifted its head to her touch.

She didn't see him rise, but she knew Palmer must have stood to kick at the fire coals that exploded, the orange embers swirling and racing.

When she returned at last to the fire, she found him reclined on the bare ground with his hat over his eyes and his arms folded and his boots crossed at the ankle. She took her same seat opposite and watched the dimming shape of him vanish with the last of the fireglow. There were no crickets where they'd camped, and no other nightsound save the rustling movements of the horse.

I'll say this but the one time, Palmer spoke into his hat crown, so listen real close. You want a baby, that's your business. But that don't make it my business, understand?

He lifted his hat to look at her, and he replaced it again.

Christ all fuckin mighty.

★　★　★

They saw the dust cloud long before they smelled the sheep, and they smelled the sheep long before they actually saw them.

There must have been over a thousand head. They spilled from the makeshift corrals and flooded the desert floor around them; a boundless, churning sea of ewes and bucks and wethers clustered tightly in bands of tens and twenties, the bleating and the tinkling of bells and the whoops of the men afoot and on horseback rising and echoing among the ocher cliffs like some hellish swarm descended.

Tents had been pitched alongside the corrals, and above their white canvas peaks, on a low rise hard by an enormous cliff-face, a two-story building stood. And though its walls were of a piece with the surrounding rockfall, its appearance in that vast and empty country was as startling as a lighthouse adrift on the open ocean.

The horse quickened its pace. The riders circled upwind, skirting the sheep and the corrals and raising a hand to the drovers they passed. They reined in at the stone building, and they sat the horse for a while longer, taking in the spectacle.

The downstairs room was dim and cool, with trowel-plaster walls and a raftered ceiling. A bench sat inside the door, and a raised wooden counter ran in a long L along both walls opposite. Behind the counter, shelves were stocked with canned goods and tins and yard goods and sundries. An old Indian man who may have been sleeping was slumped on the bench, while a raven-haired woman and a young girl on tiptoes, each identically dressed in calico skirts and loose velvet blouses, examined the shoes that were arrayed in pairs along the counter, their voices hushed in a rhythmic vocal cadence that was as strange to Lottie's ear as the bleating of the sheep outside.

Welcome, said a woman who'd emerged from somewhere behind the counter. Didn't see you come in. I'm afraid we're a little
busy today.

She was beautiful—tall and slender, with blondish hair and an
air of easy confidence, and her appearance was doubly startling for
its spare and rustic setting.

Palmer removed his hat. Beggin your pardon, ma'am. We was
lookin for Mr. Goulding.

The woman looked at Palmer, and at Lottie. She sidestepped
to an open doorway and called, Harry!

He'll be right down, she assured them, her smile radiant. He
may try, but he can't hide up there all day.

They were waiting outside when a gangling scarecrow of a
man emerged from the trading post and paused on the threshold.
He wore a checkered shirt with the sleeves rolled, and his cuffed
dungarees were cinched high at the waist in the manner of the
newly gaunt. His face was long and his hair was lank and center-
parted. He shielded his eyes with a hand to better survey the
pandemonium at his doorstep.

Hope you come lookin for sheep shit, he told them. We're
havin a special today.

Introductions were made, and hands shaken, and Lottie noticed
that although they appeared to be around the same age, Palmer
addressed the man as mister.

Fella name of Hunt up in Bluff, he told me you might have
some sheep down here to work, or maybe to lease. I guess he
wasn't foolin.

Goulding's smile was lopsided, laconic. Well. Your information
is good, but your timing is plumb lousy. The government came

in here yesterday and gave me twenty-four hours to move this flock across the river. And it looks like they're just about ready. Hey, Paul!

A young man on horseback came at a trot.

Paul, these here are the Palmers, and they're lookin to lease some sheep. You seen any sheep around these parts?

The young man tilted his hat and smiled. I say we give 'em the whole bunch right here and now for a rag dollar.

That's why you'll never make a trader, son. You about ready?

Ready as we'll ever be.

You tell Morris to take her nice and easy. Head straight for the Garden, and wait there for the wagon. I'm figuring Monday afternoon is about right. North side of Bell Butte, just south of the Lee place.

You got it. And, Harry?

Yeah?

Tell sis I want beefsteak and apple pie when we get back. And cold beer.

You get these lambs across in one piece and I'll bake that pie myself.

The boy winked at Palmer as he turned his horse. Ain't no call to be makin threats. He touched his hat to the girl. Miss. He trotted off, circling the herd and closing on the other rider.

I'd like to never seen so many sheep in my life, Palmer said as the riders called out to the drovers and a dog barked and the herd began to bunch in bleating protest.

There's near fifteen hundred head. Was a time they'd fetch a pretty penny. And I believe they will again, but first I need grass and water and time.

And a pair of trusty hands.

Goulding grunted. Tell you what. Tomorrow is Sunday. We generally have horse racing on Sundays. And just to show we ain't licked over this sheep business, I believe we'll have us a real do. That gelding of yours fast?

He's no Gallant Fox.

Well then, maybe we'll have us a chicken pull too.

And them sheep?

The woman appeared in the doorway. She pouted theatrically, and Goulding nodded and turned to watch as the flock boiled forth into the crossroads, its massive dust cloud rising and twisting like the smoke from a prairie grassfire. Like a windblown cottonfield, rippling as it moved.

You all stay and join us for supper, Goulding said, his eyes still on the sheep. It's a long ride back to Bluff.

They ate by kerosene lanterns; Palmer newly shaved and washed and Lottie in her best chambray shirt and Goulding's beautiful wife, whom he called Mike, shuttling the mutton and potatoes in steaming platters from the kitchen to the table. Goulding at the window, watching the sunset, the stone monuments arrayed behind him like a departing armada.

It sure is quiet without them sheep, he said over his shoulder. I forgot what quiet sounds like.

Mike brushed a loose strand from her face. Ten years we've been out here with nothing but the sound of our own voices. And now he's forgotten all of a sudden.

A hand-crank phonograph played faintly in the bedroom, and a yodeling cowboy song ended with silence and a rhythmic scratching. I'll get that, Goulding said.

They all sat up when he returned, and they followed his lead as he shook out his napkin and tucked it into his shirtfront.

It's always a pleasure to have visitors, he began as a kind of benediction. A man lives in raw country like this, he learns right quick to appreciate the value of good company. He lifted his water glass in toast, and the others did likewise. Mike and I love nothing better than to share our little slice of heaven with the world. Here's to a pleasant visit.

I never understood how these tradin post operations worked, Palmer said to fill the silence after the glasses were touched and sipped and set down again and the platters were being passed. The angle in it, I mean.

Oh, it ain't overly complicated. Goulding spooned potatoes as he spoke. The Navvies need their staples, like flour and coffee and sugar. We buy in bulk up in Durango, or down in Flagstaff. Potatoes and onions, crackers and candy. Salt. Canned goods. Yard goods. We either sell for cash or trade for sheep or hides or wool. And blankets, these Navajo women weave the most beautiful rugs and blankets, oh my. They earn cash money from lambs in fall and wool in spring. In between, we either trade in kind or we take pawn. Jewelry mostly, some belts and bridles. Wonderful silverwork. Mike and me, we provide a market for their wool and their weavings, and we build up a nice little flock for ourselves to take to the market in fall.

We did, his wife corrected. Back when there was a market.

Goulding nodded. Nowadays, you can't give away the sheep. Lose money just driving 'em to the railroad. But, we'll still buy one or two head from each family, just to tide 'em over. They're so god-awful poor. He cut the lamb with his elbow raised in a sawing motion. I'm kinda long in sheep just now.

167

What about this government business?

Goulding chewed. He dabbed at his mouth with the napkin.

This strip of land we're on, between the river and the Arizona state line, it used to be Paiute country. Fierce warriors, the Paiute. Gave the Mormons holy hell for years. So the big shots up in Salt Lake worked out a deal to move 'em off the strip. That was back in '23. Then the strip became public domain. The Navvies moved in, and then the wildcatters. Oilmen, some prospectors. That's when Mike and I come, back in '25. Then last year, once they finally figured there wasn't any oil to speak of, the federal government went ahead and made it all part of the Navajo reservation.

Palmer had stopped eating. And they let you stay on?

They had no say in it. This here is what's called a school section, so it never become part of the reservation. We lease it from the state of Utah. Problem is, what with this drought and all, and with the size of my flock the way it's got, there just wasn't enough forage. So a couple of judges showed up here yesterday, drove up from Shiprock with the police, and they served me with a notice.

The heck you say.

Goulding shrugged. There ain't no help to it now.

Mike stood and refilled their glasses from the pitcher. She smiled at Lottie, who smiled meekly in reply.

Palmer set down his napkin and cleared his throat.

Me and Johnny Rae here, we got us a little bit saved. Not much, but a little. What we ain't got is a situation for ourselves for the winter. When I heard you had sheep, I thought maybe we could work ourselves some kind of deal. Like maybe we'd ride herd for a percentage of the lambs and wool. Somethin like that.

I been a stockman all my life, mostly in Texas. I'm dependable, and I'm hardworkin, and I'm honest as the day is long. Oh, and a army veteran to boot.

Goulding chewed. Well, he said, scraping at his plate. I appreciate you coming all the way down here. That shows gumption right there. But I already got me a couple Navvies lined up to herd. And what with Morris and Paul on the payroll, I'm afraid there ain't much I can offer just now.

Except some fresh rhubarb pie, the woman said, rising to gather the plates.

They woke in the morning to a singsong chant that was faint at first and dreamlike in their somnolence. Each rose, blinking, to an elbow and looked across the tent floor to the other.

What the hell?

Palmer slid barefoot from his cot, and Lottie, covering herself with the tentflap, joined him in the doorway.

Look!

Far down the valley, a dozen or more riders approached in a long, single file. They were an irregular assortment on horses and mules, some alone and some with other horses ponied behind them. All appeared to be men. All sang the same lilting chant with their faces lifted skyward, and it rang high on the cliff walls, growing louder as they approached.

Looks to me like a war party. Hang on to your scalp.

Mike had emerged from the trading post, and she stood now at the threshold with hands on hips. She watched the riders for a while, then disappeared inside.

Come on, let's get dressed.

By the time they'd stepped into sunlight the chanting had

reached a crescendo. Mike was outside, as were several Indians from the little mud hogan that stood beside the trading post. A young Indian boy moved to Mike's side, and she took his hand in hers.

Hey! Get that pop set out! Goulding called from the upstairs window, and Mike and the boy hurried inside.

As the party reached the corral area, the chanting suddenly stopped. All of the Navajo men wore dark hats with tall crowns, some over bandannas, some adorned with feathers, and some with bands of quill or beadwork. They wore stiff Levi's and snap-front shirts, and some wore a kind of tunic under a belt of silver conchos. All wore skeins of red trail dust. The horses were cayuse mustangs mostly, but some of them were pintos, and a few were good-looking quarters under saddle or being ponied.

Henry, who had stood with his ears pricked at the chanting, now paced and blew in his pen. A pair of leopard Appaloosas in the pen opposite glanced up for but a moment, then returned to their hay.

When Mike and the Indian boy reemerged from the trading post, each struggling with the handle of a heavy ice chest, the two largest of the riders dismounted and handed off their reins and intercepted them in their progress. They hefted the chest and carried it on their shoulders to a table that had been set up downhill from the corrals in the shade of a thatched and sagging lean-to. Mike produced a bottle opener from her pocket and rewarded them each with a soda pop.

By now Goulding had emerged from the trading post and was speaking to the other men in Navajo. At one point several of the men looked across at Palmer, where he stood outside the guest tent. Then all dismounted, and there followed a general milling as the horses were untacked and watered and blankets were carried to the lean-to and arranged about it in sun and shade.

C'mon, let me introduce you, Goulding said as he approached the tent. Lottie hung back while Palmer followed the tall man first to the corral and then to the lean-to, where Goulding spoke and Palmer nodded and shook hands with each of the Indian men in turn.

Can I help with somethin? Lottie called to Mike as she passed, and the older woman stopped.

Why, thank you, Johnny Rae. That would be lovely.

Inside the cool of the bullben, Mike bent behind the counter and set a row of packages on the bartop.

Here. You can take these down to that table and open them and just set them out. Tell Harry I'll be down in a jiffy.

They were boxes of Tootsie Pops and Butterfingers and Baby Ruth candy bars. Lottie stacked them and carried them down to the lean-to, where the men parted and watched as she set them out and tore with her teeth at the paper wrapping. When she stepped aside, the men continued to stare at her and none of them moved toward the candy.

Go on ahead, she told them. They're for you.

Thank you, the tallest of them said as he reached for a Butterfinger, and the others crowded in behind.

Ready, get set, go!

The horses exploded at the drop of Goulding's hand, and he turned and spat in their billowing dust cloud. They were a pair of lean quarter horses, and the jockeys who rode them were the youngest and slightest of the men.

The others whooped and jostled and shouted in Navajo words

of encouragement or hex as the horses galloped neck and neck to a stake some quarter mile distant, where they braked and skidded in a churning shower of reddish earth.

Look out! Goulding called as he backed toward the onlookers, restoring the line with his bootheel.

The horses were a mirrored pair as they bobbed and dug for home, their nostrils flared and their tails aloft like battle jacks, the jockeys' quirts wheeling and cracking over and under as they thundered past the line to shouts and catcalls distinguishable to Lottie even in that strange and halting tongue.

Half of the spectators drifted toward the loser's blanket, on which coins and bracelets of turquoise and silver were scattered. Lottie and Palmer watched as the men laughed and elbowed one another and pocketed their winnings.

They do love to gamble, Goulding said as he moved to stand beside the two. You watch, after the racing they'll commence with the cooncan.

The horses had returned from their cooling trot and stood now slick and heaving, their great veins tumid over tight and rippling muscles. The jockeys slid to the ground and were variously consoled or congratulated. Then another pair of horses appeared, and the same jockeys stepped into the stirrups and turned them and moved them off at a trot.

You got an opinion on these 'uns? Goulding asked.

Palmer studied the horses. The ease of their gaits and the length of their strides. The shape of haunch and head.

These boys must know who's who. It ain't like they never seen each other before.

That's true, Goulding replied, but you watch. They'll match best to best so's to make it a fair race.

The other Indians were clustered together, drinking the grape and orange sodas and mouthing the candy bars and Tootsie Pops, licking their fingers and wiping the melted chocolate on their pantlegs. There was much discussion and chin-pointing, and soon hands were in pockets and rings and bracelets were removed and brandished like talismans.

Okay. Suppose I like that sorrel. Now what?

That's his blanket there. What's your wager?

Palmer leaned and reached into his own pocket. How about a paper dollar?

That's fine. Come on.

They walked together to where the men stood. Goulding spoke in Navajo and a discussion ensued among the others. Some shook their heads and drifted off, while others glanced at Palmer and at the girl who stood behind him and then huddled in further conference. At last one of the men bent to his bag and produced a silver ring with a band of inlaid turquoise. He showed it to Palmer and gestured with his head in Lottie's direction.

Palmer nodded. Yeah, sure. Why not.

The man, who wore looped silver earrings, crossed to the far blanket and tossed down the ring. Palmer bent and weighted his dollar among the coins and baubles on the blanket at his feet.

The horses approached the line together, their eyes rolling and their necks arched as they jigged and strained against the bit shanks, the jockeys talking to them and to each other and sawing on the horses' mouths. Goulding raised his hand again and counted again and set them off in another churning dust cloud.

These too were evenly matched. They streaked in tandem toward the distant stake, their polls bobbing like pistonheads, and as they neared the turn, the brown horse nosed in front and cut sharply so that the sorrel was forced wide and showered in its rival's dust plume. The brown horse straightened and pinned its ears and flattened out on the home stretch, and it held a two-length lead until, halfway to the finish line, it suddenly broke stride.

A cry went up from the watching men as the sorrel thundered past while the rider of the brown horse slid lightly to the ground, running and checking his limping mount and lifting its injured foreleg.

An argument erupted among the bettors, and while some ran to tend the hobbling animal, the others joined together in a circle with lowered heads and lowered voices. Grave faces, listening and nodding. Then, as the horse was led on past, the men who were huddled parted and turned, and Goulding was summoned to join them in their deliberations.

Will he be okay? Lottie asked Palmer as she followed the horse's progress toward the corral.

Looks to me like maybe a tendon. I don't think they'll shoot him. Less maybe they bet on him.

When the huddle broke again, a smiling Goulding crossed to where they stood.

Good news for you. They asked me to rule, and I ruled your sorrel the winner.

Palmer looked past him to where the losers were still talking and shaking their heads. Shit, he said. Don't seem fair to reward a poor judgment on horseflesh.

Goulding shrugged. Fair is where the fat lady sits.

Palmer left them and crossed to the blankets where he retrieved first his bill and then the turquoise ring. He stepped to the Indian in the silver earrings and pressed them both into the startled man's hand. The man tried to protest, but Palmer turned his back and walked to where Goulding and Lottie waited.

Goulding, hand to chin, said nothing. They stood together and watched as the next pair of horses was saddled and led to the waiting jockeys.

Don't worry, Palmer told him. I've always been lucky with chickens.

The Navajos were arrayed in groups of three and four wherever there was shade. Some were still eating, and some were napping, and one yet tended to the injured horse, wrapping its foreleg in a kind of poultice. Another pair loitered by the doorway of the trading post, while a quartet sat cross-legged around a jar in whose lid a slot had been cut. They dealt cards and played them on their blanket, depositing coins at long intervals into the jar slot.

Looks like some kind of rummy, Palmer observed from where they sat in the tree shade. Man could grow whiskers earnin a dollar at that rate.

Lottie sipped at her soda pop. Maybe these ones ain't the high rollers.

By God, you might be right. Maybe the big chief's on his way right now. Got himself a gold-plated Packard and big bag o' wampum.

They reclined in the shade and watched the game and watched the light shifting on the vermilion buttes that blazed beyond the players like ingots in the noontime sun. A hot breeze blew from the west, and it tousled the horses' manes and flipped one of the playing cards on the blanket. Lottie finished her pop and shifted and rested her head on Palmer's shoulder. He did not caress her, nor did he shrug her off.

Call me crazy, he said, but I think a man could hang his hat in these parts. Mike and Harry, they got a pretty sweet deal down here. And I think Harry's right about them sheep.

What about 'em?

What he said, about time and grass and water. In a couple years, that flock could be four thousand head. Once prices come back, the man that owns four thousand sheep is a rich man.

The players' heads turned toward the trading post, where Goulding had stepped again into sunshine. He sported a cowboy hat of battered straw, and he carried in one hand a hen inverted by its leg shanks. In the other, he carried a shovel.

Shit, said Palmer. I think I'm gettin the picture.

The sleepers were nudged awake, and the cards were collected and stowed. The men rose in unison and dusted their seats and drifted toward the corrals.

Goulding hefted the prostrate bird as he approached. You ever seen this in Texas?

You aim to bury that thing?

I'll show you. Come on.

They walked together onto the hot and dusty hardpan, and when they'd reached the morning's finish line, Goulding handed Palmer the hen, which flapped and settled again in helpless resignation. Goulding started to dig.

You see them stakeposts out there?

Palmer followed his nod and saw that the turnpost for the morning's races was but one of a dozen like stakes arrayed in a giant oval.

We bury the chicken up to its neck, see? Then all the riders wait in a big group over thereabouts. Each man gets a run at the bird. You pull it free, then you ride like hell, cuz they're gonna be coming after you. The man that rounds the course and crosses the finish line with the chicken's head in his hand is the winner. Give her here.

They traded. Goulding cupped the bird with both hands, its wings firmly pinioned, and he lowered it into the hole. Move some dirt, cowboy.

Palmer carefully backfilled the hole, and together the two men pressed and smoothed and stamped the ground until only the chicken's head and neck were visible, rooting and twisting like some hatchling newly born.

They returned to where the Navajo men had formed into a circle. Goulding spoke to them in their language, and with a shuffling of feet a place was made for Palmer to stand among them. At the center of the circle lay an empty pop bottle, and when all were finally in place, Goulding stepped into the circle and bent and spoke again and spun.

The bottleneck when it stopped was pointed at one of the jockeys. The smiling boy stepped away and hurried to the corral.

They continued in like fashion, repositioning themselves around the circle after every spin, every departure less enthusiastic than the last. Palmer was the eighth thus chosen, after the man with the silver earrings, and as he walked from the circle to his horse, Goulding's voice called out behind him.

Cinch her tight, cowboy! Once the racing starts, it's no holds barred!

Mike appeared from the trading post in new dungarees and a white and ironed blouse that seemed oddly formal to the occasion. She carried a patterned blanket under her arm, and when she'd descended to where the riders were clustered, she laid it on the ground and spoke a few words in Navajo. Goulding stood beside her and spoke again at length, and there followed a lively discussion among the men on horseback. Then, one by one, each rider removed some piece of jewelry and held it aloft and tossed it onto the blanket.

Goulding moved to stand alongside Palmer's stirrup.

You got five dollars?

Palmer frowned. He leaned and dug into his pocket. I suppose I should've asked before you got me this far.

Goulding chuckled. Winner gets the rug and everything on it. Them's big stakes in these parts.

He took the bill from Palmer and walked it to the blanket and set it down with great ceremony. Mike then bent and gathered up the corners and carried the rug and its weighty cache to the shade of the lean-to.

One by one the riders turned their horses, and when they'd regrouped at a distance, Goulding stood alone at the start line with the chicken's neck worming luridly between his boots. He called out a name, and the younger of the two jockeys removed his hat and flung it and rolled back from the others. He circled at a trot, then roweled his big pinto forward at a gallop.

I can't bear to watch this, Mike said to Lottie, and she turned and walked toward the trading post.

Four strides from his target, the boy gripped the saddle horn with his left hand and dropped his weight to the offside, his right hand cupped and trailing, and as he lunged at the twisting bird, the other riders pulled rein, their horses backing and squatting.

The boy missed. Whoops of derision went up from the mounted gallery, and the horses relaxed again. Then another rider removed his hat and flung it to the ground.

The pattern repeated. As each of the riders swooped and missed his grab, there was a chorus of jeers, followed by a reordering within the group as legs were hitched and cinches already tightened were tightened yet again.

The garden of hats grew to half a dozen before a rider, the second of the young jockeys, grabbed enough neck for the hen's back to hump. The bird was squawking now, one wing partly exposed, her throat and hackles twisting and flailing wildly.

When the brave with the silver earrings whooped and flung his hat, the others began jostling in earnest. The rider circled and gathered speed and came at a jerking gallop. As he swung low and lunged at the easy target, the bird exploded from the ground in a welter of dirt and feathers, and the waiting riders burst forth like a swollen levee breached.

The lead brave's horse was a line-back mustang, short and compact, and he rode it low over the pommel with his shoulders rolling and his topknot bouncing wildly. The flapping bird he held aloft like a bagful of money. His lead, which was eight to ten lengths at the outset, narrowed with every stakepost as the others, kicking and whooping, closed the distance behind him.

The first to reach him, midway down the backstretch, were the two young jockeys. They flanked and crimped the fading mustang, and as arms flailed and hooves clacked, a plume of red blood burst from among them, spattering Palmer where he leaned, dusty and blinded, a length behind the leaders.

Palmer reined to the outside as a cry went up and the horse that was before him stumbled, horse and rider pitching forward into the piston-churn of hooves and hocks. From this new vantage Palmer could see the outside jockey holding firm to the leader's wrist, with the chicken, or what was left of the chicken, flapping raw and bloody over the outside jockey's pommel.

The horses leaned through the final turn and thundered for home. Palmer kicked and cursed and gained on the outside as Henry's ears flattened and the trailing horses one by one began to fall away.

Slowly, gradually, Palmer inched the bay horse forward, until he was nearly abreast of the trio. Then, with a hundred yards to go, he made his move.

Swapping the reins to his outside hand, he leaned and clapped the fist that gripped the flaccid birdneck, then he used his thumb to pry the fingertips away, one by one, until the prize was in his grasp.

He jerked it free as the horses crossed the finish line, and he held it aloft as he stood in the stirrups, dirty and bloody and grinning crazily, loosing a warbling parody of an Indian war cry.

The huddle was again in session by the time Palmer had cooled his horse and pulled his saddle and returned still grinning from the corral. Only this time it was Goulding who appeared vexed, glancing over at Palmer as he argued with the others.

We got a problem?

Palmer spoke to Goulding's back, and to the wall of baleful stares that encircled the taller man.

Goulding sighed without turning. Seems like Mr. Cly here thinks he crossed the line with the bird still in hand.

Palmer looked to the man in the silver earrings. His arms folded and his jaw set, obsidian eyes glinting under his dirty hat brim.

That a fact.

What's more, it seems the others agree with Mr. Cly. I'd have to say they're downright settled on the subject.

I thought you was the referee. What do you say?

Goulding turned to face him. I'd say you want them trinkets, you'll have to shoot your way out of this valley.

Hell, there's a good fifty dollars of loot in that blanket.

Goulding nodded. And then some.

The Indians stood shoulder to shoulder, joined as in arms to repulse some threat to their sovereignty.

Palmer leaned and spat. Fuck it, he said as he turned. They want it that bad, they can have it.

He marched toward the corral and took down his saddle and carried it to the tent, where Lottie stood watching in the doorway.

What're you lookin at? he snapped, and she nodded over his shoulder.

Look behind you.

The man in the silver earrings stood apart from the others, and when Palmer turned to face him, the Indian walked forward and reached into his pocket and proffered the bill that Palmer had wagered.

That's mighty white of you, Chief, Palmer said as he reached for the bill. But the Indian snatched it away and turned to where the others watched, and all of them burst out laughing.

Goulding stared into the fire. I don't know what to say.

Palmer plucked a brand from the fire and lit his smoke. Don't worry. It ain't the first time I been poorly used, and I'm guessin it won't be the last.

Still.

Palmer shook out the flame and leaned back and looked off down the valley, where the shapes of the giant monuments appeared only as darkness torn from the surrounding starlight.

What I don't understand is you trustin these people with your sheep.

Mike rose and lifted the coffeepot from the fire and topped the mugs all around.

Come on, Johnny Rae. Let's us girls powder our noses.

Lottie followed the slender woman into the bullpen, then through a back passage to the wareroom, then up the narrow stairs. A kerosene lantern burned in the kitchen, and Mike filled the coffeepot from a pitcher.

I've been wanting to thank you for all your help today. It's been nice having a woman around the place.

Yes, ma'am.

Mike turned to face her. You're not much of a talker, are you?

Lottie shrugged.

That's all right. I'm not either. Not really, anyway. It's been my experience that the more a woman talks, the less she seems to say.

Lottie smiled. Yes, ma'am.

How long have you and Jimmy been married?

I don't know. A few months, I reckon. Seems like longer.

Mike nodded. Not that it's any of my business, but isn't he a little old for you? Harry and I thought you two were Mormons at first, but . . .

Lottie looked at her with no expression at all.

Like I said. None of my business.

Mike wiped her hands on the apron that hung by the basin, and she lifted the pot by its handle.

We'd best be getting back.

Twenty-three years.

The woman stopped.

That's how much older. I figured it from papers I seen.

Mike set down the kettle.

Are you happy, Johnny Rae? That's the only thing that matters. When I followed Harry out here, my family all said I was crazy. But they didn't know Harry, and they didn't know how I felt about him. She touched the girl's cheek with her long and slender fingers. Does Jimmy make you happy?

Lottie turned to the window. To the scissored cameo of two men paired by a fire, black shapes brightly haloed against a larger backdrop of nothingness.

He may not always act like it, but Jimmy needs me.

That may be, but you didn't answer my question.

Lottie faced the woman. Yes, ma'am. She nodded once. I guess he makes me happy. Some of the time, anyways.

Lottie woke to the creak of a buckboard wagon.

She slid from her cot and crossed the empty tent to the door in time to see a gray-haired Indian seated high on the springseat behind one of the Appaloosa horses. In the bed behind him was a canvas tarp lashed to the gunwales with lengths of baling twine, and behind that stood the second Appaloosa haltered and half-hitched to the back of the rig, all of them standing in near relief in the cool light of dawn.

The Indian sat with his head turned toward the trading post. He raised a hand, and Goulding in the doorway responded in kind. Palmer stood beside the taller man, and when the wagon rolled and tilted forth into the crossroads, the two men turned and disappeared inside.

They were seated at the upstairs table when Lottie entered from the stairwell. Mike rose and smiled and crossed to the kitchen to fetch a plate from the warmer.

Morning, honey. I hope you like pancakes.

Goulding watched the girl eat. Palmer smoked, his eyes out the window. When Mike returned, Palmer stubbed his cigarette onto his breakfast plate and pushed it away.

Well. We could look in on 'em at least. If that would ease your mind any.

Goulding nodded, still watching the girl. I'd be obliged.

If this Oliver is as hard as you make him out, there could be trouble.

Goulding frowned. I don't mean to give the wrong impression. Bill Oliver is a fair man. A tough man, but fair. If they find water, and if they stay out of John's Canyon, there shouldn't be cause for trouble.

And if there's no water?

Goulding sipped his coffee and set the mug down on the table.

Let me tell you a story about Bill Oliver. He must be pushing seventy-five now, but he was sheriff in these parts for a good many years.

Wait a minute. His wife name of Mary Jane?

You know her?

Palmer glanced at Lottie. We met her one time in Blanding.

Goulding nodded. Well, back in nineteen and twenty-three, they had a spot of Indian trouble hereabouts. The Posey War, some call it now. The last Indian war in the West.

War, Mike snorted, clearing Palmer's plate. Foolishness is what I call it.

It all got started when a couple of Ute kids name of Sanup's boy and Joe Bishop's little boy got into a fracas at a sheep camp. Killed some sheep, set a bridge on fire. That sort of thing.

Mike returned and took her seat at the table as Lottie chewed and listened.

Anyways, Oliver arrested both boys and brought 'em to stand trial up in Blanding. And old Posey, he come into town with some of his braves to keep an eye on the proceedings, him being head troublemaker and all. There weren't no love lost between Posey and them Mormons, I can tell you that. It was a powder keg is what it was.

Mike snorted again.

The trial was held in the basement of the old schoolhouse there. Then, at the lunchtime recess, all the good Mormons went home to break bread with their families, leaving Oliver in charge of the two prisoners and a crowd of hostile Indians. Which, if you'd ever met Bill Oliver, you'd have to say was about a fair fight.

If he's seventy-five now, he couldn't have been no spring chicken in '23.

Goulding grunted. Like I said, a fair fight. Anyways, Joe Bishop's boy had him some kind of wooden crutch, and just as Oliver was mounting up outside the schoolhouse, why, he went ahead and bashed Oliver with the crutch and grabbed for Oliver's gun.

Palmer grinned and leaned back in his seat. No shit.

One of two things happened next, depending on who's doing the telling. Either Joe's boy got the gun and pulled the trigger on

Oliver, or Oliver squeezed on the prisoner before losing his gun. Whichever it was, the gun jammed. So Joe's boy hopped onto a little racing pony that Posey's boy Jess just happened to have saddled up and waiting, and off he went with Oliver in pursuit. Only now Joe's boy got the gun to working again, and he turned and shot Oliver's horse out from under him.

What about that other boy?

Sanup's boy, he took off with Posey. They run straight to Westwater and warned the other Utes to get ready for a shooting match. Well, sir, that started a stampede for high ground, with a posse on their tail and old Posey fighting a rearguard with his thirty-aught-six Springfield rifle.

Palmer shook his head. Sounds like a goddamn jackpot.

That night in Blanding, all the good Mormons turned out with their torches and pitchforks. Then the next day, while another posse set out to scout for Posey, Bill Oliver had the bright idea of rounding up every Ute man, woman, and child he could find and holding them hostage until Posey surrendered. And that's what he done. First in the schoolhouse, then they built a big stockade out of barbwire, smack in the middle of town. He held over eighty prisoners under armed guard for nearly a month.

I guess he didn't take kindly to havin his horse shot.

Goulding sipped his coffee. By now the whole area was crawling with Mormon rifles. Not to mention U.S. marshals, and newspapermen, and every crackpot vigilante in riding distance of the Four Corners. Hell, there was even talk of bringing in airplanes with machine guns.

Mike took her husband's plate and carried it to the kitchen. Like I said, plain foolishness.

So what all finally happened?

Well, let's see. Joe Bishop's boy got shot dead. Some say it was the posse, and some say it was Posey himself, upset over him starting all the ruckus. The rest of the Utes eventually surrendered and went into the stockade. It wasn't for a month or so that they finally found old Posey's body, hid up in a cave. Turns out he'd been shot on day one, only nobody knew it until a federal marshal discovered the body. Only then did they let them other ones loose.

Palmer lit another smoke. And what about Oliver?

Oh, he retired, eventually. Went back to his cattle. Him and his boy Harrison run their herd out there in John's Canyon. Near as I can tell, the years haven't mellowed him one bit. He sees sheep in that canyon, someone's liable to get himself ass-kicked. Or worse. He's not a small man.

Them Injuns of yours know to give him a wide berth?

Goulding grunted. They been warned. There ought not be a problem this time of year, since that there is winter range for cattle. He sighed, pushing away from the table. But come September, things could get mighty interesting.

They set out after breakfast, riding double and following the sheep track northbound out of the valley. In late afternoon they met the Knee brothers south of the Mexican Hat bridge. Paul, the younger, reined his horse and crossed his hands on the pommel.

We miss any horse racin yesterday?

Afraid you did. Palmer nodded toward the distant monuments. And a chicken slaughter to boot.

The boy turned to his brother. You hear that? Shit.

Harry said to say if you really want beer with your pie, then you'd best pick it up at Spencer's.

The boy again looked to his brother, and his brother looked over his shoulder to the little mud trading post, small across the river.

Up to you.

Shit, the boy said. I ain't about to start goin backwards.

The next rider they met, miles beyond the river, was the old Indian drayman on the Appaloosa saddle horse. They saw him from afar, where a wagon track split off from the Bluff road. Palmer stopped and nodded at his approach, and the old man nodded in reply but did not stop and continued clopping down the road toward Mexican Hat without ever once looking back.

The track from which he'd come was narrow and rutted by rains long past, and it meandered for miles through a surreal landscape of jagged spires and sandstone buttes. They could tell where the flock had bedded by the buckbrush and black sage, stripped and trampled, and by the telltale remnants of wool clinging like Spanish moss to the bare and broken branches.

Not until dusk did they finally catch sight of the sheep. Palmer walked the bay horse onto a rise and studied the spectacle of the whole flock fanned and tinted pink by the churning dust that hung roseate in the fading sunset.

The buckboard was nowhere in sight. The drovers were a man and woman afoot, moving the flock westward with a dog zigging and heeling the wandering bunchquitters.

Palmer leaned and spat. I reckon Shitface got enough exercise for today.

Lottie rested her head on the flat between Palmer's shoulders. What're we doin out here, anyways?

He fished a smoke from his shirt pocket and cupped it and

bent into the flame. When he'd straightened again, the flock had faded farther into the distance.

I don't know about you, but I ain't seen grass enough to feed a milk cow in these parts, let alone a sign of water.

So?

So I got me a feelin them dumb sonsobitches is already headed for that canyon.

Palmer lifted his leg over the pommel and dropped lightly to the ground. He mouthed the smoke and reached for Lottie to ease her off the bedrolls. They stood together and stretched beside the streaked and breathing horse.

I think it's best we stick around awhile. Ain't no tellin what harm might come to them poor souls in country such as this. He slapped the horse's flank. And if somethin did happen, who would there be to look after all them hungry sheep?

On the night of the following day Palmer rose from their fire and crossed to his soogan and felt there for something unseen. They had spent the day mounted, trailing the flock westward at a distance in the shadow of Cedar Mesa through shad scale and beaten greasewood, then along a narrow roadway that wound through boulders big as houses, and then through a gated bottle-neck where the trailside fell away to the dizzying cliffs of the San Juan River gorge. Farther on, the canyon had opened onto a sea of summer grasses—grama and galleta, Indian ricegrass and Western wheatgrass—newly parted by the trampled path that led them, in the cool of late afternoon, to the waters of a caprock pool.

Now, some six hours later, Palmer's shadow passed across the rockface as he moved to where the horse was hobbled, and Lottie heard beyond the firelight the creak and clink of the saddle.

Clint?

He didn't answer. She stood and moved into the blackness and there was startled by the sudden advent of horse and rider stepping toward her as from some darker place beyond.

What're you doin at this hour?

He stopped the horse in a stance defined by the play of firelight on spur and buckled bridle.

I'll be a whet. You go on to bed.

You'll break your neck in this pitch, she told him, but he was already moving, down the clattering scree to the canyon floor below.

She retired to the fire, and long after the embers had died, to her bedroll. She listened, wide-eyed at first, to the faint bleating of sheep and the soft tinkle of distant bellwethers giving way to the closer nightsounds of coyote and owl. She closed her eyes to listen, and then, after a time, to sleep.

At the sound of the first gunshot, she sat upright. The moon was newly risen, and it bathed the canyon floor in a wan and bone-colored light. She stood. From the edge of the escarpment she could make out the shape of an old line shack, but nothing else beyond. Not horseman nor buckboard wagon nor the night camp of the Indian drovers.

The second gunshot was met by the barking of the sheepdog, and at the third gunshot, the barking stopped.

Chapter Eight

A BIGGER FIRE THAN THIS

BY MR. PHARR: You were how old when you learned you were pregnant?

A: Thirteen.

Q: Your mother had died when you were three years old?

A: Yes, sir.

Q: You were raised by men? No women with whom to discuss matters such as pregnancy or childbirth?

BY MR. HARTWELL: Leading.

THE COURT: Overruled.

A: Yes, sir, that's true.

Q: You were frightened, I should think, to learn you were pregnant?

A: Yes, sir. A little.

Q: Living in a strange place?

A: Yes, sir.

Q: Your father missing?

A: Yes, sir.

Q: This man Palmer, whatever his coarse and reprehensible conduct, your only link to the world you knew?

A: Yes, sir, that's true.

Q: Is it any wonder then that you clung to him? A mere
child, alone and frightened and pregnant and orphaned—

BY MR. HARTWELL: Objection, Your Honor.

THE COURT: Order. We'll have no more of that.

Lottie paged through the mail-order catalog while Mike hummed tunelessly, absorbed in her knitting. Outside, Goulding's and Palmer's voices wafted up through the stairwell as they hauled provisions from the wareroom out to the bed of the creaking buckboard.

I sure would like me a doll someday, Lottie confided, folding the page for Mike to see.

The woman paused and studied first the page and then the girl, the latter's face tanned and earnest under the tilt of her cowboy hat.

Honey, you'll have a real live doll soon enough.

Lottie smiled and Mike smiled in reply, until the girl's eyes returned to the page and the woman's smile faded quickly and altogether.

They sat that way in silence, the woman furtively examining the girl and the girl examining with unguarded wonder the offerings of Montgomery and Ward.

We certainly are lucky that you and Jimmy checked on those sheep.

Yes, ma'am. Lottie licked a finger to turn the page. Jim says he thinks somethin musta scared 'em off. Like maybe they seen a panther or somethin. Jim says you can't trust them Injuns for nothin.

Let's go! called a voice from downstairs, and Lottie returned the catalog to the table.

Thank you for the picnic, Mrs. Goulding. The girl's eyes rolled upward. And for the hat.

Mike set her knitting aside. You take care of yourself out there. And if there's trouble, you get to Mary Lee, understand?

Yes, ma'am.

You tell her I said so.

All right.

You promise?

I promise.

And keep that sun off your head. And don't overdo yourself, or smoke or drink any alcohol.

Yes, ma'am. You sound like my mama.

The woman picked up her knitting. You go on now, she said, waving the girl off with a hand. Don't keep your man down there waiting.

The gypsy sheep spent the rest of that summer in the bottleneck canyon, where the grass was high and the water abundant, and where the towering cliffs of the mesa gave shelter both from wind and beating sun. The spring lambs thrived and fattened, and Lottie hailed them each by name as she led them in child games of her own devising, laughing and telling them that she would soon be fattest of them all.

The days were long and languid as she and Palmer napped in the shade of the cottonwoods, or lay in the water pink and naked, or combed the canyon floor like sleepwalkers searching for potsherds and Stone Age arrowheads. They climbed among red boulders to read there, scratched in black varnish, the ancient missives of an ancient people: the spirals and squiggles, the tracks of animals, the effigies of goats and of men with heads of birds, their meanings lost to modern man by the endless passage of time. They played at rummy and at pitch, and they ate from the wagon, and they slept in the company of Cassiopeia, and under the watchful eye of Vega.

If I'd known sheepherdin was this easy, Palmer told her on one such night of starry repose, I'd of quit cows and roosters years ago.

But the days were growing shorter, and the sun flatter, as the angle of the shadows on the sheltered bed ground tilted inexorably toward the coming equinox. And thus Palmer, turning to survey the old line shack and its copse golden cottonwoods, announced his plans for a dugout.

What all for?

On account of winter, that's what. In case you ain't heard, it snows around here.

But what about Mr. Oliver?

What about him?

Ain't this his land?

Palmer crouched and snatched the stem from his mouth. Hell, no. He's maybe got grazin rights, but this here is public domain, and you and me is the public same as anyone else. Anybody can live out here that's got a mind to.

Are you sure?

Course I'm sure. Why, we could build right next to the old man's shack if we took a notion. Palmer stood again, regarding the cabin. Wouldn't that be a hoot? We could hang us a big ol' sign out front. He framed a square with thumbs and fingers. Posey's Hideout.

She giggled. Keep Out.

No Lawmen Welcome.

This Means You.

Asses Kicked, Inquire Within.

She lay back and laughed, and he squatted beside her and rested his hand on her belly where her shirt rode up, and where the sun shone warm, and where his hand was like some nut-brown flaw on purest alabaster.

It's got like a sourdough biscuit, he said in wonder.

She rested her hand on his.

More like the whole loaf, she replied.

Lottie followed the tracks from the dead lamb up into a side draw, only to lose them there amid rock and rubble. The lamb was called Emily, and her mother stood bleating over its torn and twisted carcass, indignant at the impassive ruminations of her nearby bandmates.

I'll be right back, mama, don't you worry, Lottie assured the forlorn ewe as she hurried off in search of Palmer.

She found him at his excavation, shirtless despite the chill, his hands composed on the handle of his shovel. She started to speak but stopped when she followed his gaze to the canyon mouth, where three figures on horseback were skylit at the edge of the river gorge.

Go on to the tent, he told her.

Who is it?

I don't know, but I can guess.

The men came forward and reined their horses at the point of the escarpment where the canyon opened wide. They clustered again to confer. One of them pointed, and Lottie turned to see with a stranger's eye the spectacle of fifteen hundred hungry sheep scattered in bands and bunches across the beaten and stubbled grassland.

The men came on at a lope.

What should we do? Lottie asked, but Palmer only slipped into his shirt, his eyes still on the riders.

The riders halted again at the line shack, where the eldest of them dropped heavily from his saddle and handed off his reins and approached like a gathering storm to the clash and clang of jingle spurs. A huge man, slab-faced, with a low brow and small eyes burning over a heavy, gray mustache. He was, Lottie noted, the smallest of the three.

What in God's name, the old man sputtered, the sweep of his arm completing the indictment, the gesture encompassing the fresh excavation and the felled timbers beside it and the trampled grassland beyond.

Afternoon, was Palmer's reply, calm as a shopkeeper. Prime day for a ride.

The man's face reddened. Listen, you! I'll give you ten minutes to get yourself packed and get these goddamn sheep movin off my range. After that, we'll start layin in mutton.

This last pronouncement was punctuated by the sound of a shell levering onto the Winchester rifle that the middle rider held upright, the stock butt resting on his thigh.

Palmer stood his ground. No, mister, you listen to me. You show us a legal paper on this range, and we'll move them sheep. But until then, we aim to do just like we're doin, and if you don't like it, you can piss up a goddamn rope.

The old man was about to respond when he noticed Lottie or, rather, noticed her condition.

He removed his hat.

Son, the old man said, extracting a pocket watch from his vest. I don't know who you are or what it is you think you're doing, but I got two hundred head comin in on the trail in less than two hours, and those sheep are down to eight minutes.

Palmer pitched the shovel. He stepped toward the man, but the man did not budge, and they stood that way, face-to-face in mismatched apposition.

The rider with the rifle turned to the youngest man and snickered.

Less you got a paper on this range, Palmer repeated, them sheep ain't goin nowheres.

The man replaced his watch and half-turned to the riders.

Harrison.

The mounted gunman shouldered the rifle and took aim at the nearest of the lambs.

Wait! Don't!

Lottie rushed forward, into the line of fire. The rifleman looked over his gunsight, and his father turned once again to Palmer.

I'd say it's your call, sonny.

Palmer darkened. He grabbed Lottie by the arm and pulled her, stumbling, toward their makeshift corral, where, under the watchful eyes of three Mormon generations, he cursed and kicked and hitched the big Appaloosa to the buckboard.

There played out, in the weeks that followed, a game of cat and mouse. Whenever the cattlemen would quit the line shack for the comfort of their Blanding homes, Palmer and Lottie would drive the sheep back through the bottleneck, there to graze and water thirstily among the lowing Seeps Ranch angus.

When they were lucky, the sheep were out of the canyon and back on the open range by the time the cattleman returned. When they were not, trouble followed.

Oliver threatened the sheep, and he threatened Palmer, and he rode his big bay walking horse into Monument Valley to personally comfort Harry Goulding. He lodged a formal complaint at the county seat in Monticello. And, true to his former calling, he took to wearing his old sidearm, a single-action Colt revolver, in a tie-down leather holster.

Palmer divided his time between helping Lottie with the sheep and working alone on the dugout; between their roving camp outside the canyon and their future home within. He too traveled to Monticello, a three-day pilgrimage on horseback to file his own claim on the canyon. He too began carrying his pistol for the other man to see.

Goulding first sought allies among the Mormon stockmen of the area, and finding none, he traveled to Monticello to plead his case to the authorities, citing the hardship attendant to his forced vacation of the Strip. He carried chuck and gear and updates to Palmer and Lottie, urging them to do what they could to avoid further conflict, but insisting they do what was necessary to keep the flock alive.

Lottie, for her part, tended sheep. She rose before dawn to fix breakfast, and at first light she moved the bleating flock to what little browse there was over the next hillock, beyond the next arroyo. With the sheep thus bedded, she returned to break their camp and move the buckboard wagon. Then, at long day's end, in the violet light of dusk, she gathered wood and built their fire and set up camp again.

The forage in the Garden of the Gods, thin even in summer, grew scarcer still as the flock's migration in and among the buttes and spires doubled back upon itself. By mid-October the grass was all but gone, and the greasewood and the shadscale all but stripped, and the incessant bleating of the lambs took on a new and poignant urgency.

As old man Oliver despised the sheep, and the shepherd, so he pitied the girl, and under one guise or another would ride out to watch her, small on the vast horizon, driving her buckboard or waddling after her charges, ripe with child and as helpless looking in that desolate rockscape as the feeble lambs she tended.

And so it was that, on a cold and moonless evening in early November, the old sheriff appeared without warning at their campsite.

They'd heard no hoofbeats, yet there he sat astride the walker, his collar upturned, horse and rider sudden and rippling in the orange fireglow. Palmer, oblivious to the apparition, dropped his plate when the old man finally spoke.

I see you eat about like you build.

Palmer scrambled to his feet, his eyes moving to the rifle stowed in the buckboard.

There's some would say it's customary to offer a night visitor some coffee.

What do you want? We ain't done nothin.

Oliver stood down from his walking horse, leather creaking and spurs chiming, the eyes of the animal glowing beside him like a pair of stolen embers. He brushed past Palmer and sat on the ground where Lottie sat, his canvas duster fanning like a carriage robe beneath him, his Colt pistol winking in the firelight.

Here, Lottie said as she leaned for the coffeepot. That's a clean cup right there.

Much obliged, the old man said as Lottie poured. There are few things in this world to top the smell of fresh-made coffee over a wood fire.

He held the cup with both hands. You're gonna give me a sore neck like that, he said without looking at Palmer, and after a moment, Palmer sat.

Somewhere beyond the firelight, a lone coyote cried, ragged and plaintive, and the sheep around them stirred. The horse turned its head; two red eyes becoming one, then none, then two again.

Frost this morning, Oliver spoke into his cup. Expect you noticed that. Snow soon, the Lord willing. His chin lifted slightly. Even if you get a roof over that thing, you'll freeze come Christmas. That ain't a suitable shelter, son, that's just a fact. And as for living out here, I've seen grown steer froze to the ground in open country like this.

I reckon we'll make it, thank you very much.

Oliver's eyes held on Palmer where he sat cross-legged on the ground. Diminished, somehow, under the bigger man's gaze.

Maybe you will and maybe you won't. Far as you're concerned, I can't say that I care. But I can guarantee one thing, and that's this right here. You keep on like you're doing, and you'll lose this baby here.

It must be a comfort, Palmer sneered, knowin all there is to know.

The old man nodde, his hat brim, underlit by the fire, a burnished crown of light.

The good Lord has blessed me with seven children and sixty-three grandchildren. Over fifty great-grandchildren by my last count. I reckon I know a thing or two about childbirth.

The good Lord, Palmer said. There ain't no escape from it.

The old man tasted his coffee.

You just said a mouthful, son, whether you know it or not.

You'd be well counseled to put more faith in the Lord than you do in that hogleg you been carrying.

You seen that, have you?

I'll tell you what I seen. I seen a dozen of your kind come through here over the years, all mouth and no trousers, mistaking a gun barrel for a backbone. If you think I'm the kind that bluffs easy, you got a lot to learn about people.

Palmer's smile was reptilian. You think I'm bluffin, you go right ahead and call me.

The old sheriff shook his head, returning his eyes to the girl.

What I come to say tonight is this. Me and Jake—that's my Alice's boy—we can make camp at the Seeps. That old oil shack ain't much, but it's got a woodstove and a floor and two beds off the ground. He turned again to Palmer. That's one for each of you.

Palmer stood, his face dark above the firelight. We can shift for ourselves, thank you. We don't need your Christian charity.

Oliver nodded. He swirled his dregs and pitched them into the darkness. He placed a hand on his knee to rise.

I'm obliged for the coffee, ma'am. He stood and bent and set down the cup. We'll be out of that shack come morning. Be a shame if it went to waste.

He turned and brushed past Palmer, his huge shape receding into darkness, his crown dimming to nothing.

You and your man are welcome! his voice rang as he mounted and turned the horse. Afraid them sheep are not!

The snow when it came was wet and heavy. It slanted off the mesa, muffling the frantic bleating of the sheep as they turned from it en masse, surging southward toward the roadway and the river gorge beyond. By the time Palmer had saddled Henry and reached the first of the stragglers, he could see pockets of fleece like drifted snow packed into the draws and arroyos where the sheep had wedged in their panic, and where the living were bleating and scrambling for purchase on the muddy backs of the dead.

God damn it to hell!

His hands were nearly frozen. He slid from his saddle and waded, arms paddling, into the wet and roiling scrum. He slipped in the mud and fell. He tugged at the screaming sheep and wrestled their heads and was kicked to the ground in return. He sat on the muddy embankment, soaked and filthy and numb with cold, and he covered his ears with his hands.

Lottie found him thus when she arrived in the buckboard, and her screams were lost in the swirling snowfall as she climbed down over the wheel. She scrambled into the wash, and fell, and rose again before Palmer caught her and pulled her to him, holding her though she struggled against him, the wind howling and lashing their union.

Just let it go, he told her quietly. There ain't nothin to be done.

By dawn the skies had cleared, and the red mud in the arroyos had congealed into a thick and viscid clay, and they walked out together to tally their losses. Fifty-three sheep were dead in the snowstorm, plus four who'd been wounded beyond doctoring, and those Palmer had shot. The rest they herded back toward the mesa, where they built a bonfire by which to warm the living and in which to incinerate the dead.

I seen horses last night, Lottie told him, still shivering in her blanket.

Where?

Comin out the canyon.

How many?

Two.

Palmer stood from the fire. The view, both south and east, was to the ocher buttes of the Garden, their shoulders mantled in the newly fallen snow. Palmer cupped his hands and blew. He hadn't shaved for a week, and neither man nor girl had bathed in over a month.

The hell with this, he told her. The ones that ain't froze are gonna starve soon anyways.

He crossed to their sagging tent, and when he emerged again, it was with Goulding's coyote rifle.

What if they come right back?

Palmer slid the rifle into the scabbard. He led Henry, dark and winter-shaggy, through the throng of muddy sheep.

They'll come back all right. But if these ones don't get some grass and water soon, we'll need us a bigger fire than this.

Lottie woke to the sound of a motorcar. She thought at first it was a fever dream, but the sound persisted as she rose from bed and crossed on swollen ankles to the frosted windowpanes.

The stovemouth was ash; the shack still dim and bitter cold. Palmer lay snoring in his single bed. Outside, sheep and cattle grazed together in the new sunshine, the ground fog of their mingled breaths melting the frosted grass tips.

The engine sound faded.

Clint, she whispered. Wake up.

He rolled and laid an arm across his forehead. What's the matter? What time is it?

I heard a car.

What?

A car.

It's just a dream. Go back to sleep.

It come from up the canyon, I swear it.

Palmer sat upright in his blankets. You see anything?

She shook her head. Just the stock.

He was wild-haired and blinking when he joined her at the window. Rank in his woolen union suit.

You wait here.

She dressed when he'd departed, pulling on the jumper that was Mike's and the sweater that was hers and that covered the swell of her belly. The long johns she wore were Palmer's, old and torn and baggy-waisted. She sat on the bed light-headed, waiting for the room to still.

She was donning her cowboy hat when the door opened and Palmer high-stepped into the room on a blast of frigid air.

It's them all right. They're dressed like for a funeral and headin this way.

He shed his blanket and hopped into his trousers. He crossed to the doorway and lifted his rifle from the gun rack, then put it back again.

He's like to pitch a fit, she said.

Palmer was pacing now, raking his hair with his fingers. Okay, here's the deal. The spring was froze and we had no water. Then you took sick. Then we had some sick lambs, and—

There was a knock, but before they could answer, the door opened with a bang, dust sifting from the rafters as the old sheriff ducked through the doorway. He wore a dark hat with a suit of darker wool under his long and tawny duster. A string tie under a starched collar. He was freshly shaved, and the white of his mustache glowed against the red rage of his face.

By God, he seethed at Palmer. You ungrateful little whelp.

Hello, Mr. Oliver.

His flint eyes softened when they shifted to the girl.

Good Lord, child, you're pale as a ghost. He removed his hat and set it on the table. Fever?

She nodded. Yes, sir. I think so.

He placed an icy hand on her forehead. How long?

About a week.

A week? He turned and glared at Palmer. And I suppose you've been cooking and cleaning for this one the whole time? Of course you have. Sit over there.

The old man turned to the doorway. Jake!

The boy who entered was older than Lottie but younger than Palmer and bigger than both of them combined. His face was freshly shaved. He too wore a necktie, and a vested suit, and a starched and strangling collar. He carried with him a fatted pullet, plucked and pink in a tin roasting pan.

What the hell's that?

The boy hefted the pan. Don't you know what day today is?

From the look of things, I'd say it was Sunday.

No, sir, the boy said as he set the pan on the table. Today is Thanksgiving Day.

Jimmie Rodgers played softly on the phonograph, and Lottie listened through "The Brakeman's Blues" and "In the Jailhouse Now" and "Blue Yodel No. 3."

When the music finally stopped, she heard voices outside, and she slipped from her bed and crossed into the front room, to the window that overlooked the corrals. Paul and Morris were there, wiring crossrails to a fencepost, and Morris stopped and lifted his head in the manner of a dog hearing a silent whistle. He looked to the trading post and saw the girl there framed in the upstairs window.

Mike! he called to his sister. She's up again!

Lottie was settling into bed when Mike appeared in the doorway, wiping her hands on her apron. Her hair was up, and she blew a wayward strand from her face.

You're fixing to wear one of us out. Are you warm enough?

Yes, ma'am.

Would you like a glass of water?

No, thank you.

Mike crossed to the bed and sat and placed a hand on the girl's forehead.

I know it's hard, honey, but the doctor says you've got to stay put. It's for the baby's sake.

I know it. I just get fidgety is all.

Are you sure you don't want some water?

I'm sure.

Mike rose again and smiled at the girl, who smiled warmly in reply. Each of them was the object of the other's longing: Mike the mother of Lottie's shadow memory, and Lottie the daughter Mike would never have, and whose own unborn daughter, or son, was to both of them a shared adventure.

I'll bring you up a magazine. And some tea.

She got as far as the doorway before the daily question came.

Did Harry go for the mail today?

Yes, honey, the woman answered without turning. But nothing came for you.

The arrival of December marked the seventh month of Lottie's pregnancy and the second week of her forced quiescence in the little guest bedroom of the little stone trading post where she lay pale and hidden like some bone-shard relic, consecrated and fragile, in the vast and red cathedral of Monument Valley.

She watched from her sickbed aerie as parcels began to arrive, hauled up from Kayenta by Paul on horseback, or down from Durango by Morris or Harry in the Chevrolet touring car. Old blankets and jackets, or used shirts and shoes, all of them opened and clucked over and stored in the big guest tent for the coming holiday.

When on the seventh day of December a piñon pine went up in the bullpen, Lottie was allowed downstairs to witness the trimming. Mike and Harry solicited her opinions from the bench where she sat swaddled in her blankets, and Lottie, for her part, directed their ministrations with an odd and poignant gravity. And on the very next morning, amid a cacophony of Navajo chanting and generalized commotion, the parson Sunshine Smith arrived.

His battered Ford truck was a wobbling parade float, a kind of motorized Conestoga that was both marvel of engineering and paean to the nomadic life. Lanterns were clanking and pots banging, and four roped Herefords trudged wearily behind. Rocking chairs rocked and water jugs sloshed, and the scalloped edges of a green canvas awning rilled like piano keys in the cold desert wind.

Lottie watched, transfixed, as the truck and its trailing entourage of Navajos afoot and on horseback snaked into view. First the Knee brothers appeared below her, followed by their sister. Then Mike retreated inside, her voice ringing in the stairwell.

Harry! Shine's here!

Goulding appeared in the doorway, a towel around his neck.

Ain't you supposed to be in bed?

He moved to stand beside Lottie in the window, and together they watched the spectacle unfold.

He does make an entrance.

Is he really a parson?

Goulding dabbed at his chin. I don't know about parson. Preacher is more like it. Or missionary, I suppose. He was a Presbyterian once, but him and the church, they never got eye to eye on the Navajo question. Or the liquor question, I reckon. Now he's more like what you'd call a hand-trembler. He glanced at the girl. A medicine man.

Do you think he'd ask a blessin? I mean, for my baby?

Well, I reckon he could. Course there's no telling where it might get heard. Christian god or great spirit. Might be like one of them party lines on the telephone that gets all mixed up in transmission. Bound for heaven, and then it hits the wrong relay and winds up on Navajo Mountain. Maybe jumbled up with some other prayers, half English and half Navajo. Ain't no telling what kind of blessing might come back.

Lottie was a remote observer of the Christmas preparations. First the magic truck was off-loaded, its parcels and bundles removed to the tent for storage. Then a huge pit was dug, and a mountain of firewood gathered. Then there rose a makeshift abattoir of poles and canvas sheeting to which each of the tethered steers was led, alone and blindfolded, to be slaughtered.

Lottie watched and slept and rose to watch again. By day the Indians came and went in tidal fashion, sometimes dozens, sometimes only four or five seated in a circle, playing at cards or passing between them a shared can and spoon. By night the abattoir glowed from within, and the smearing of the skinners and the spattering of the skinned read from her high vantage like painted runes on an outsize Japanese lantern.

Day and night there was chanting, and on the third night rhythmic drumbeats and stuttered dances performed by firelight.

Mike would visit her each evening to recount the day's events, only to admonish her for having witnessed firsthand the events that were recounted.

On the eleventh day of December, after her breakfast tray was cleared, Lottie heard voices in the stairwell. They spoke in English, and in Navajo, and were followed by the clatter of footsteps.

Three men entered her bedroom. Two were Navajo elders in velvet shirts, each heavily ornamented in earrings and necklaces of silver and turquoise, their faces blotched and shriveled. Each wore his hair—long and lamp black and shot throughout with gray—in a loose and greasy bun. The senior of the two wore a beaded shoulder bag, and the other a tall black hat that he removed and placed with great ceremony on the chair inside the doorway.

The third visitor, by accident of parentage, was a white man. He wore over his frayed cleric's collar a jacket of fringed buckskin and a large silver crucifix centered with a single blue stone. His face was red and parboiled, and his eyes were hewn of the selfsame veined and sky-blue turquoise.

She guessed that the parson Sunshine Smith was half the age of his companions. It required no guessing to know that he'd been drinking.

Well, he told her, you must be Johnny Rae.

He placed one cold hand on the swell of her belly while cupping the other as if to hold some unseen object. He spoke briefly in Navajo, his eyes lifted to the ceiling, while the elders stood stiffly behind him, splenetic and silent.

I'm much obliged, she said when he'd finished and the elders had knelt to rummage their bag. I guess I was expectin a Bible readin or some such.

The parson fixed her with his raw and terrible eyes.

Many are those who've found comfort in the good book, he said. And for each of them a thousand more whose cries of anguish echo yet in the dark hallways of history. In every tongue known to man, and in others strange yet to our ears precisely because of what is written there.

Lottie blinked.

I know what you're thinking, the man continued, fingering the gaudy cross. Why then does he don each day the very trappings of the oppression and subjugation which he so passionately deplores? The Diné have a saying, child, perhaps you have heard it. They say you cannot wake a man who only pretends to be asleep.

He looked to her for some sign of understanding.

In Coleman, he told her, they called me reverend. In Flagstaff, they call me parson. In Blanding I'm yet known as a man of the Christian cross. But these are mere guises, my child. Props and costumes, to suit the actor's purpose. And it is my purpose, indeed, it is my calling, to help the helpless, to clothe the naked, and to feed both physically and spiritually the hungry victims of my forebears' terrible genocide.

He removed the heavy cross, lifting it over his head and stashing it in a pocket.

Your host, Dibé Nééz, understands this. He is a wise man, unburdened by the white man's superstitions. And Leone is a fine woman, strong and true. In their fellowship, at least, you are blessed.

On the floor behind him, an oblong crystal lay prismed in the window light where the old men knelt beside it. One spoke in Navajo, and the parson listened and translated.

My friend asks whether you are the woman of Little Sheep, the man who tends his flock near the Garden of the Gods.

Yes, sir.

Again the old man spoke to the crystal.

My friend asks whether the baby that causes your sickness is the child of Little Sheep.

She did not answer. The old man spoke to his cohort, and they nodded and rose together in a complex girdering of hands on knees and arms on shoulders until the three men all now standing conferred in low voices, the parson glancing at Lottie where she lay. Then the parson stepped aside, and the old men stood paired at her bedside, druid apple-crones wreathed in the wig hair of Halloween window puppets.

One of them held her wrist in his small and leathery hand. His eyes rose to the ceiling, and he began a low chant. The other, his eyes tightly closed, soon joined in.

The chanting quickened. Lottie looked to the parson, but his eyes too were fixed on the ceiling. She felt suddenly light-headed. She felt her throat constricting as the room closed in around her.

As the old shaman's wrist-grip tightened, his arm began to vibrate, and an electric charge ran from Lottie's forearm to her elbow to her shoulder. Thence to her entire body. She opened her mouth to speak but she could not speak. Her legs tingled. Her feet tingled. The room began to blur.

She felt her arm rise. Then, as the old man released his grip, the chanting ceased and the room snapped into focus. Her arm, still tingling but dead now to her conscious mind, grew rigid. She watched, powerless, as the arm that was hers and yet no longer hers fell to the bed and rotated as by some force unseen to ten on the clockface, her finger stiff and pointing.

She heard herself scream. She heard, as through a heavy curtain, the voices of the men in conversation. As if debating the meaning of what they had seen. Of what it foretold.

Her arm ached. She tried again to bend it, and this time it bent.

The men regarded her with detachment. There were rapid footsteps on the stairs.

What all happened? she asked, her voice a whisper.

The parson touched a hand to her forehead. My friends wished to know the whereabouts of their people who went missing in the Garden of the Gods. They asked the great spirit to enter you, that you might show them the way.

Lottie felt sweat beading on her forehead, and a sudden wave of nausea, just as Mike burst forth from the landing. She stopped in the doorway and clapped a hand to her mouth, strangling a cry.

Lottie, still oddly quiescent, followed her eyes. To the bed. To the blankets below the rise of her belly. And only by sitting upright could she see the darkly crimson wellspring as it pooled between her thighs.

PART THREE

Chapter Nine

HARD TWISTED

BY MR. HARTWELL: Miss Garrett, just so we're clear on this, you never saw Mr. Palmer kill the alleged deceased, is that correct?

A: You mean my daddy?

Q: That's precisely whom I mean.

A: Then that's true.

Q: Or take an ax to him?

A: No, sir.

Q: And you never saw this skeleton that the state claims to be the remains of the alleged deceased until . . . when was it? Last week?

A: Yes, sir.

Q: And that was with Mr. Pharr and Sheriff Newton both present?

A: Yes, sir.

Q: And which of them told you that the skeleton belonged to your father?

BY MR. PHARR: Objection.

BY MR. HARTWELL: I'll rephrase. When Mr. Pharr first took you to see the skeleton, tell the gentlemen of the jury exactly what it was he said you were going to go look at.

She called out in darkness, and after a long while the door opened and a quadrate beam of bright light climbed the wall where she lay. Within it, the black and graven silhouette of a woman. Then all was dark again.

When next she awoke, it was daylight. The door to the hall-way was open and she heard the distant tapping of a typewriter. Her head was throbbing. She tried to sit up but could not, and she vaguely apprehended through an ethylene fog that her wrists were bound to the bedrails.

On her third awakening she found herself unbound and attended by a woman of middle years. The woman was seated, her hair severe and tightly pinned. She leaned and touched a hand to Lottie's cheek.

How are you feeling, dearie?

Lottie's tongue was thick.

I'll bet you'd like some water, the woman said, rising and crossing to the door. Don't worry, I'll be right back.

The room was sparsely furnished. Other than the chair just vacated, there was a small table on caster wheels, and a painted radiator beside it. A porcelain pan resting on the table. The room's lone window was small and without curtains, and she could see from the sunlight on the worn linoleum that the window glass was inlaid with a fine wire mesh.

The nurse returned with a tray. She set it on the table and carried to the bedside a drinking glass with a straw.

Here. Try some of this.

Lottie tried to sit, but her pain was hot and stabbing, and in its radiant clarity she remembered that she'd been pregnant, at the same moment she realized that she no longer was.

On the third day of her convalescence, the doctor appeared. He was a precise man with a trimmed mustache and steel-rimmed spectacles. He set his calfskin bag on the table, and the sight of it, its familiar shape, was to her as a millstone tossed to a drowning woman.

Where's my baby? They keep sayin I got to wait for the doctor.

The doctor shot a cuff to expose a wristwatch. He sat.

Mrs. Palmer, he began, with a demeanor whose gravity took the last of her breath. Please try to relax. You've had a very difficult time. You've lost a great deal of blood, and it's only through God's healing grace that you're with us still.

The doctor rested his hand on hers where she held it balled against her thigh. His touch was cold and light, like a settling moth. Like the shadow of the angel of death she knew him to be.

Your baby was born alive, but prematurely. I'm afraid it's very small and very, very weak. The odds of its survival are almost nil. I'm terribly sorry.

Where's my baby? I want to see my baby!

The doctor pressed her down by the shoulder, and the sunlight from the window toggled his spectacles. Clear. White. Clear again.

I'm afraid that's not advisable. Or even possible.

I got a right to see my baby! I got a right!

The doctor stood. Again he checked his watch.

Just tell me, please. Is it a boy or a girl?

The doctor crossed to the table and lifted his valise.

A boy or a girl, damn you!

He turned to regard her for a final time. I'm sorry, he said again.

Two days after the doctor's visit, Lottie was encouraged to walk. Made to walk, in fact, though bent and shuffling with the nurse soothing and steadfast at her elbow. Once, twice, down the long hallway to the picture window with the view of Blue Mountain, the new snow white on the alluvial cedars like confectioners' sugar.

The next day she was called to the telephone, where Mike's words were hollow and distant, as though coming to her through a long stovepipe.

Johnny Rae?

Where are you?

We're in Flagstaff, honey. We came down for New Year's, but we're heading home tonight.

How was Christmas?

Christmas was fine. We all missed you. We saved you some cake, and there's still a gift under the tree with your name on it. Johnny Rae? Are you there?

I'm here.

Listen, honey, I can't talk for very long. Harry and I were thinking, maybe you'd like to stay with us for a while. Until spring, maybe. Or longer. It's really up to you. What do you think about that?

Silence.

The nurse said we could come up next week and take you home. To the trading post. Maybe on Tuesday. How does that sound? Would you like that?

Yes, ma'am.

Mike.

Ma'am?

Call me Mike, honey. Or Leone.

All right.

All right then. Are they taking good care of you?

Yes, ma'am.

Is there anything you'd like us to bring?

I don't know. Maybe some clothes. I'm not sure what they done with my clothes.

All right then. We have to run now. Harry sends his best. And, Johnny Rae?

Yes, Mike?

I'm so sorry about the baby.

On the day next following, Lottie was asked by the nurse to sit with another patient, an elderly man who'd fallen from his roof while shoveling snow. He'd been found by neighbors the next morning, frostbitten and delirious.

Man and girl sat opposite one another on hard wooden chairs. The man wore flannel pajamas and a tattered robe of no determinate color. His nose was purple and bulbous, and he talked to Lottie in a gravel voice of the crossing at Hole in the Rock, and of Indian wars and range wars, and of the founding of Bluff City. He talked to her of horses he had owned, and dogs, and of wives and children born and buried, and he moved his tokens on the checkerboard with stubbed and bandaged fingers.

Of the baby, nothing more was said. Lottie knew it was a boy, and she knew from her conversation with Mike, and from the faces of the Mormon women, that her baby boy had died. Just as she knew from the old man at his checkerboard that death and childbirth were, in that cold and windswept Zion, but two faces of a coin.

Two days later, as Lottie stood at her window watching the mallards circle over the bare cottonwoods, she heard a familiar voice downstairs.

She left her room on stocking feet and crossed the cold linoleum to where she could see him leaning unsteadily, hat in hand, over the woman at the desk. And as she appeared above him, silent at the balustrade, he stopped in midsentence and turned and lifted his face.

He reeked of firesmoke, and of bourbon whiskey. They rode together in Harrison Oliver's Model A Ford, in a silence as frozen as the black macadam, and when the pavement ended, Palmer reached for the glove box and opened it and removed a stoppered bottle. He offered it to her, and when she did not respond, he bit the cork and tilted his head to drink.

You're skinny as a bedslat, he told her. I guess there's that at least.

She watched the frosted plain and the white and twisted cedars, and in the bleary door glass she watched Palmer as he drove.

The winter had aged him. His skin was raw and mottled and there were crow's-feet at his eyes and slack now in the line of his jaw. His eyes were yellowed, and bloodshot, and he had neither shaved nor bathed.

I got a surprise, he told her.

What surprise?

He grinned drunkenly. The sheep are fine, thank you, in case you was wonderin. Oh, and we got us a new horse. Only that ain't the surprise.

What horse?

He drank again and set the bottle between his legs. Let's just say a stray showed up one day, all cold and hungry-like, so I give him a good home. I been breakin him to the stock. He ought to be just about right for you in a couple weeks. And guess what? He's a pinto!

He cackled crazily as he turned to regard her. Ah, you ain't foolin me. I know you always wanted a pinto.

The snow outside Blanding was mostly gone, and what little remained had been plowed from the red-clay roadway into low drifts that appeared as the bloodied dressings of some ghastly wound laid open. Palmer leaned forward and wiped the fog from the windscreen with his shirtsleeve.

I want you to tell me somethin, she said, breaking their long silence. The truth. I want you to tell me what really happened to them Indian herders.

What?

Them two Indians was working for Harry.

I already told you. I run 'em off with the gun. Why?

Cuz they got friends down at Goulding's was askin after 'em, that's why.

Askin what?

Askin did I know where they'd gone to.

Christ, I already told you. They just moved on. Or maybe they fell into the goddamn river. How the hell should I know?

They arrived in John's Canyon after dark. They parked the car by the line shack, and Palmer bade her wait as he disappeared into the frozen night. After a while returned with a lantern.

The sky outside was starless. He took her arm and led her to his old excavation, where a humped mound now rose in the yellow lamplight like some ancient tumulus. He lifted the lantern to reveal a low stone facade framing a small crate-plank door.

Surprise! he told her.

Lottie crawled forth into the bitter dawn with her blankets still around her. She stood, blinking and shivering. Frost was on the car and on the roof of the line shack, and a vast and glistening sea of frost blanketed the canyon floor, broken only by the smoking hulks of the cattle.

From the lee of the shack rose a wisp of woodsmoke, and she heard after a moment the thin and tinny melody of a harmonica.

She walked toward the sound, moving quietly, and upon rounding the corner saw the broad back of Jake Shumway, the old sheriff's grandson. He sat before the cookfire with his sheepskin collar raised, his head wreathed in semaphores of breath frost as he played a song of delicate beauty that contrasted starkly with his brute size and with his bleak and empty theater.

She listened for a long time. Until, although she'd made no sound, the playing stopped abruptly and the boy stood as though bitten and turned to face her in blank and wordless wonder.

He removed his hat.

The ground was black and trampled where the sheep stood bleating near the canyon narrows, and although their winter fleece was thick, she could see that the animals were thin, and listless, and that many of the yearling lambs were gone.

Ain't there any better forage than this? she asked Palmer, who sat the new pinto horse with the new JP brand, smoking and watching the flock.

Yeah, he said. Right through that pass yonder.

How long have they been out here?

Palmer took a final drag and flicked the glowing butt, startling the horse. They brung the car on Friday. That makes it four days.

You reckon they'll be goin anytime soon?

He fished his makings from his shirtfront.

They been tradin off the watch. The old man stays a few days, then Harrison, then the kid. Sometimes they overlap. They was all gone for Christmas, but now they're back at it. He chuckled mirthlessly. I'm startin to think maybe they don't trust me.

Lottie slacked the reins and rose from the seat of the old buckboard wagon and gathered the blankets to her chin. These sheep need water, Clint. They need food.

You think you're tellin me somethin I don't know? The horse backed at the rise in his voice. You think I got stupid while you was off layin in a warm bed havin breakfast brought to you on a tray?

He sawed the horse and kicked it, hazing the sheep as he went.

When Lottie woke the next morning, the Oliver car was gone. She walked behind the line shack to where the cattlemen's firepit lay black and cold, and she shielded her eyes to count the horses moving loose among the beeves.

As she circled back to the dugout, a shape draped on the shack's door handle stopped her. It was, she realized, a coat. A heavy, sheepskin coat.

By the time Palmer crawled from the dugout disheveled and blinking like some wild thing undenned, Lottie had already groomed their horses and built a fire and started the coffee. Now she stood looking westward, her shadow long before her on the hard and frozen ground.

What'd you do, skin a bear?

She was all but lost inside the coat, which hung from her shoulders and sheathed her hands and almost trailed the ground.

They're gone.

He looked to the shack, then he looked to the girl.

What's the matter? You get your heart broke?

What?

Don't give me what. He flapped his arms over the fire. I was born of a night, but it wasn't last night.

You don't know what you're talkin about.

I'll tell you what I know. Two days you been back, and I ain't had so much as a hug from you. He crouched and blew into his hands. I reckon that's the thanks I get for freezin my ass out here, mindin them sheep and buildin you a nice home.

I didn't ask you to build no home.

But you'll sleep in it though.

Maybe I will and maybe I won't.

By God, would you listen to this. You'd think she'd gone and growed a backbone in that hospital.

Maybe I did. Maybe when you was too busy to pay me a single visit or write me a single letter, maybe you just didn't notice.

Write you a letter? How? With what? And who'd be mindin them sheep if I went off to go visit?

Seems like when it's somethin you want to do, you always find a way.

I told you that baby was your own damn affair!

She turned and stalked off toward the buckboard.

Hey, where you goin? I ain't done with you. Hey!

He grabbed her by the collar, yanking her backward. She struggled and thrashed as he pulled the coat from her shoulders and then from her grasp, walking it to the fire.

You think you're too good for me now, is that it?

He held the coat over the flames until the shearling caught and crackled and the flames rose almost to his hand. He dropped the smoking heap onto the fire.

You're a bastard! You're a no-good murderin bastard!

That's right, sister. You finally got me figured out.

He kicked at the coat, and the coat flipped over, and the fire flared anew.

And I'll tell you somethin else. You even think about tryin to leave me out here and I'll kill you. And I'll kill every last one of them lambs. And then I'll kill that boyfriend of yours just for the fun of it.

You're crazy.

He laughed. Damn right I'm crazy. I been crazy all my life.

Three days later, Palmer reined the pinto horse as twin plumes of dust rose thin and soundless from among the distant monuments. He lit a smoke and watched for a long time as the cars came into view.

Who is it?

Damned if I know.

The cars as the riders approached them had stopped on the roadside with their doors open, and three figures now stood waiting in the wind. Lottie recognized the Goulding Chevrolet and the Oliver Model A Ford behind it. She trotted Henry up beside the pinto and brought him to a halt.

Mike Goulding held her fluttering kerchief at her chin.

Hello, honey! We missed you at the hospital! We ran into Mr. Shumway on the road, and he told us you were out here!

That was right thoughtful of Mr. Shumway, Palmer said as the boy Jake removed his hat and stood a foot on the running board.

I'm sorry, Lottie said. They was supposed to tell you.

Goulding stepped forward to stand beside his wife.

How you making out with them sheep?

Fair to middlin, Palmer replied, looking again to the boy. Given the limits of the situation.

How's your chuck holding out?

Palmer spat. Could use some tobacco.

Oh! Mike said. I almost forgot!

She hurried to the Chevrolet and returned with a package wrapped in paper that she handed up to the girl.

Merry Christmas, honey.

Lottie held the box with both hands and rested it on the pommel. She looked at Mike and shrugged. I ain't got nothin for you.

That's all right. Maybe you can come visit soon, and that'll be gift aplenty. In fact, maybe we could wait right here while you run and—

That's enough, Goulding told her.

The wind gusted and the pinto horse backed and fidgeted and Palmer walked him in a circle.

Go ahead and open it, baby.

Lottie tore at the paper. She opened the lid and lifted a baby doll pink and naked from the box and pressed it to her shirt-front.

Do you like it?

She nodded, her eyes tightly closed.

What do you say? Palmer chided her as Mike turned with a hand to her mouth and ran back to the car.

Goulding kicked at the ground. Well, he said, I guess we'll be getting on. I'll put tobacco on the list.

He walked to the driver's door and stopped there and nodded once to Palmer, who nodded in reply. When the doors had closed and the engine started, the Chevrolet swung wide in the roadway, leaving in its wake a swirling cloud that when it cleared left only the boy still standing with his hat in his hand and his foot on the running board.

It was a Thursday late in February when the coast was next clear and they drove the bleating sheep in through the bottleneck, Lottie on Henry and Palmer on the little pinto, and no sooner did she close the gate behind them than the snow began to fall.

She trailed the flock into the canyon with her collar raised and her hat brim lowered as the sheep jostled and cried and fell away in a mad rush toward water, leaving her alone with no sound but her horse's footfalls on the frozen hummocks and these yet muffled by the lightly falling snow.

The ride was several miles along a narrow bench shaped to her left by the horseshoe bends of the river gorge and to her right by the red mesa rising from its steep buttresses of talus. She passed by tilted boulders pocked with ancient petroglyphs, and she passed the old Seeps campground where stone dolmens stood as mammoth cairns to mark the river's progress.

By the time she'd reached the dugout the storm had already passed, and she dismounted and moved among her charges counting heads. She shooed the bellwethers and divvied up the subherds and noted the various markers. When her count was finally finished, she walked to where Palmer sat huddled and shivering by the fire, like something swept in with the flock.

They's four missin, she told him.

Four? You sure it ain't three? Or six?

Speckles' bunch is missin one, and Blackie's bunch is missin one, and—

All right already, you're givin me a headache.

He'd fished his makings from his pocket and was rolling a smoke with stiff and frozen fingers.

I'll take the wagon, she told him. I'll need help if they's one needs liftin.

Shit! He flung the half-rolled cigarette and stood and wiped his nose with his sleeve. I said I was comin, didn't I?

Back outside the cattle gate, Lottie drove the buckboard north and east along the mesa while Palmer, riding Henry, cut a straight path eastward toward the Garden. The snow had already melted and the ground was soft in places and she looked for tracks or sign left since the thaw. The buckboard rasped and sawed as the Appaloosa horse marked a steady pace with Lottie rising at intervals to scan the broad horizon.

She was almost to Bell Butte when she heard the engine sound. She whoaed the horse and stood again listening. Then she sat and clucked and turned the wagon back again toward the canyon.

Palmer and Henry were stopped and listening, skylighted on a low rise. She rolled to a halt beside them, and he nodded in the direction they faced.

You hear it?

It sounded like Mr. Oliver's car.

Palmer leaned and spat. That's what I thought. Shit.

What're we gonna do?

You got the rifle back there?

I think so.

He stood down and loosed the catchrope and tied Henry to the back of the wagon.

Move, he said as he climbed over the wheel with the pistol in his hand. He laid it on the floorboards by his feet.

Put that away before you get us both shot.

Shut up.

He hawed the Appaloosa forward, and they crossed the rolling plain tilting and jostling in the direction of the roadway. From there they headed westward, and as they wove their way along the escarpment, they came at last upon the open cattle gate. Farther on they encountered the first of the sheep streaming outbound from the canyon.

Goddamnit.

Soon the sheep were flowing past on both sides of the wagon. Farther still they saw the old sheriff on his walking horse, cutting and shouting and swinging a lariat.

You son of a bitch! Oliver bellowed as the wagon pulled abreast. He dropped a loop and swung the rope, lashing at Palmer's face. Palmer ducked, blocking the rope with his arm as he bent for the gun.

Don't!

Palmer came up firing.

His first shot blew a pink cloud into the air and onto the neck of the walking horse. Lottie screamed as the Appaloosa reared in its traces, sending the other shots wild.

The walking horse bolted. Palmer turned and reached for the rifle, and when he found it, he jumped clear of the wagon.

More shots rang out behind her. Lottie grabbed the reins,

turning in time to see Palmer in a firing crouch and Henry backing on the catchrope and the Oliver horse snubbed and twisting as the sheriff drew a rifle from his scabbard. The old man tried to turn his horse, but his arm fell limp and his lone shot went wide as he toppled from the saddle.

Clint!

The echo of the final gunshot died among the boulders. The only sounds remaining were the bleating of the sheep and the tinkling of bells and the wind in the river gorge below them. Palmer rose and wiped his face with his shirtsleeve.

You see that? He gestured with the rifle. Whoo!

He sauntered toward the walking horse, which stood now with its head lowered and its reins trailing beside the fallen rider.

Lottie clambered down and rushed to where the sheriff lay splayed on his side. Palmer rolled him with a foot. Blood was everywhere.

Is he dead?

The old man's forehead was scraped where he'd fallen. His mouth was open and his eyes were senseless and red mud was caked in his mustache and on his eyebrow.

He's dead all right. I guess he wasn't so tough after all.

Palmer's eyes scanned the trail by which they stood.

You seen what happened. Self-defense is what it was.

He left her stunned and staring, and he walked back to the buckboard. He returned holding his pistol by the barrel.

Take it, he said.

What for?

I want to see you shoot him.

What?

Shoot him. Hit him right there in the chest.

She backed a step. You're crazy.

Maybe I am and maybe I ain't. But I'm not stupid.

What are you talkin about?

I'm talkin about you and me are in this together. Here. Take it.

She would not take the gun. He set down the rifle and grabbed her arm and marched her forward to where the body lay. He pressed the gun into her hand, and when she would not grip it, he closed his fingers onto hers and sighted the barrel and squeezed off a shot.

Her eyes were closed and she was already crying when she felt the cold steel of the trigger and the buck of the second shot; heard the loud report and its lesser echo ringing across the gorge.

She found herself on her knees. The gun was gone and Palmer was standing beside her.

Get up, he told her. Don't be a goddamn baby.

The lariat rope lay coiled by the roadside. Go get that, he told her, and he shoved her, and she ran stumbling for it as Palmer belted the pistol and sheathed the sheriff's rifle in its scabbard and walked the sheriff's horse to Palmer's own rifle on the ground.

Give it here. Hurry up.

He handed off his rifle, and the reins, and then he bent and paired the old man's boots, working a loop around the ankles. He played out the rope, backing as he went, until he stepped into the stirrup of the sheriff's horse, swinging his leg over the saddle.

You pick up anything falls off him.

He dallied the rope and put the horse forward. When the slack caught, the sheriff's body jerked and dragged into the roadway.

Palmer rode slowly with his tiptoes in the stirrups, and Henry backed and blew as first the bloody horse and then the bloody body with its arms raised in a futile show of surrender slid past the wagon.

Lottie stowed the rifle as she climbed into the buckboard. She popped the reins, and the Appaloosa followed the grisly procession, clopping for a hundred yards or more until Palmer left the trail again, angling the walking horse toward the river gorge.

Go on ahead, he called to her as he dropped from the saddle. I'll be along in a minute.

She watched him as he worked the rope and freed the dead man's feet. Then he bent and leaned and dragged the lifeless body toward the precipice.

He rode in at a gallop to find Lottie still in the springseat with her head bowed and her hands between her knees. Henry turned his head to watch as Palmer skidded to a halt and dismounted the bloody horse.

Lottie looked down at him where he stood, man and horse both wild-eyed and hard-breathing and damp despite the chill.

You had no cause, she said quietly.

Palmer stripped the bridle and the saddle, leaving them in a heap where they fell. He smacked the horse across the flank, and the horse bolted and bucked once on its way to join with its fellows out among the cattle and the smattering of sheep that still grazed within the canyon.

Listen to me, Palmer said, grabbing her wrist and pulling her sideways on the seat.

You're hurting me!

You don't know the meanin of hurt, sister. Not till you been to prison and lived in a cage and had your head stove every day and your ass whipped every night for night on end. And I'll tell you one thing that you'd better believe, and it's this right here.

He pulled her farther across the seat until their faces almost touched.

If I go to prison, then you go to prison. But lucky for both of us, I ain't goin back to no prison.

She fell as he released her, tumbling and landing hard and scrambling wet and muddy to her feet. She ran for the dugout. She slammed the door behind her and knelt in the darkness, watching through the door crack as Palmer retrieved the rifle and levered a shell. He walked to the line shack and kicked the door open.

He emerged moments later, the rifle on his shoulder. He climbed atop the Oliver car to scout the canyon east and west, then he climbed down again, sheathing the rifle in Henry's saddle scabbard and bending to work his fingers at the catchrope.

She crawled back into sunlight.

What're you doin?

He cursed the knot and drew his jackknife from his pocket.

Where you goin?

He swung into the saddle and sawed the horse in a circle.

The old man wasn't alone! Looks like your boyfriend's on the loose!

Palmer ate furtively with the rifle across his lap. His back was to the dugout, and his eyes, alert and unblinking, swept the canyon floor until the light faded, and then he sat apart from the fire until the fire died and there was no light at all. When the moon rose low and cloud-veiled in the east, shadows reappeared among the stock, and when Lottie saw him again, it was his dark shape moving among the cattle like an Indian.

When she'd finished her cleanup, she walked out to where she'd seen him last and called into the darkness.

Clint? C'mon, Clint. It's freezing out here!

Shhhh!

The sound came from behind her. She turned to see him moving toward her in a crouch, the rifle in both hands. Like the soldier he once was. Or claimed once to have been.

You can't stay out here all night.

Beats gettin knifed in your sleep.

She looked where he was looking, up the darkened canyon toward the bottleneck.

What're we gonna do?

I don't know about you, but I figured to wait until sunrise and then hunt his ass some more.

That ain't what I meant.

I know what you meant. You just go on to bed and let me worry about it.

She lay in the dugout wide-awake like some Lazarus interred. Seeing in the darkness the old sheriff's body. Feeling the cold weight of the gun. Hearing the report. Smelling the blood, and the death.

She closed her eyes, listening for any sound but that of her own breathing, and if she slept at all, it was the brief and dreamless sleep of the condemned.

At the first hint of daylight she sat upright.

The morning was cold, and clear, and when she crawled forth from the dugout, she found the sheriff's walker tied to the buckboard with both rifles fitted to the saddle.

Clint?

The horse lifted its head.

Clint!

Hands grabbed her from behind. She shrieked and spun to see Palmer grinning crazily in the half-light, the pistol in his waistband and his eyes glowing in the new dawn like fox fire.

Come to wish me luck?

She grabbed hold of his shirtfront. Listen, Clint. Just listen a minute. It was self-defense like you said, and there ain't nobody but you and me to swear to it. We could ride out to the Lees or down to Mike and Harry's. Right now, we could ride.

He pried her hands away.

You're forgettin a thing or two, darlin.

Like what?

Like we already throwed his body over a cliff, remember? Like he used to be the sheriff. Like ever juror in a hundred miles of here is his goddamn cousin. Like these horses is stole, and we's fugitives from two states, and we been all this time usin phony names.

I'm scared, Clint. I'm scared real bad.

He glanced up-canyon, to where the sun lay low over the vermilion cliffs.

Most important thing you seem to have forgot is your boyfriend Jake. The reason he ain't come back is cuz he's hidin somewheres. Yonder's his horse. That means he's afoot, and he's just waitin for us to leave so's he can ride out and turn us in. That's what ought to be keepin you awake.

Maybe we could talk to him.

Talk. Palmer leaned and spat. A little late for talk. We got no choice but to see this all the way through.

He released her wrists. Then he unhitched the walking horse and swung into the saddle.

Pack up that car, he said, positioning the rifles. Take whatever we'll need for three days' drivin. I shouldn't be too long.

He turned the horse, and pressed down his hat, and set off at a canter.

The noon breeze carried hints of the spring to come.

Lottie had laid the bedrolls side by side and had placed upon each of them a single change of clothes. To his she'd added his satchel and his bridle and some food items from the wagon. To hers she'd added her Christmas doll and her father's leather Bible. She'd knelt and rolled them both, then tied them off and carried them to the backseat of the Oliver car.

She'd next walked among what sheep were there, calling to them by name and telling them each good-bye. That they were the lucky ones, here inside the canyon. That soon they would be reunited with their bandmates.

When noon had passed without sign of Palmer, she'd found the knotted hackamore and retrieved Henry's saddle from the car and tacked the faithful horse for what she knew would be the final time. She'd stood before him and offered him her shirt-front, but the horse had bent instead to crop the grass at her feet.

She was twenty minutes in the saddle when she heard a sound that might have been a gunshot. She kicked Henry forward, riding hard until at last she could see movement up ahead among the distant boulders of the Seeps camp, and there she brought the horse up short.

What she saw were the shapes of a man and a horse, both now still, both small against the tumbled rocks.

And then the man was holding something in his hands.

And then the man was chopping at something on the ground.

Chapter Ten

AS LONG AS IT AIN'T HERE

BY MR. PHARR: I'm hot in Utah?

A: Yes, sir.

Q: To which the old man replied, You're no hotter in Utah than you are here?

BY MR. HARTWELL: Hearsay, Your Honor, and grossly prejudicial.

BY MR. PHARR: An adoptive admission, Your Honor.

THE COURT: Counsel will approach.

(A CONFERENCE WAS HELD AT SIDEBAR.)

BY MR. PHARR: What did the accused say when the old man told him you're no hotter in Utah than you are here?

A: He didn't say nothing.

They followed the dry wash of Gypsum Creek, keeping where they could to the hard and rocky parts, and in the morning they entered Monument Pass from the east with two tires flat and one wheel bent and wobbling.

When they reached Goulding's trading post, only the old Chevrolet was parked under the thatched lean-to. A trio of horses were hitched to the corral. A thin thread of smoke hung over the stone building.

Palmer drew the pistol and checked it and told her to stay put, but she ignored this and opened her door, so he warned her not to speak once they were inside.

The door to the trading post was open, the bullpen empty. Palmer called into the wareroom, and then they climbed the stairs together to find them all at breakfast, Mike standing by the cookstove and Harry in his usual seat and a woman in a dime store cowboy hat staring openmouthed at the dirty and wild-eyed man with the gun.

A word, said Palmer to Goulding, gesturing. In private.

They descended to the empty bullpen, where Harry stood with his long arms folded and Mike waited behind him, backlit in the doorway.

What the hell's going on? Goulding demanded. Who's minding the sheep?

Had us a patch of trouble, Palmer told him. Oliver's dead, and so's that Shumway boy.

Mike raised a hand to her mouth.

Afraid there wasn't no help to it. The old man trampled the sheep, and then he hard-twisted Johnny Rae. When he drew down on me, I shot him off his horse and drug his body over the cliff. The boy too. We left the wagon and the horses in the canyon. The gate's open, so my guess is the sheep are back inside by now.

Goulding felt for the counter, slumping his weight against it.

That old man was askin for it from day one. Well, by God, he finally got it.

Goulding looked to Mike in the doorway. What do you want from us?

We'll need to borrow that Chevy if you don't mind. And

some gasoline, and a little motor oil. And whatever cash you got, I'll take in settlement of wages. That's a hell of a deal for you.

Goulding moved as in a dream. He circled behind the counter, touching Mike's shoulder in passing. He bent for the strongbox and set it on the counter and opened it and counted out the bills.

Mike stepped down to where Palmer and Lottie waited.

Listen, Jimmy. Running away won't solve anything. You need to stay and explain what happened. If it was self-defense like you say, then you need to drive up to Monticello and turn yourself in to the sheriff.

The new cowboy hat appeared in the doorway, and Palmer pointed the gun, and the doorway cleared again. He tilted his own hat with the muzzle.

Look, Mike. You and Harry been square with us right down the line, so I ain't gonna lie to you. Even if it was self-defense, there ain't a jury in Utah would let us walk from this. You know it and I know it. I'm sorry, but that's just the way it is.

Here, Goulding said. Forty-three dollars.

Palmer swept the bills and stuffed them into his pocket.

Johnny Rae could stay. Mike turned to the girl. She's just a minor. She didn't kill anybody. You could run, and she could stay, and we could vouch for the both of you. We could hire a lawyer if we had to.

Palmer turned to the girl. He shook his head.

We appreciate the offer, but we gotta get movin. Harry, you come and give us a hand.

He waited for Goulding to pass before him, then he led the girl by the arm until she stopped in the doorway and shrugged him off and turned to the woman whose face was but a blur to

her through the sudden welling tears. She removed her cowboy
hat and set it on the bench.

Lucile, she said.

What?

Lucile Garrett. That's my name.

They were three days in the Goulding Chevrolet; south to Kayenta and Tuba City, then on to Flagstaff, where they met Route
66 and followed it eastward into Gallup.

They minded the speed limits and took the back roads through
the bigger towns and cities, and they swapped their Utah license
plate outside Albuquerque. They watched their gas and they
watched their oil, and they stopped to fill up only at night. Always they watched for the police.

They ate in the car and slept in the car and bathed but once,
in the cold Pecos River near Santa Rosa, New Mexico, where
Palmer gave Lottie his cowboy hat and sent her into the post office to scout the walls for his picture. Then, outside of Wichita
Falls, Texas, they passed three girls on the roadside standing with
their hips cocked and with their thumbs out all in a row.

What are you doin?

Palmer swung hard to the gravel apron and watched the girls
come running.

Hell, we could use a little company. Help to keep me awake.

The giggling girls crowded the driver's window. Two were
plain and towheaded, and the third was a redhead with a too-
tight sweater. They dipped their heads and studied man and girl
and set again to giggling. Lottie guessed they were all of sixteen.

Where you all headin? the redhead asked.

Wherever you're headin, darlin. Move that stuff and hop in.

The two girls who may have been sisters wrestled the saddle atop the bedrolls and squeezed into the backseat beside it. The redhead circled the dusty car and opened the passenger door, and Lottie lifted the satchel onto her lap as she shifted to the center.

I'm Helen, the redhead said once the doors were closed. She wore snug jeans and pointed boots, and she smelled of cigarettes and chewing gum. And these here juvenile delinquents are Mavis and Mary Sue.

Look who's talkin, said Mary Sue. Or possibly Mavis.

Palmer nodded at the mirror. Dick Garrett, he said. Pleased to make your acquaintance. This here is my daughter Lucile.

Are you all with the rodeo? asked a backseat voice as Palmer worked the gearshift and eased back onto the roadway.

No, darlin, we're just a couple outlaws on the run and wanted for murder is all.

I was hopin you was with the rodeo.

She wanted to see if you could stay the eight seconds.

Shut up, Helen.

You shut up.

Hey, there's a rifle back here.

There's two rifles.

Hey, are these loaded?

Can we shoot at somethin?

Put that down, darlin, before you blow your brains out.

Mister, ain't nobody shoots that good.

Shut up, Helen.

You shut up.

Wichita Falls to Henrietta to Bellevue. The girls chattering and Palmer laughing and newly animated and Lottie watching the roadway front and back. As they rolled into Bowie, the backseat girls begged Palmer to buy them liquor, and he parked by a road-side store.

They watched him through the window. After a while the backseat girls announced that they had to pee. They held hands as they skipped through the parking lot, the redhead watching with a look of bemusement that Lottie could read in the door glass.

Are they your friends?

We go to the same high school is all. Their brother thinks he's my boyfriend.

Ain't there no school today?

She turned her face to Lottie. Oh, there's school all right. Only Mavis has her period, so we took us a trip to see the falls. And guess what? There ain't no falls in Wichita Falls. Ain't that a pip?

What grade are you all in?

They're both in the tenth, and I'm in the eleventh. What about you?

I ain't in no school.

You're lucky, the girl said, watching again for her friends. I swear I get stupider every day I'm around the likes of these.

A Packard pulled into the lot, swinging a tight arc and parking by the door.

You're real pretty, Lottie told her.

The redhead shrugged. When my daddy was around, he said I had the face that launched a thousand ships.

What does that mean?

I don't know. It's like Shakespeare or somethin.

Where's your daddy now?

He lives in Philadelphia. My mama's got her a new husband. He's a real prize.

The girls reappeared and cupped their faces to the store window and ran stumbling and giggling to the car.

Your daddy's cute, the first one said as they slid into the seat. Is he really a outlaw?

Nah, he's just a cowboy. Sheep and cattle and such.

I had a sheep once, for the 4-H. Only it died.

It probably kilt itself.

Shut up, Helen.

What about your mama, Lucile?

She's dead. I don't remember her real good.

You're lucky. I wisht my mama was dead.

Has your daddy got a girlfriend?

Does he want one?

Does he want two?

The girls were still giggling when Palmer returned with a paper sack in each hand.

Okay, ladies. Coon Hollow or Old Grand-Dad?

Didn't you bring no pop?

Did you ask for pop?

Aw, hell.

It's okay. We'll take that Coon.

How much do we owe you?

You don't owe me nothin, darlin. You done paid for it already with the pleasure of your company.

Thanks, mister.

Yeah, thanks.

The door opened, and the backseat girls tumbled out.

Come on, Helen.

Yeah, we ain't got all day.

The redhead stared at her reflection. She turned to Palmer. Would you all mind if I rode for a while?

Heck, no. We'd be happy for the company. Ain't that right, Lucile?

You don't even know where we're goin.

That don't matter, the girl said, settling back in the seat. As long as it ain't here.

Lottie dozed in the lap of the new girl, waking only when the car had stopped and the driver's door opened. She sat up to the sound of crickets and the smell of wet grass in the moonlight.

You was talkin in your sleep, the redhead told her.

What all did I say?

Nothin I could make out. But you was mumblin a blue streak.

Where are we?

The girl shrugged as she turned. Dick's gone to fix somethin in back.

They watched Palmer's shape rise up and move to the rail of the bridge on which they idled, and they watched him fling something over the side. When he returned to the car, his eyes were barely open. He rubbed his face and took a pull from the half-empty bottle.

We's gettin close.

Where are we?

He adjusted the mirror. We passed Emblem just a ways back.

What time is it?

I don't know. Past midnight, I reckon.

The gate was open when they reached the Palmer farm, and he followed the drive with the headlamps off, crunching to a stop at the old barn. At the slamming of the car doors, a light came on at the back of the house.

Come on.

The old man met them in the parlor, pale and shrunken in an outsize robe, a bony hand clutched to his throat. Squinting. His hair wispy and wild.

Hello, Pa.

Hell's bells! I thought maybe that was you. He leaned toward the other shapes in the room. What the hell're you doin in Texas?

I'm hot in Utah.

You're no hotter in Utah than you are right here. Wait a minute.

He disappeared in back and returned like some wizened seaman in black galoshes and a slicker slung over his robe. A woman's voice called something from the bedroom.

Come out here a minute.

Palmer followed him onto the darkened porch, where the two men stood in close conversation. Shit, they heard him say to his father.

What's goin on? the redhead whispered.

You should get quit of us. If they's trouble, you don't want to be accessory.

What kind of trouble?

Law trouble.

The redhead watched the shadow men. Is Dick really on the run?

I reckon we both are.

I knew it. Hot damn!

★   ★   ★

They'd off-loaded the saddle and the bedrolls and most of the tack, and now they sat three abreast in the front seat with the rifles standing upright between them. They traveled north and east in the Goulding car, following its headlamps through a moonless maze of back roads and farm roads and dirt tracks, zigging their way toward the Oklahoma border.

What happens when we get there?

Hell if I know. They got the cabin watched, that's for sure. We could maybe make it across to Arkansas.

What's in Arkansas? the redhead asked.

My mama lives in Little Rock. We could maybe hole up there for a spell.

Lottie turned to face him. Your mama?

We could go to Mexico, the redhead said. She shimmied and snapped her fingers. You could be Ricardo, and we could be Helena and Lucilla. We could open us a little cantina, and you could be bartender and grow a big mustache, and we could be bar girls and dance on the tables with roses in our teeth.

Palmer grinned madly at the image. Damn, I like the way you think!

There was a loud thunk as the headlamps rocked and the road fell away beneath them. Then a splashing sound as the car was momentarily afloat. The engine sputtered as the headlamps flickered and died, and the car's back end drifted in a slow and silent arc, stopping again on a mudflat facing east with the engine drowned.

Palmer tried the starter and tried it again. He pounded the steering wheel with his fist. Shit!

Now what?

They sat in silence, listening to the water. Palmer lowered his window and leaned outside and boosted himself into the frame. He spoke some words they could not hear. Helen rolled her window, and the car was filled with the gurgling sounds of the creek.

What?

I said if we push her just over to there we could get across!

The redhead turned to Lottie. Who does he expect to do the pushin do you suppose?

It's too dark! the girl yelled out the window. You can't see the end of your nose!

Palmer wriggled inside and sat again with both hands on the wheel. Like a child pretending to drive. He drummed his fingers.

Okay then, here's the deal. It's a couple hours yet till sunup, and I'm dog tired anyways. Let's grab some shut-eye, and we'll push her across come dawn.

He climbed over the seatback and adjusted the blankets and was already snoring by the time Lottie and the girl had removed their boots and arranged themselves in front with their heads propped and their legs overlapping. Lottie listening to the water and staring at the darkness until, after a while, she could make out the soft shape of the sleeping girl and the hard lines of the rifles leaning upright beside her.

She woke two hours later, sideways to the wheel with her neck stiff and the sun still down and a whispering sound coming not, as first she had thought, from the water outside, but from the seat directly behind her.

Don't.

You know you like it.

Shhhh.

Shift over.

Not here.

Come on, darlin.

Stop it.

What are you scared of?

Shhhh.

Lottie pretending to sleep but wide-awake with her neck aching all the more that she feared to move.

You're wearin me out.

Behave yourself.

Come on.

You're bad.

I am bad.

Shhhh. Just quit talkin.

At daybreak the new girl climbed carefully over the seatback, and Lottie watched through hooded eyes as she straightened her clothes and settled against the passenger door. Then, moments later, Palmer made a show of waking and yawning and spreading his arms.

Rise and shine! he announced, thumping the seatback, and the redhead sat up rubbing her eyes and Lottie did likewise, all of them performing their assigned roles like actors in a parlor farce.

The car was half off the road, and the view through the windscreen was to a grassy bank some twenty yards upstream. Beyond the bank were trees, and beyond the trees lay the open expanse of a field.

We's sittin ducks out here. You two need to get out and push us over thataway.

What about you?

Someone needs to steer and work the starter. Go on.

I ain't got no change of clothes, the new girl protested.

Then take 'em off, stupid. Both of you, hurry up. Let's shake a leg.

The girl looked at Lottie and shrugged and peeled the sweater over her head. She twisted and scooted and stripped to her underwear, then sat and waited as Lottie worked her legs from out of her jeans.

Your daddy's a dirty old man, the girl said, smiling into the backseat.

Hurry up.

They climbed through the windows, the water thigh-deep and oddly warm and sulfurous. They waded to the rear quarter panel where the car was lowest, and there they set their feet and squatted and pushed on the fender. Then they waded to the rear bumper and turned their backs to it and leaned with their legs braced until the girl slipped in the mud and disappeared, surfacing again ten yards downstream soaked and coughing and all but naked.

Forget it! she called. It ain't moved a inch!

Shit!

What now?

That looks like a farm just yonder. You girls go see if he's got a tractor or somethin to pull with.

You're crazy! the girl said, standing now to examine herself. I'm all wet!

Go on. He'll think he's died and gone to heaven.

The girls held hands like paper dolls as they crossed the flowing water with their arms raised. The morning air was cold and the redhead hugged herself as they ran from the bank through the field to the old farmhouse. A dog barked at their knock, and the old man who appeared behind the screen stood dumbstruck as the redhead explained their predicament through chattering teeth.

Palmer tossed her sweater through the window, and the girl caught it and removed her wet brassiere and flung it at him, both of them laughing and the girl's round breasts swaying and Lottie watching them both in stony silence.

When the farmer finally appeared, he was leading a white-faced mule. The mule wore a kind of leather surcingle, and the old man carried with him a bundle of rope on his shoulder.

I got my doubts! he called.

Palmer leaned through the windowframe. We'd be obliged if you'd give it a try!

While the man busied himself with his mule, Lottie waded to the window where Palmer sat watching him.

Maybe he's got a car we could borrow.

Maybe you could shut up and let me do the thinkin.

The farmer positioned the mule and handed the rope ends off to the waiting girls, who waded out like magician's assistants to flank the car and tie off to the wheelhubs with Palmer leaning and giving orders like a ship's captain run aground.

Ready, professor!

The man raised a hand and walked the mule forward. The mule leaned and strained, and the ropes rose taut and dripping from the water until one of the ropes detached with a loud report, raveling into the water.

Jesus Christ, Lucile! Can't you tie a goddamn knot?

The farmer waved her off and waded himself into the river, the water shearing over the legs of his overalls. He checked the redhead's knot, then he circled behind the car to where Lottie stood hugging herself.

The farmer bent and tied the rope as Palmer leaned from the window opposite, bantering with the girl. When the farmer straightened, Lottie touched his arm and gestured with her head, and the old man followed her eyes to where the rifles were leaning upright on the seatback. The man's eyes widened, and Lottie nodded once with great solemnity.

How about it, pops? We about ready?

The man waded back to where the mule stood like a puppet mule unstrung and grazing now on the streambank. He took up the lead and walked the animal forward and the ropes rose as before and the mule strained as before but again the car did not budge. They let the mule rest and then tried again, but with the same result. And then a car horn sounded on the roadway behind them.

The redhead ran waving with her sweater bouncing and her panties sheer and clinging, and the new car skidded to a halt. The driver was a ham-faced drummer in a straw hat who thumbed it back and gaped at the vaguely lurid spectacle of girls and car and old man and mule, all of whom, including the mule, were turned now and looking at him in the new sunlight of Sulphur Bottom.

We got ourselves in a jackpot, the redhead explained. Think you could give us a push?

The driver looked at her, and at the angled car, and he appeared to consider the geometry.

I might scratch your paint job.

Heck, mister, she told him. You wouldn't be the first.

The redhead clapped theatrically as the dripping Chevy lurched forward before the new car, over the culvert and around the narrow bend to where the road again widened. There the new car backed and pulled up alongside, and Palmer thanked the driver and offered him a dollar for his trouble, but the man declined on the ground that he'd got his dollar's worth already. He advised it would take an hour at least for the starter to dry, and then only if they parked in the sun with the engine cover open. Behind him, the barefoot girls were picking their way up the road, and the farmer and his mule were hurrying in the opposite direction.

The girls were dressing as Palmer laid open the engine cover and frowned at what he saw.

Shit.

It leads a girl to wonder what kind of outfit she's signed on with, the redhead said.

The snakebit kind.

How long you reckon it'll be?

Man said a hour.

I'm hungry, Lottie said.

You're always hungry.

The redhead pointed to a house farther up the road. We could ask these good folks right here for some breakfast.

Go ahead.

I believe I will.

She'd already started up the road when Palmer called her back.

Hold on a minute, and let's get our stories straight. He tilted his hat and scratched. Okay. I'm Dick Smith, and you two are sisters, Lorena and Helen. And both of you keep your yaps shut and let me do the talkin, you hear?

Yes, Daddy, the girl said. She winked at Lottie. If I talk, do I get a spankin?

Mr. and Mrs. O. P. Nations were only too happy to aid a young family in distress. They were all in the kitchen, hosts and guests alike, with the woman presiding over the stove as the old man said grace and the redhead said, Amen, looking to Palmer and covering her mouth with a hand.

They ate fried eggs and fried potatoes and fried ham, and when the man asked Mr. Smith his business, Palmer told them he was a private detective tracking the outlaw Clint Palmer, and that he wanted to know everything his hosts had heard about the case.

The only reason I hate to trace him down is on account of his poor old daddy, Palmer said sadly, lighting a smoke. I don't think his daddy had anythin to do with the murder, but he might've helped to put him in that cave and put the brush over him.

Could be, Mr. Nations agreed. 'Bout scared the bejesus out of them boys what found him.

Did you all go down to the courthouse and see the skeleton?

We did not, the woman said firmly. It was right unchristian, in my opinion, to do such a thing with that poor man's remains.

That's right, said her husband. And besides, it was always too damn crowded.

The car started on the first try. The old farmer leaned into the windowframe and with the angling of his hands described a shortcut to the county road, and they thanked him for his hospitality and waved to the woman on the porch and were off again with the sun now high above the treetops whose shadows dappled the roadway as it curved through the ordered and malachite fields.

They'd gone but a mile past the sign for Franklin County when they heard the sirens. Faint at first, the sound rose and faded and rose again from deep in the hollows behind them. Palmer cursed and floored it, and the redhead rose to her knees and climbed over the seatback to watch with Lottie through the little rear window.

I see one!

Make that two!

Hang on!

The car swerved and the girls were thrown as it bounced into an open field. When they regained their knees, they saw three police cars emerging into sunlight with the drag car all but shrouded in the leaders' billowing dust.

There's three now, and they're comin hard!

Hang on!

They burst through a wooden fence, bounding onto a rutted one-lane roadway. They fishtailed and straightened, speeding past trees and open farmland with the engine straining and Palmer cursing and the sirens gaining precious ground behind them.

You want your gun, Dick? You gonna shoot it out?

Shut up!

They passed an oncoming truck that skidded as it swerved, and they sped through a blind curve until the roadway straightened again, narrowing at a bridge.

Palmer braked hard, and the car yawed and nearly rolled. He spun the wheel and punched the accelerator, launching them forward into a tangle of streamside creeper and saplings, but the bank fell away beneath their weight and the car tipped sideways and all within slammed hard against the door glass with Lottie landing sprawled atop the redhead, the blankets and rifles tangled up between them.

Listen to me! Palmer shouted over the siren sound. You two is sisters and you ain't never seen me before till Bowie. After they turn you loose, you come back and visit me and bring me a hacksaw blade, you hear me? Lottie, you hear me?

The sirens crested and car doors slammed and six men surrounded the listing car, four on the bank and two to their knees in the muddy water and all with rifles pointed.

Police! Come out with your hands in the air!

Palmer scooted upright, showing his hands through the passenger window.

I ain't armed! Don't shoot!

Come on out!

He raised a foot to the steering column, pushing himself upward where he was seized and lifted free and swarmed by three men, who wrestled him face-first in the briar with a knee in his back.

A rifle muzzle showed in the open window, and Lottie heard a voice call for calm before the door above them opened and a lawman reached a hand and she took it and was pulled upward into sunlight, where she saw the three cars with their doors open standing at haphazard angles in the bosque.

They don't know beans! Palmer yelled from where he was being handcuffed. I just picked 'em up this mornin!

The redhead was the last to be rescued. She stood blinking on the streambank with a deputy's hand on each arm, and she looked at Palmer where he lay with his face bloodied, and at Lottie on her knees being handcuffed, and at the rifles and the hard faces of the other deputies.

She broke into a grin. Hot damn! Wait till they hear about this in Bowie!

Chapter Eleven

PUT NOT YOUR TRUST
IN PRINCES

THE COURT: In this case the state relies upon circumstantial evidence for a conviction, and you are instructed that in order to warrant a conviction of a crime upon circumstantial evidence, each fact necessary to the conclusion sought to be established must be proved by competent evidence beyond a reasonable doubt. All the necessary facts to the conclusion must be consistent with each other and with the main fact sought to be proved, and the circumstances, taken together, must be of a conclusive nature, leading on the whole to a satisfactory conclusion, and producing in effect a reasonable and moral certainty that a homicide was committed and that the accused and no other person committed the offense charged. But in such cases it is not sufficient that the circumstances coincide with, account for, and therefore render probable the guilt of the accused, and they must exclude to a moral certainty every other reasonable hypothesis except the guilt of the accused, and unless they do so beyond a reasonable doubt, the accused cannot be convicted.

Her cell was on the second floor, with a view onto the parking lot and the courthouse just beyond. The courthouse stood some five stories tall, like a storybook castle in pink granite and red sandstone with Romanesque arches, while the jailhouse was a squat rectangle of plain brick, and their juxtaposition served as a kind of metaphor, or at least as a declaration of values, by the founding fathers of Hopkins County, Texas.

A crowd had gathered at the news of their arrest, and by nightfall the parking lot had filled with cars and with men afoot and on horseback, milling and drinking, and with entire families picnicking on blankets with baskets packed for the occasion. Fires had been set in trash cans, and she heard guitar music and breaking glass and Palmer's name shouted along with drunken epithets long into the night.

When the deputy sheriff came for her three days later, he placed her in handcuffs and led her down the hallway by the arm. Faces darkened the judas windows of the other holding cells. Typewriters quieted, and office doors inched open that the jail personnel might get a look at the skinny girl in the baggy, gray shift and the backless canvas shoes that made a slap-slap-slapping sound on the cold linoleum.

Sheriff W. C. Reneau had jet-black hair and a stiff and military mien. He gestured to the chair opposite the desk at which he sat, and the deputy steered Lottie there and looked to the sheriff, who nodded once. The deputy bent to unlock her handcuffs.

The room had no windows. There was a wooden coatrack and a wooden trash can on pedestal feet and three wooden chairs along the wall, two of which were empty. Occupying the third chair was an earnest young man in a suit and tie with a briefcase in his lap and a writing tablet atop the briefcase and a pencil poised above the tablet. He nodded at Lottie and smiled.

The sheriff studied the girl. He leaned to his jacket where it hung beside him and removed a pack of Pall Malls. He shook the pack and offered her a cigarette.

Suit yourself, he said, removing the cigarette with his lips and lighting it off the front side of the desk. Get me an ashtray, he told the deputy, who straightened and stepped into the hallway.

A manila folder was on the desk, and the sheriff opened it and flipped a page and closed it again and pushed it aside with his finger.

October tenth, 1920?

Yes, sir.

That makes her fourteen, he told the other man, who made a note on the tablet.

Oh, this is Mr. Fannin. He's the county prosecutor.

Hello, the young man said.

Hello.

The deputy returned with a ceramic ashtray that he set on the desk. Check on that other thing, the sheriff told him, and the deputy looked at the girl and left the room again.

The sheriff tapped his ash. He ran a hand over his face.

I ain't gonna lie to you, miss. There's folks around here say you was in on it from the get-go. There's some say you must've been the brains of the outfit, cuz that Palmer boy ain't got no brains of his own to speak of. The sheriff opened the folder again. I read your grand jury statement, and I got to tell you, it raises more questions for me than it answers. But we'll come to that in a minute. Bill?

The man in the suit cleared his throat.

Miss Garrett, have you got any money to hire a lawyer?

No, sir.

If you did have the money, would you want to hire a lawyer?

No, sir. I don't need no lawyer.

The men exchanged a look.

This Uncle Mack of yours, is he your closest kin?

Yes, sir. I mean, he is now.

Mack Garrett?

Yes, sir.

And he lives in Oklahoma?

Yes, sir. Or he used to.

The young man made another note on the tablet.

Sir?

The sheriff glanced up from the ashtray. Yeah?

You said you got questions. I'd be glad to answer 'em, cuz I'd as soon get this over and done with quick as I can.

The men shared another glance.

All right, the sheriff said. He flipped a page. Let's see then. You told the grand jury that Palmer first took advantage of you when you were driving together to New Mexico, is that right?

Yes, sir.

Against your will, you said.

Yes, sir.

You said that happened in a rooming house, and then it happened again a few nights later in some camp with Mexicans. Is that your story?

Yes, sir, that's what happened.

The sheriff looked up from the page. And yet you never once tried to run away or ask for help the whole time you were in New Mexico or Colorado or Utah, is that right?

She looked at the floor.

Yeah, you think about that.

Well, sir—

Look at me.

Well, sir, I don't rightly know how to say it. Clint was on the run, and he got beat up real bad. And he said my daddy would get in trouble if I run away, or if I went to the law for help.

Oh, God. Here it comes.

Hot tears streaked her face. It ain't like I had no place else to go. And I knowed I'd already missed my time of the month.

Look at me, I said.

She smeared her face with her wrist. Clint said it didn't matter whether I was innocent or not, that the police would charge me with accessory anyways.

Accessory to murder, you mean.

No, sir. Not murder. I didn't know my pa was dead then, I swear it.

But you must've thought something was fishy when you got that letter.

He told me about accessory before that.

Who told you?

Clint. Clint told me.

The men shared another glance.

Go on.

That's about it. I know it don't sound right to you, but you wasn't there. You wasn't there, and you wasn't me, and you wasn't with him.

The sheriff leaned back in the chair. All right. It don't make no sense, but that's all right. It never does. He closed the file and lifted it and dropped it onto the desk. Bill?

Lucile, did you and Mr. Palmer ever go through any kind of a wedding ceremony?

No, sir.

Did he ever give you a ring?

Uh-uh. No.

Did you ever think in your own mind that the two of you were actually married?

No, sir. He told folks we was, but I knowed we wasn't.

There goes your bigamy charge, the sheriff said.

Yeah, but there goes his privilege claim. The lawyer made another note. I'll take that deal any day.

Sir?

And when you got back to the Palmer place in Peerless, you heard him say to the old man . . . Wait a minute. The lawyer opened his briefcase and removed some papers that were clipped together and he flipped through the pages. You heard him say, I'm hot in Utah. And the old man said, You're hot here too. Is that about right?

That's what I heard. Yes, sir.

And what did Palmer say after his father told him that?

Nothin. They just went outside together and talked.

After the old man went and got dressed.

That's right.

And the Smith girl, she heard this as well?

I reckon. She was standin right there.

The lawyer made some lengthy notes and then he looked to the sheriff and shrugged. The sheriff snuffed his cigarette and rose with his keys jangling and walked to the door and called into the hallway.

Sir?

Yes, Lucile?

I was wonderin how long I got to stay here in the jailhouse.

The lawyer looked to the sheriff in the doorway. For right now, you're what's called a material witness, Lucile. That means you've got to stay until after the trial at least. Clint Palmer's trial.

Okay.

And then I guess it depends on what happens. Whether you cooperate or not, and whether he's convicted. Cuz if he's not convicted here, there's folks up in Utah want to get their hands on him real bad.

A different deputy entered the room and stood behind her and placed her in handcuffs, and nobody spoke again as he lifted her by the arm and steered her to the door.

They passed back through the hallway to her cell, and there he removed the heavy cuffs and she sat down on the cot and rubbed her wrists as the door clanged shut and the bolt slid home with a sound that made her jump.

Five days after her arrest she was told by the matron that a motion to change venue had been granted, and that Palmer's trial for the murder of her father would be held not in the courthouse across the parking lot, but at the Hunt County courthouse in Greenville.

Nine days after her arrest she was led in handcuffs once again to the same windowless room. Awaiting her this time were the sheriff and four other men, all of them seated in a semicircle around an empty chair. A typewriter sat on the desk, and once she was herself seated and her handcuffs removed, the man behind the typewriter nodded.

The justice of the peace introduced himself as Mr. Wyatt and asked her to stand again and raise her right hand to be sworn. Then Sheriff Lawrence Palmer and District Attorney Donald

Adams, who had driven together from San Juan County, Utah, questioned her each in turn.

They were young and earnest men, and they queried her at length about her time in John's Canyon, and about all that had happened there. The typewriter clattered as she spoke. She told them the truth, or such truth as might be gained from the story of a girl who was herself no longer the girl of her story.

Over the course of her interrogation, Lottie learned that both of the cattlemen's bodies had been recovered from a ledge overlooking the river gorge, and that Norris Shumway, the boy known to her as Jake, had died of a gunshot wound to the face, and that he'd all but been decapitated with an ax.

If the men who questioned her knew anything about the missing Navajo herders, they did not care enough to ask.

At the end of their questioning, which lasted over an hour, they told the local sheriff they were returning the Goulding car to Utah, and when Lottie asked that they let Mike and Harry know that she was all right, the Utah sheriff said he didn't plan on speaking to either one of them, either now or in the future, not if he had any say in the matter.

A month after her arrest Lottie was taken in handcuffs to a room on the ground floor of the jailhouse. Men spoke in the anteroom and watched her through the open doorway as a typewriter tapped and papers were shuffled and stapled and stamped. From there she was handed a blanket and led outside to a waiting car.

A deputy leaned on the fender. He folded his newspaper and tossed it onto the passenger seat. Then he opened the rear door and eased her inside with a hand pressed to the crown of her head.

Where we goin? she asked as the engine started, but the man did not answer.

They drove past planted fields and running creeks and trees that dappled the windscreen. The day was sunny and warm and farmers were in the fields and trucks and other cars on the road. At a crossroads in Commerce, the deputy honked and waved to a filling-station attendant, who raised a hand in reply.

The ride took almost an hour, and the driver never spoke.

The Hunt County courthouse filled an entire city block. On the sidewalk, heads turned to watch as the handcuffed girl in the blanket and slippers clap-clapped her way up the wide concrete steps. Once inside, Lottie was taken to an office where sheriff's deputies in green uniforms were waiting, and where the driver removed her handcuffs, and where another deputy replaced them with handcuffs of his own.

Watch she don't slip through them bars, the driver said as he left.

They sat her in a chair by the door. A deputy spoke on the telephone and a typist glanced at her and smiled. Soon a uniformed matron appeared, and documents were exchanged, and together the matron and the girl rode the elevator up to the fifth floor where the women's cells were located.

It was the first time Lottie had ever been inside an elevator.

The cell doors in Greenville were open bars, and she could see the other prisoners in their street clothes pacing or sitting or lying on their cots. The corridor smelled of cigarette smoke and shit and perfume, and when they passed the cell of Helen Smith, the redhead sprang to her feet.

Lucile! Hey, it's me! Hey!

The girl continued shouting, but her voice was drowned by a

chorus of other voices that told her to shut up or said Fuck you and Stupid white whore.

Lottie's cell was at the end of the row, and through her window bars she could see the street below, and the rooftops of the brick buildings opposite, and the green expanse of trees and fields that stretched for miles beyond the city limit. After nightfall, when the outer dark was absolute, the lights went off in the cellblock and the women called to one another and called to her by name, saying, Lucile! Oh, Lu-ceel! but she did not answer them.

The day after Lottie's arrival in Greenville the matron brought to her cell her old boots and her old clothes newly laundered and folded and stayed to watch her dress. She was then led without handcuffs down the corridor and through an iron gate to a stairwell, and from there down a wide hallway to a conference room on the third floor where she sat alone listening to the sounds of people milling in the hallway. Some of them laughing. A child crying. And then, after almost an hour of waiting, the door finally opened and two men entered.

One was a lawman in a crisp green uniform with stars on his collar and a gun holstered low on his hip. The other was a lawyer in a vested suit and rimless wire spectacles. They each carried cups of heavy ceramic, and the man in the suit had an extra cup for her.

Miss Garrett? How do you do. I'm Henry Pharr, and this is Sheriff Newton. I hope you take it black.

They sat on either side of where she stood at the head of the table. The sheriff removed his hat and set it on the table and blew into his coffee. Your show, he said to the lawyer as Lottie sank into her seat. The lawyer showed his teeth.

Miss Garrett, I don't know how much you've been told, so let me take a moment to bring you up to speed. Our trial is scheduled to start on Tuesday. That's April the ninth. Mr. Palmer's lawyers have filed a motion for a continuance and a motion to quash the indictment, but I expect those to be denied. That means with any luck we should have you on the witness stand by Thursday afternoon. Friday morning at the latest. How does that sound to you?

Lottie blinked.

I've read your witness statements and I've spoken with Bill Fannin at some length, and I want you to know right up front that we understand the predicament you were in, and that nobody here blames you for what happened to your father or for any of that business up in Utah. As far as we're concerned, you were just as much a victim of Mr. Palmer as any of them. You believe me, don't you?

Yes, sir. She nodded. Thank you.

Excellent. Now Mr. Palmer has already confessed to the two murders he committed up in Utah, but none of that matters here in Texas. If we're to win a conviction here, we'll need your full and complete cooperation. You understand that, don't you?

The sheriff leaned sideways. The man asked you a question.

What do you want me to do?

The lawyer smiled again. It's very simple, Lucile. Just tell the jurors exactly what you've already sworn to in your statements.

Can't you just read 'em the statements?

I'm afraid it's not that simple. You see, your statements are what we call hearsay evidence. They can only be used for impeachment purposes.

Sir?

Impeachment. So for example, if you were to lie or to change your testimony, then I could use your statement to show that you lied. But that would be foolish, because lying to the court is a crime. In fact, it's just about the stupidest crime a witness can commit. You understand that, don't you?

Yes, sir.

All right then.

Will Clint be there at the trial?

Yes, he will. He'll be seated at the defense table with his lawyers. But don't worry, you don't have to look at him. In fact, I'd prefer that you don't.

So what do you want me to say?

Let's don't worry about that just now. We'll have a chance to go over all of this again before you actually testify. But there's one thing we need you to do for us first. And by that I mean today. Right now in fact.

What is it?

The lawyer glanced at the sheriff as he sipped from his cup.

Without getting overly complicated, it will be the state's burden to prove that Mr. Palmer was the killer. But before we can even get to that, it's also the state's burden to show that your father, Dillard Garrett, was the victim. We expect the defense to challenge that fact by arguing that the skeleton that was found up in Peerless wasn't your father's at all. Or at least that we can't prove it was your father's beyond a reasonable doubt. They may try to claim that your father is still alive, for example, and that the skeleton belongs to somebody else altogether. Do you understand what I'm getting at?

I guess.

Good. Very good. Now, what we'd like to do today is to take

you downstairs and show you the skeleton. I know that may be difficult for you, but I'm afraid we have no alternative. We've got a doctor from Baylor College who's an expert in these things, but all he can say for sure is that the skeleton belongs to a male of a certain age and height, and that the head was decapitated while the victim was still alive.

The girl blanched. The men shared another glance.

I'm sorry, Lucile. I thought they told you.

They waited, both watching the girl.

Are you okay?

I guess I never thought about it is all. How he done it.

That's all right. The lawyer checked his watch. You just take your time. But if you're up to it, we'd like to go downstairs right now. Is that all right with you?

The matron was waiting outside the door. The two men flanked Lottie as they walked, with the matron following behind them. Heads turned in the hallway and on the staircase. An attendant rose from his stool as they reached the basement landing, and a windowless door was opened with a key on a chain. The matron and the attendant waited outside.

The sheriff threw the lights. The room was a kind of store-room, with a low, raftered ceiling and shelving on the walls and in stacks that ran in long and ordered rows. It smelled of dust, and mildew, and old cardboard.

They threaded their way toward the back, to where a table lay covered in a thin white sheet, the caged bulb overhead imparting a topographic grid onto the contours of what lay beneath it.

The men did not speak as they flanked the table, each taking a corner. Then the lawyer nodded and they lifted the shroud and walked it to where the girl stood waiting at the foot of the table.

What she'd expected to see was a Halloween skeleton of clean white bones and hollow eyes and clenched and grinning teeth. What she saw instead beneath the shroud was the kind of jumbled game skeleton she might have found in the spring woods of her childhood, the kind with clumps of hair and naked tendons and brown and shrunken hide that clung yet to the twisted bones like something melted in a fire.

She vomited onto her boots. Her knees sagged, and the lawyer's arm was around her and helping her to a chair, where she sat with her head lowered and where the smell of her own sickness caused her to heave and vomit once again.

Christ almighty, she heard the sheriff say.

The lawyer eased her upward from the chair. They walked together, to the open doorway where the matron stood frowning, and where the sheriff soon returned with a thin Negro woman, and behind them both the attendant bearing a mop and heavy pail.

We'll wait out here, the sheriff told them.

Lottie breathed the courthouse air that smelled of floor wax and polished brass. She leaned over double with her hands on her knees. Papers lifted from a bulletin board as a door opened somewhere down the hall. The fresh air helped to revive her.

I'm sorry, she finally said.

That's all right. We should have warned you.

When the two inside at last emerged, the Negro woman stopped and bent and swiped at Lottie's boots with a rag.

There you go, chile, she said. You all better now.

When they reentered the storeroom, the dust and cardboard

smell had been supplanted by the ketone scent of disinfectant, and at the long table in back, the light shone brightly on the newly wetted floor. They stopped and waited a moment, and then when Lottie had breathed and nodded, they stepped forward and assumed their places as before.

I'm afraid the clothes are missing, the lawyer said. Burned, we suspect.

She nodded.

Did your father have any distinguishing features that might still be evident? A tattoo, maybe? Or a broken bone?

His finger. Lottie pointed. His pinkie finger was all broke and crooked.

Both men leaned closer to inspect the ivory pegs of metacarpal and phalanx that formed the skeletal hand. They raised their faces in unison.

Bingo, said the sheriff.

She attended the prison chapel service on the Sunday morning next, held in what appeared to be a cafeteria, a dozen or more folding chairs arrayed in rows with women on the left and men on the right and guards between them in the center aisle. The minister facing them all on a low wooden riser. He paired his hands and spoke to the prisoners of hope and redemption, and he read to them from Psalm 130:

I trust in the Lord;
my soul trusts in his Word.
My soul waits for the Lord
more than sentinels wait for the dawn.

★   ★   ★

On Monday afternoon she was escorted to the visitors' area, where she sat in a hard chair at a scarred wooden table and faced across a framed wire screen her uncle Mack, who rose at her entrance and who sat again and set his hat on his knee.

Look at you, he said. All growed up and haired over.

Tears ran hot on her cheek. She looked away, down the long table to where a young Negro man, the day's other visitor, held an infant child aloft for its mother's inspection.

I knew I should of never let you go with him, her uncle said, fingering his hat. He was never cut out to be no father.

It weren't your fault.

Hell.

I'm the one's to blame. I'm the one took up with that no-account—

Hush. You just hush your pretty mouth.

They watched together as the baby wriggled and drooled, the mother leaning forward with black and shining eyes.

I'm goin to hell. I know that much at least.

You are no such thing.

I am. I know I am.

Lucile, you listen to me. Your grandpa Garrett never had a day of school in his life, but I reckon he was just about the smartest man I ever knew. And he used to say that folks would do a lot more prayin could they find a soft spot for their knees.

She wiped at her face with a sleeve.

Have they said how long they're gonna keep you here?

She shrugged. I never did ask Mr. Pharr.

Mr. Pharr. Her uncle shook his head. I don't know about you, but Mr. Pharr strikes me as the kind of lawyer whose most important case is the next one.

Sir?

Never mind. I'll talk to him myself. The way I see it, he'll owe us both before this thing is over.

Yes, sir. Thank you.

Again they watched the baby.

It don't really matter, Lucile. You understand that, right?

Sir?

Even if that little bastard walks, they'll just hang him up in Utah. Helpin to convict him here is the best thing you can do for yourself. And maybe for him too.

She nodded.

Right?

They say I got to face him in the courtroom.

Hell, that ain't nothin. I'm guessin you've faced worse than that. A lot worse than that, thanks to him.

She nodded.

Come on, Lucile. Don't you go weak north of the ears.

She smiled. No, sir, I won't.

All right then. Meanwhile, is there anythin you need? Women's things? They's a drugstore just down the street.

No, sir. They give me all of that for free.

All right then. What's still botherin you?

She shrugged. I don't know. Daddy's Bible, I guess. I had it in the car when we got arrested. It was wrapped up in my bedroll. I'll bet if you was to ask Mr. Pharr, he could get it for me.

The baby had begun to squall. They watched as the matron came to shush it and the man jerked his arm and words were exchanged. Moments later, a guard stepped from the door behind the man, tapping a truncheon in his palm.

Her uncle rose from his chair.

Put not your trust in princes, he told her, donning and leveling his hat. I think you'll find that writ somewheres in old Dillard's Bible.

She knew that the trial had begun by the hubbub in the street. Cars arrived and parked and then others double-parked. Horns honked. Pedestrians streamed from the train station and crowded the courthouse entrance and queued up in a line along the sidewalk. She saw the flash-pop of photography and heard the milling of the crowd. And in the afternoon, she watched the entire process play out again in reverse.

The matron brought her a newspaper the next afternoon, the *Greenville Morning Herald*. The headline read 11 JURORS SECURED IN 'SKELETON' MURDER IN HOPKINS. She said it was from Mr. Pharr.

Lottie sat on her cot and read. The article stated that the defense motions had all been denied, and that eleven of the twelve jurors had already been selected. It said that

questions propounded by District Attorney Henry Pharr indicated that the State would demand the death penalty. The defense, on the other hand, will challenge the attempted identity of the skeleton found in an isolated spot last December as that of Dillard Garrett.

The matron appeared again on Thursday morning, this time with an oblong box under her arm. She set it on the cot. Lottie opened the string and folded back the paper and held to her chin a long, blue dress with a ruffled collar.

It's from Mr. Pharr, the woman said. Wish he'd send one to me.

She was led down the corridor to catcalls and wolf whistles from the cells of the other women. A crowd was waiting for her on the other side of the gate, and newsmen called to her by name in the stairwell amid jostling and shouting and a frenzied crush of bodies.

She walked a narrow gauntlet in the third-floor hallway. A man lifted a child onto his shoulders. A woman reached a hand to touch the hem of Lottie's dress.

Four men were waiting for her in the conference room. Henry Pharr rose from the head of the table as the door closed and the noise of the hallway died out behind her.

Lucile. He crossed the room to take her hand. These are my colleagues Mr. Lowrie and Mr. Norwood. And you already know Mr. Fannin.

The men all nodded as he led her to an empty chair. Pharr consulted his watch as he returned to the head of the table.

We've only got a few minutes, so please listen carefully. When we leave here, you'll go with Mr. Norwood. On his signal, you'll walk into the courtroom from a side door and you'll go straight to the witness stand. That's the chair between the jury box and the judge's bench. Remain standing to be sworn, and then sit down. I'll take over from there. I'll take you through your sworn statement, and all you have to do is answer my questions fully and truthfully. You think you can do that?

She looked at the other faces.

If you have any questions, now's the time to ask them.

Is it true Clint's gonna hang?

The lawyer chuckled. No, he won't hang. That I can guarantee. If the jury returns a prison term, he'll go to Huntsville. If the jury returns a death sentence, and if the verdict is upheld on appeal, then he'll go to the electric chair. That's a perfectly humane and painless way to die, I can assure you.

She did not respond.

What's the matter?

Nothin.

Don't be shy. Say what's on your mind.

It's just that I was learned that only God says who should live and who should die.

Pharr shifted in his seat. He glanced at the others. Well. If only Mr. Palmer had been so enlightened. Then we wouldn't be here, would we?

Wedding, said the man named Lowrie.

Oh, yes. There will be a motion made by the defense to bar your testimony on the ground that you are the common-law wife of the defendant. In the state of Texas, a wife can't give evidence against her husband. The judge will deny the motion, subject to what we call an offer of proof. So once you're on the stand, I'll ask you straight out whether you and Mr. Palmer were ever married. The answer is no, I hope.

There were more chuckles around the table.

All right then. Once I'm finished with my questions, then a defense lawyer will cross-examine. Mr. Hartwell, in all likelihood. He'll try to chip away at your testimony and look for inconsistencies. But there won't be any, because you're going to tell it just like you did in your statement to the grand jury. Isn't that right?

She nodded. All right.

Good girl. Anything else before we go?

How long will it take?

All day would be my guess. But don't worry, there's a lunch break at noon.

And what happens when it's over?

Well. When it's over, with any luck, we'll have a conviction.

More chuckles, and another shifting of bodies.

I meant to me. What happens to me?

Oh. Well, assuming your cooperation, then your attachment as a material witness will be vacated at that point. Right, Bill?

Should be.

Vacated?

Exactly. Any other questions?

But the district attorney was already standing, and the others were standing, and the three men moved as one, straightening ties and buttoning jackets. Pharr turned to her and winked. Then the door opened and they were gone, swallowed by the tumult in the hallway.

The hallway had emptied by the time she left the conference room. She could see the entrance to the courtroom, where a uniformed guard was posted, and a where a cluster of men jostled for a view through the window. She recognized, on a bench along the wall opposite, the ordered profiles of Helen Smith and Lonnie Kincaide and old Mrs. Nations.

They turned right, then left again down a dimly lit side hall where a sign read COURT PERSONNEL ONLY. Norwood raised a finger and went on ahead. He opened a door and he peered inside and then he closed the door again.

Okay, come on.

She heard her name called, and when she stepped through the oaken door, she was awash in lights and in a sea of eager faces. Of the judge and the jurors. Of the bailiff and the clerk and the stenographer. Of the lawyers huddled at their tables. And of the murmuring spectators who filled the wooden benches to over-flow beyond the gated railing. All of them watching her. All of them already judging.

The judge rapped his gavel. Pharr stood and gestured with his head and she half-turned and walked to the empty chair and sat and then stood again when the clerk approached with a heavy Bible that he held out before her.

Please raise your right hand. Do you solemnly swear that the testimony you are about to give in the cause now pending shall be the truth, the whole truth, and nothing but the truth, so help you God?

Lottie nodded. Yes, sir.

Please be seated.

Not until the clerk had stepped aside and the room had settled and sharpened into focus did she notice Palmer where he sat.

His hair was neatly barbered, and his face was shaved, and he wore a pressed gray suit and a silk necktie with a matching blue handkerchief, looking for all the world like a banker, or like another one of the lawyers, or like some honored guest at whose behest all around him had assembled.

His eyes, blue and unblinking, locked on to hers.

Lottie raised her chin and met his gaze and held it. And after a long moment Palmer looked away again, the smile fading to nothing at all.

EPILOGUE

THE VERDICT CAME ON SATURDAY.

She heard the commotion in the street, and she rose from her bunk to watch as the crowd that had gathered outside the courthouse surged and parted and formed again like quicksilver. Umbrellas tilted and flashbulbs popped and men ran splashing down the sidewalk, and Lottie knew from the shouts and the sirens and from the blaring of car horns that Mr. Pharr had won.

The details she learned at the afternoon mess. How toward the end of Pharr's closing argument, when the judge had warned the lawyer that his time was almost up, Palmer had stood and said, Give him all the time he wants, Judge! My conscience is clear! And how, when the verdict had been read and Hartwell had thanked the jury for its consideration, Palmer had stood again to say, It's all right for you to thank them! You don't have to serve the ninety-nine years! They're sendin an innocent man to prison!

By afternoon, the rain had grown heavy. It darkened the sky, and it darkened the cellblock, and it darkened the hearts of all who dwelt within it.

By evening puddles were in the street, black holes where the storefront neon bled in twisted reds and greens, and where sodden trash pooled and floated in a rueful denouement to all that had been witnessed. To all that had transpired.

Lottie lay on her cot in the dark with her eyes closed and her fingers laced, listening to the rain. Thinking about Palmer, and about her father, and about her own life to come. Later, after the rain had stopped and all had grown quiet, her thoughts returned yet again to the question of love.

First, she decided, there was familial love, which seemed to her the most fragile of love's embodiments, random in its origins and destined by nature to fade as life in its endless recycling begins anew with aught but memory and heredity tying one generation but loosely to the next.

Then there was spiritual love, the love of God the Creator that transcended generations and dwelt in the hearts of all men.

And lastly, she thought, there was romantic love, or carnal love, which she herself concluded to be the most tangible and enduring love of all, as it was no mere accident of birth or genetic imperative, and was neither predestined nor presumed, but rather was a thing of human choosing. And how each, for having chosen, was thereby and forever altered.

And for having betrayed, condemned.

Lottie wept that night, and all the next day. Whether tears of regret or of relief, none could tell.

And she least of all.

On April 20, 1935, Clint Palmer's motion for a new trial was denied by the Honorable Charles Berry of the Eighth Judicial District of Texas, and his sentence—imprisonment for a term of not less than two and not more than ninety-nine years—was formally pronounced. His conviction was affirmed by the Texas Court of Criminal Appeals on February 5,

1936. On March 1, 1936, he entered the Texas State Penitentiary at Huntsville, where he died on January 13, 1969.

Lucile Garrett was tried as a juvenile and convicted of associating with a known criminal. She was sentenced by the Honorable S. S. Bullock to serve in the girls' reformatory until her twenty-first birthday. She entered the Texas Girls' Training School in Gainesville on May 23, 1935.

AUTHOR'S NOTE AND
ACKNOWLEDGMENTS

Hard Twisted, although based upon real people and true events, is entirely a work of fiction.

My first exposure to the saga of Clint Palmer and Lottie Garrett came in somewhat dramatic fashion when, on November 26, 1994, while hiking with friends in the remote recesses of John's Canyon, in San Juan County, Utah, I stumbled upon a pair of human skulls.

Frozen under a pewter sky, muffled in the stillness of a late-autumn snowstorm, we bent to inspect our macabre discovery. As we did, a rolling thunderclap shook the ground under our feet.

They were old Indian skulls, we knew, judging by the shape and the dental condition. Navajo or Ute or Paiute, from the location. But how had they got here? And what of the jagged fractures, suggestive of bullet holes, that were visible on the backside of each?

That chance discovery began a personal odyssey that would play out in fits and starts over fifteen-odd years, setting me onto the trail of what I would come to regard as one of the great, untold stories of the American West.

The first leg of that journey took me to Mexican Hat, Utah, and to the doorstep of the incomparable Doris Valle—octogenarian, amiable curmudgeon, and erstwhile proprietress of the Valle Trading Post, a remote and windswept vanguard hard on the banks of the San Juan River. Her history of the region, *Looking Back Around the Hat* (1986), provided me with my first account of the murders of William E. Oliver and Norris "Jake" Shumway, an incident she styled the Tragedy in John's Canyon. As Doris put it:

There are as many versions of the John's Canyon murder story as there were adults in San Juan County at the time of the tragedy. Historical research involves shifting through reams of material and all available versions of any story. When the researcher is ready to write, the facts are presented to the best of the writer's knowledge and belief. The writer cannot state categorically that one thing is true and the other false. Ultimately, only God knows the truth.

I had the unique pleasure of hiking with Doris in and around Mexican Hat, throughout the Valley of the Gods, up on Cedar Mesa, and in John's Canyon itself, and I am deeply indebted both to her and to our frequent hosts Gail L. Goeken and R. Lee Dick, the founding owners of the Valley of the Gods Bed & Breakfast at Lee Ranch, for introducing me to this most beautiful slice of the American landscape. Without them this book could not, and would not, have been written.

A second, tantalizingly brief reference to the John's Canyon murders appears in *Tall Sheep* (1992), Samuel Moon's excellent interview-cum-biography of Harry T. Goulding, the legendary trader, promoter, and pioneer who famously brought Hollywood director John Ford to Monument Valley. It is largely upon this source, and my visits to Goulding's Trading Post Museum, that the book's depictions of Depression-era life on the Paiute Strip are based. Moon's book was also, along with the late H. Jackson Clark's memoir, *The Owl in Monument Canyon* (1994), my introduction to the truly larger-than-life character Sunshine Smith.

Yet another version of the John's Canyon tragedy appears in Helen N. Shumway's "The Ingredients of Violence in the Murders of William E. Oliver and Norris Shumway" (*Blue Mountain Shadows* 1 [Fall 1987]). While this account cannot be squared in all its particulars with that of Ms. Valle, it is nonetheless noteworthy in several respects, including its familial insights and its quotations from the diary of the late William Oliver.

Sheriff Oliver was, as *Hard Twisted* suggests, one of, and perhaps the last of, the legendary frontier lawmen. For my account of his role in the Posey War, I relied upon several sources, most notably Robert S. McPherson's "Paiute Posey and the Last White Uprising" (*Utah Historical Quarterly* 53 [Summer 1985]) and Steve Lacy and Pearl Baker's *Posey: The Last Indian War* (2007).

A trove of material describing pioneer life in San Juan County, including firsthand recollections of the John's Canyon murders and the Posey War, resides in the archives of the Southeast Utah Oral History Project, a vast collection of interviews and documents amassed and maintained by the Center for Oral and Public History at California State University, Fullerton, under the direction of Professor Emeritus Gary L. Shumway. I am indebted both to Dr. Shumway and to archivist Stephanie George for allowing me access to these data.

All of these sources, together with multiple visits to the communities of Bluff, Blanding, and Monticello, time spent in the archives of the *San Juan Record*, and trips to the local library, cemetery, museum, and historical society—thank you, LaVerne Tate—provided the framework on which the book's Utah-based narrative hangs.

John's Canyon today remains little changed from the secluded landscape described in *Hard Twisted*. While the oil company line shack that served as seasonal headquarters for the Seeps Ranch cattlemen is long gone, the Palmer dugout remains. And those of a more adventurous bent can still visit the boulder cave in which Norris Shumway spent his final night, and where he etched his own epitaph, N.S. FEB 28 1935, deep into the Navajo sandstone.

I would be remiss if I did not, before departing Utah, offer a tip of my hat to the late David Lavender, that sage and prolific chronicler of all things Western, upon whom I relied for a rudimentary understanding of the methods and practices of Depression-era sheepherding, gleaned from his own epic memoir, *One Man's West* (1943).

The red-rock country of southern Utah—with its canyons and mesas, its monuments and gorges—is among the most beautiful and, paradoxically, among the least populous regions in all America. That the life of a Texas drifter would, over a few short months, intersect with those of historic figures such as William Oliver and Harry Goulding is a testament to the remoteness of the area. Which brings me to another intersection, not mentioned in the book, but that is worth noting here.

On the same day—March 7, 1935—that the *San Juan Record* first reported the John's Canyon tragedy in a banner headline proclaiming DOUBLE MURDER SHOCKS COUNTY, it also reported, in the adjoining column on page one, the disappearance of a young, unnamed artist who had last been seen in November of 1934 near the Escalante River, where "planes were used to try and locate the artist's camp and succeeded in finding what they thought to be the pack burrow [*sic*] which he used. No camp or other sign of the lost man have yet been found."

That missing artist was none other than Everett Ruess, whose disappearance in the Utah wilderness remains one of the enduring mysteries of the twentieth century. Author Jon Krakauer, in his bestselling *Into the Wild* (1996), recounts a conversation with former Escalante River guide Ken Sleight (upon whom Edward Abbey, in his novel *The Monkey Wrench Gang*, modeled the character Seldom Seen Smith) in which Sleight claims to have seen Ruess's trademark NEMO graffito carved into the wall of an Anasazi granary near Grand Gulch, on the northern bank of the San Juan River, some forty-five miles due east of Ruess's last known location at Davis Gulch. (A claim subsequently confirmed to me by Southwest historian Fred M. Blackburn, author of *The Wetherills, Friends of Mesa Verde* (2006), who has traced and compared both the Grand Gulch and the Davis Gulch carvings.)

That discovery puts Everett Ruess less than twenty miles from Clint Palmer's dugout in John's Canyon, and has Ruess headed in Palmer's direction at a time (December 1934) when Palmer was known to have been alone, heavily armed, and dangerously psychotic.

Although reams have been written about the life of Everett Ruess, by notables ranging from John Nichols to Wallace Stegner, no historian has, to my knowledge, yet posited a connection between the disappearance of the man Stegner called an "atavistic wanderer of the wastelands" (Ruess) and the nearby presence of a man who would, a few months later, reveal himself to the world as a ruthless and predatory killer (Palmer).

★　★　★

My journey on the trail of Clint Palmer and Lottie Garrett next took me to the Red River valley, where I visited each of the principal locales described in the book, including Hugo and Roebuck Lake in Oklahoma, and Arthur City, Peerless, Sulphur Springs, and Greenville in Texas.

For an understanding of the events that presaged the John's Canyon tragedy, I relied heavily upon newspaper accounts of the 1935 "skeleton murder" trial of Clint Palmer, in which the testimony of the prosecution's star witness—Lucile Garrett—was thoroughly reported. Of particular utility was the coverage provided by the *Greenville Morning Herald*. For the judicial proceedings leading to and following Palmer's conviction, I consulted all of the extant court records from the Hopkins County District Court, the Hunt County District Court, and the Texas Court of Criminal Appeals.

The most informing of all the official Texas records, I found, surprisingly enough, not in the courthouses or archives of the Lone Star State, but rather in Salt Lake City, at the Utah State History Museum. These included transcripts of the grand jury testimony of Lottie Garrett and H. P. Palmer, as well as transcripts of the statements given both by Lottie and Harry Goulding to the Utah authorities who traveled to Texas as part of the John's Canyon murder investigation. My special thanks to Michele Elnicky, historical collections curator, for her invaluable assistance.

Dillard Garrett's remains were discovered in a shallow cave near Peerless, Texas, on December 29, 1934, seven months after his brutal decapitation murder, by a group of young boys out rabbit hunting near the Palmer farm. The skeleton was thereafter placed on public display at the courthouse in Sulphur Springs, which event, combined with the notoriety surrounding Palmer and Lottie's dramatic capture, resulted in a change of the trial venue to Greenville on the grounds that

> wide publicity has been given to the finding of said skeleton and that the same was on exhibition for many weeks in the court house of Hopkins County, and was viewed by thousands of citizens . . . causing a large amount of discussion . . . and that the arrest of the defendant was published widely in the newspapers of Hopkins County and on the day of his arrest large numbers of citizens . . . gathered around the jail of the said county discussing fully the facts or alleged facts pertaining to the cause.

The notoriety attendant to Palmer's trial is best illustrated by the news accounts of the day. They describe a scene in which hundreds of citizens, including a government class from Wesley College, mobbed the courthouse on the morning Lottie Garrett was to testify, such that, as the *Greenville Morning Herald* reported, "it was necessary to lock all doors early in the day, and they were locked until the court recessed for the day late Thursday afternoon."

Since Palmer's postconviction appeal was prosecuted solely on the clerk's record, and since no reporter's transcript of his trial survives, all of the excerpts that appear in the book are fictive except for the last, which is taken verbatim from the jury instructions given by Judge Berry at the trial's conclusion. Also, since Lottie's subsequent prosecution was conducted in a juvenile proceeding, no public record of her trial or conviction exists. Indeed, only a short newspaper account from May 24, 1935, attests to her sentence, and to her having "left today for the Texas Girls'

Training School at Gainesville" in the custody of Deputy Sheriff Jeff Branom, almost one year to the day from her first, fateful encounter with Clint Palmer.

Readers will be cheered to know that Lottie Lucile Garrett survived the ordeal of her childhood, married at age twenty-one, and raised a son named Dillard. She died on November 21, 1991, in Irving, Texas, at age seventy-one. My thanks go to Lottie's son, Clyde Sconce, and his wife, Linda, for sharing with me, a complete stranger, such a difficult part of their family history.

Clint Palmer was a sexual predator and a career criminal who when he first encountered young Lottie Garrett in May of 1934 was only four months removed from his latest incarceration, a three-year stint in the federal penitentiary at Leavenworth, Kansas, for kidnapping, statutory rape, and violating the Mann Act. For a physical description of Palmer, I relied both upon a lone photograph that appeared in the July 1936 issue of *Startling Detective Adventures*, and upon the records of the Texas State Penitentiary at Huntsville, which describe him as five feet six inches in height, 135 pounds in weight, and as having size seven shoes. Readers might also be interested to know that Clint Palmer was born in 1897, was a Baptist, had five years of formal schooling, and claimed as his former occupations ranch labor, rodeo, and farming. I thank the Texas Prison Museum in Huntsville for these details.

For a complete catalog of Clint Palmer's extensive criminal exploits, I thank the archivists at the United States Penitentiary in Leavenworth, Kansas, whose records describe a young man first arrested in Texas at age eighteen for rape and assault (two years at Huntsville), then arrested in Oklahoma at age twenty-three for forgery and white slavery (three years at McAlester), in Oklahoma at age twenty-eight for statutory rape, in Colorado at age thirty-one for rape, in Arizona at age thirty-one for forgery, in Montana at age thirty-two for grand larceny, and, finally, in New Mexico at age thirty-four for white slavery (three years at Leavenworth).

The Leavenworth records also describe Palmer as a manipulative psychotic, a toothless syphilitic, and, most prophetically, a "menace to society."

As for my efforts to capture the culture, language, and general flavor of the Red River valley circa 1934–35, I am indebted both to the late Bill Owens for his terrific memoir of Texas frontier life, *This Stubborn Soil* (1966), and to Donald Worster for his *Dust Bowl, the Southern Plains in the 1930s* (1979).

Closer to home, I am deeply appreciative of the encouragement and support provided by my dear friends Pati and David Temple of Cortez, Colorado, and of the invaluable feedback I received from my brother Dan Greaves and his daughter, filmmaker Katie Greaves, both of whom were kind enough to read and critique *Hard Twisted* in its early manuscript form. My thanks to you all.

While still in manuscript, *Hard Twisted* was named Best Historical Novel in the SouthWest Writers 2010 International Writing Contest. With the help of my extraordinary literary agent, Antonella Iannarino of the David Black Agency in New York, it was then acquired for publication by senior editor Anton Mueller of Bloomsbury USA, who nurtured it into print. Thank you, SWW; thank you, Antonella; and thank you, Anton and all the crew at Bloomsbury, including, without limitation, Rachel Mannheimer, Nate Knaebel, and Steve Boldt (USA) and Helen Garnons-Williams (UK).

Lastly, I wish with all my heart to thank the inimitable Lynda Larsen, my wife and muse of the last quarter century, who was there when this long journey began, was there when it ended, and was with me every step of the way.

As there are no hard-and-fast rules for confecting fiction from historical fact, the guidelines I imposed upon myself in writing *Hard Twisted* were these: First, that the story must remain true to the known factual record in all but its most mundane particulars. Second, that no fictional action, event, or depiction appearing in the story may contradict a material fact known to be true. And lastly, that any actions, descriptions, or events created to fill gaps in the historical record must remain true to the general character and behavior of each of the actors to the extent that the same are knowable.

In accordance with these guidelines, and except as noted below, all dates and general time frames described in the book are true to the extent that they are known. All persons named in the book are real, with the exception of a few minor characters imagined for the purpose of advancing the plot in areas where the historical record is entirely silent. All of the places traveled by Palmer and Lottie, and the general sequence in which they are portrayed, are accurate, again to the extent known.

Conversely, all of the book's dialogue is fictitious, with the exception of a few phrases gleaned from oral histories or from news accounts of the Palmer trial. So too are any thoughts, motives, or emotions that I attribute to Lottie or to any other character acting within the purview of my limited authorial omniscience. Also, in the service of narrative, I shifted historical time frames in a few instances, but never in a way that might distort or misrepresent the material facts.

Finally, in writing *Hard Twisted*, I was acutely aware that the historical record leaves open for interpretation the exact nature of the relationship between Lottie Garrett and Clint Palmer, and that any surviving testimony in respect of that relationship must be viewed through the compound lens of circumstance, alibi, and self-interest. That Lottie was Palmer's victim—not to mention a victim of her upbringing, and ultimately of the criminal justice system of her day—is beyond dispute. Whether her victimhood arose from seduction, coercion, force, or some combination of all of them, or from some misguided or manipulated collaboration, is entirely problematic.

It is in this last respect that *Hard Twisted* is most purely and unequivocally a work of fiction.

Charles Joseph Greaves
Santa Fe, New Mexico

A NOTE ON THE AUTHOR

C. Joseph Greaves is a former L.A. trial lawyer. His 1994 discovery of two human skulls in a remote Utah canyon would lead, eighteen years later, to the completion of *Hard Twisted*, named Best Historical Novel of 2010 in the SouthWest Writers International Writing Contest, in which Greaves was also honored with the grand-prize Storyteller Award. Greaves is also the author of a Los Angeles–based mystery series; the first installment is *Hush Money.*